D0592601

SHINING MOUNTAINS

**Center Point
Large Print**

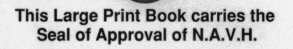

**This Large Print Book carries the
Seal of Approval of N.A.V.H.**

SHINING
MOUNTAINS

STEVE FRAZEE

CENTER POINT PUBLISHING
THORNDIKE, MAINE

This Center Point Large Print edition
is published in the year 2003 by arrangement with
Golden West Literary Agency.

The text of this Large Print edition is unabridged. In other
aspects, this book may vary from the original edition. Printed in
Thailand. Set in 16-point Times New Roman type by
Bill Coskrey and Gary Socquet.

ISBN 1-58547-315-4

Library of Congress Cataloging-in-Publication Data.

Frazee, Steve, 1909-
    Shining mountains / Steve Frazee.--Center Point large print ed.
        p. cm.
    ISBN 1-58547-315-4 (lib. bdg. : alk. paper)
    1. Large type books. I. Title.

PS3556.R358S45 2003
813'.54--dc21

                                                                        2003040957

To Pat

CHAPTER 1

THE CLAWS OF WINTER were still hooked into the earth this day in early April, 1866. Wind was sweeping the cold of ten thousand feet above sea level against a man standing on a hill above the blot of Oro City, Colorado Territory.

To Jonathan Romig there came no chill from ice crystals against his clothing, or from the sight of granite marching down the sky four thousand feet above him. Eyes half blind with thought, he looked at beauty that was new to him and yet so old the understanding of its oldness lay beyond reason.

Out from the mouth of California Gulch, beyond the tiny mark of the Arkansas in the snow flats, the trees marched up and up until there was no air for life. It was the shining summits that held Romig.

He was a hawk-nosed, powerful column of a man, with dark-blue eyes that now looked light against his snow tan. His voice, some claimed, had staggered cavalry sergeants at twenty paces. Four years he had served as a chaplain in the Seventh Indiana Infantry. Before the war he had preached three formal sermons—and afterward, one.

He was finished now with preaching.

Around his home in Ohio and in the Romig section of Vermont, his dereliction had come as no surprise. His father had wandered with trappers in the West for ten years before settling down on the Ohio; even after that he had been a restless man, that dark Jedediah

Romig. It was said that at every sunset he had stood with a gone expression, not hearing words addressed to him, just staring west.

Since young Jonathan had thrown away his creed to dig gold, it was easy to recall another Jonathan Romig, only six generations before. That one, in 1750, had given up law practice overnight to wander in the woods around the English Lakes, returning to Vermont five years later with a big-nosed solemn child, half Seneca, half Romig. Then, having made his bow to orthodoxy by bringing the boy to the advantages of a superior civilization, the father had gone back to the Indians and had never been heard of again.

Now this descendant of the solemn child of 1755 stood looking at mountains until his brain rebelled at merely seeing beauty without classifying it. He became aware then that his boots were wet, that the wind was bitter.

He went down the hill toward Oro City.

Two miles high, the camp had been the largest in the Territory when the war began. No one would ever know how many millions in gold ten thousand men had gouged and washed from California Gulch, but now the gold was gone, and Oro City was dying like a savage old renegade with a glare for the death watch. Bough huts, the first habitations, were skeletons now. The cabins had a rusty look. Along the largest sluice warped boards rose above the snow like the ribs of a Viking ship buried in sand.

Near the lower end of town two die-hards were thawing ground with fires.

Still the name of California Gulch had been strong enough to draw two parties of gold-seekers—and a third group that was there for unknown reasons. With twenty-two other Union men, Romig had come from Independence, Missouri, striking the Arkansas far out from the mountains and then following it all the way.

Already in Oro, when the Unions arrived, was a party of twenty former Confederate soldiers who had come by way of Denver, through the drifts of South Park, and then up the river the last thirty miles. The third group was small: two women Romig had not seen, a tight-lipped Irishman named Sull, and a lad of twelve or thirteen whose brains were addled.

There was shelter of sorts for everyone, even for sick mules. But there was no gold. The few regular inhabitants admitted that, although some of them claimed they owned ground where a few ounces might yet be washed. And so the two parties of gold-seekers, having come far to find nothing, camped and scratched their beards. The citizens of Oro warned against trying any of the passes so early in the year—and there was no other way out of Oro except retreat down the river.

It was futile to say the war was over. These men were still Confederates and Federals. Quite likely, Romig thought, either group, if it had been alone, would have backed out of this blind alley quickly; as it was both groups found significance in the fact that chance had put them here at the same time. Each figured there must be gold somewhere close, or else the other party would leave.

Idleness and a saloon had not helped the situation.

There had been minor fights. There would be more, Romig was sure, before Young Malcolm Alexander, unofficial leader of the Southerners, or Bruce Ruthven, to whom the Unions looked for guidance, decided that withdrawal was not a mark of weakness.

At least the two women had added no complications. Romig neared their quarters at the uphill end of the street. One of the few structures in Oro that had a window opening, the cabin had been first pre-empted by East Tennesseeans of the Union group, who had relinquished it to the women when they arrived at dusk three days before. "Too fur from the saloon anyhow," Ezekiel Davis, one of the former occupants, had said.

Romig was crunching snow fifty feet away when the door opened, and a woman in a white woolen *capote* came out. She glanced at him, then went around the corner of the cabin to the lee side so quickly that his main impressions of her were the *capote* and blue mittens.

She was standing with her back to the logs when Romig came abreast. He made a slight bow, spoke a formal greeting, and would have passed.

"Good afternoon, Mr. Romig."

The magic of his own name stopped him. He saw the woman studying him with a frankness that would have been called boldness a thousand miles east. She was young, about twenty-four, Romig estimated; a tall woman with bronze lights running in her hair.

"You put me at a loss, Miss—"

"Charity Megill."

The door of a hut close by swung out on leather

hinges. Sull, the hard-mouthed Irishman, stood in the opening with a knife in one hand, a piece of board in the other. He nodded without expression when Romig spoke, and then he began to whittle the board.

A wheyfaced boy tried to push past him.

"Old Sull's making me a sled, Miss Megill! Old Sull's whittling—"

"That's fine, Timmy," the woman said.

Sull pushed the boy behind him, saying, "Now be a good lad and stay out of the cold." He began to shape the board, his eyes rising, between strokes of the knife, to Romig's face.

"I've watched you on the hill, Mr. Romig," Charity Megill said. She glanced at peaks standing like frozen grenadiers. "You stare out there as if looking for something you had lost."

Her words, cutting so close to the truth, threw Romig momentarily within himself.

From inside the cabin a woman called a question which Romig did not understand. Miss Megill went toward the door. "Will you please ask your friend, Dr. Arnold, to come up here?"

Still thinking of her previous words, Romig nodded. He saw the door close behind her. Sull kicked shavings from his doorstep and went inside, banging the door to make it rise above mud and ice on the log sill.

Air cold enough to sear lungs bristled through three lone jack pines behind the cabin. Romig stood a moment looking at Charity Megill's door, and then he went down the street to find Heber Arnold, a Mormon who had joined the Union party at Pueblo, a hundred and fifty miles downriver.

Excitement had struck the camp. Three men ran from a cabin, stopping briefly to shout before another cabin that soon disgorged two members of the Northern party. Four Southerners staggered over waste piles in the gulch as they left the thawing fires and ran toward Dill's saloon.

Romig was passing a dirt-roofed hut when Heber Arnold brushed past a blanket hanging in the doorway and came into the street. The Mormon was a stocky, brown-bearded man who had not talked a great deal since joining the Union party. He stood squinting at snow glare, his ragged mackintosh unbuttoned. He nodded absently.

"Another?" Romig asked.

"One of the Kentuckians." Arnold shook his head. "There's no oxygen up here, Romig. In two days pneumonia can take a horse of a man."

Here was another not driven by desire for gold, Romig thought, although like Romig himself, Arnold had used gold as an excuse to be where he was. The Mormon was about forty, the oldest man among the Unions. He had marched with the Mormon Battalion during the Mexican War, refusing to send back his pay when Brigham Young's collector visited the camps on the way to San Diego. That, and dereliction in California, where Arnold had stayed awhile to mine gold after his discharge from the army, probably had caused him trouble when he finally did rejoin his brothers in Deseret.

This last was only Romig's guess, for Arnold had

never told why he had stayed just two weeks in the Salt Lake Valley. He had been curt about the Civil War also, mentioning only that he had seen some of it, and he had refused to enlarge on a statement that he had once studied medicine in Philadelphia.

At Pueblo he had come to the mule corrals when he heard that a party was headed into the mountains. He had asked to join the group. He was a miner, he said, and he knew his way around the Territory.

Arnold had no medical instruments. He did not claim to be a doctor, but he was practicing medicine now, without tools and with very little medicine.

"Miss Megill would like to see you, Heber."

Arnold buttoned his coat. "It's the woman with her." He glanced at the hut from which he had just come. "Two more down the street who won't make it till morning."

"What ails the woman?"

Arnold shook his head. "Nothing—just sick of the snow and vastness up here."

"Miss Megill, that Sull—what are they—"

"I never asked their business here. I did inquire about the boy. It seems his parents abandoned him in Denver after a horse kicked him in the head and they realized that he never would be right again." Arnold smiled faintly. "You saw Miss Megill, I presume. In case you're wondering about the second woman, she is not at all like the first. She lacks the fine bone structure, the wrists and hands—"

Romig's laugh filled the air with vapor. "Wrists and hands! You're seeing her holding a plough in the Salt

13

Lake Valley."

"She could do it, Romig. You and I could do it, too; then perhaps we wouldn't have room in our heads for some of the things that trouble us."

With the wind riffling tears in his coat, Arnold went up the street.

After a moment Romig kicked the logs beside the blanketed doorway. A hoarse voice told him to enter. The room seemed hot, although the fireplace, crumbling away from log ends, held only ashes that gusts of wind were drifting across the dirt floor. The dead Kentuckian was a long lump under a Confederate blanket on one of the pole bunks.

Bitterness lay on the dark face of a long-boned man facing the door with a jug of whiskey in his hand. Black hair slanted across his forehead. He was one of the Kentuckians who had formed a little subdivision in the Southern party, Romig knew; he tried to remember the man's name.

"The Yankee preacher, huh?" Dark Indian eyes looked Romig up and down, as the man drank from his jug. "I ain't no hand for Yanks, or preachers neither, but it may be that Jim's ma will feel better when she knows he went under with a preacher handy to say a few good words."

The Kentuckian raised the jug and drank again, wiping his mouth on his shoulder. He shook the hair from his forehead, and it fell right back again. "You'll say the words?"

"I will, but I came to see if you needed any other help, digging the grave, writing a letter to his folks—

anything I can do."

"We can take care of all that, if you'll just do the mumbling. Not that I give a damn. Your words won't help Jim none, but—"

"Not that I give a damn either. The words will be to make his mother feel better."

Some of the bitterness left the Kentuckian's eyes. He lifted the jug slowly and held it toward Romig. "Rutledge is my name. I heard you was a damn' funny preacher, about half decent. Have one for Jim." Rutledge watched Romig drink, then nodded. "You handle a jug like a preacher, all right enough."

Romig had an honest drink, and one would be enough, for at this altitude whiskey was like an explosion in the muscles. "Young Malcolm has some extra canvas, I suppose?"

Rutledge nodded.

"We have a sailor in our party, Christian Muchow, who can sew a decent sack."

Rutledge repeated the name soundlessly. "We can handle our own canvas, but I'm obliged." He followed Romig outside. "Maybe you *would* write the letter, though?"

"Gladly." Romig nodded. "Was he a relative?"

"No kin. Neighbor boy. We went together in the Ninth Kentucky." Rutledge began to curse savagely. "He had to tramp all the way up here to die, after sleeping in the mud and ducking Minié balls and starving for years! Where's your God in a thing like that?"

"I don't know." Romig started away. "Send word

when you need me." He went toward the saloon, thinking of two friends from his home who had gone across the river in a borrowed boat, one to join the Rebel Ninth Kentucky Infantry, the other to join the Union Tenth Kentucky. Both were dead now.

Dill's saloon had been a gambling hall once, built on one end of a rich claim so the owners of the ground had not been inconvenienced by walking up a hill, or even down a hill, to lose their daily take of dust. The log building had two squares of four-paned windows set side by side, but there was little light getting beyond the glass when Romig forced his way inside. Men, tobacco smoke, and the smell of men were all mixed together. Remnants of blue and gray uniforms were touching by necessity. It was several moments before Romig's eyes adjusted to the gloom so that he saw clearly the man who was speaking, but had there been no light at all he would have recognized a French accent and a bear story when he heard them.

"When she rains upon the Blue, the rivair she is muddy—not with the mud—but with the yellow gold!" The Frenchman cupped hairy hands, presumably to illustrate the quantity of gold washed into the river by each raindrop. He was a jovial, murderous-looking rascal, enjoying himself fully before an appreciative audience.

Romig saw Christian Muchow's sharp face break into a grin. The sailor winked at someone and asked the storyteller, "You don't have to pan, huh? You just swish a seine through the water?"

The Frenchman nodded gravely. "That will catch some of the beeger nuggets, *oui!*" And then he rocked with laughter. He poured a drink of whiskey, rimming the glass with two fingers, while Dill, the saloonman, scowled.

"Tell us the truth about the Blue, Frenchy." That was Bruce Ruthven, leader of the Union party, a big deep-chested, black-haired Scot with eyes deep set under the dark bars of his brows. He was a quiet Pennsylvanian whom Romig had liked at first sight when they met in Independence.

The Frenchman drank his whiskey, sucking the excess above the rim before he tossed the rest. He licked his fingers, wiped his curly beard with the tassel of his cap, and grinned. "I will tell about me and the bears and gold upon the Blue."

He was a storyteller, at that, Romig thought, the vastness of his lies fitting the land, and he certainly followed the established principle that a bear story is no good if it can be believed. Midway in the yarn Romig asked the man next to him, "Where'd he come from?"

"I dunno," the man said hastily. "He just got in." Unwilling to miss a single expression of the Frenchman's face, he did not look at his questioner.

Half listening to the tale, Romig looked around him. He saw old Malcolm Alexander standing with his son, the Young Malcolm. Several times in the last few days Old Malcolm had stopped to talk to Romig. The old Scot—he must be nearly fifty—had come with the Confederate party, but he was not one of them. He had his eye out for trade in some flourishing mining camp;

and Romig suspected the other eye had come along to be kept on Young Malcolm, who at sixteen had run away from his Illinois home to join the Confederate cavalry.

Old Malcolm's face was a picture of Scotch disgust as he listened to the Frenchman.

". . . upon my back I have two hundred pounds of the gold when the first big grizzly bear, she sees me. I am not a man to run from bears, but . . ."

Romig grinned and watched expressions. He saw Hans Leibee beside a wide fireplace that threw heat up the chimney and smoke into the room to mix with the man smell and whiskey reek. Stout, aggressive, the stocky German batted impatiently at smoke rising past his fair, snow-blistered face. He was intent upon the Frenchman, but now and then his eyes wandered, and Romig saw in them something of the same look he had seen in the eyes of the boy up the street with Sull. Leibee's war had been fought inside the stockade at Andersonville after gray cavalry knocked him from his horse in Powell Valley.

On the way across the plains he had told Romig of that, but mostly the German—crouching beside the fire and working his hands as if they were already crumbling land he owned—had talked of rich bottomland in Iowa. Gold would make a dream come true for Leibee. Romig thought of his own rich farms in Ohio, land left him by his father, but the thought was merely fact without any stir or leap to it. He had no feeling for land, any more than his father had had. The soil was something that could be whipped and subdued and made a slave; then it turned sullen and had to be coaxed back to usefulness.

But if Hans Leibee or any other man could find peace in so simple a toy as ownership of land or ownership of anything, let it be so.

The Frenchman's voice was running on. "I throw this second grizzly bear one—two—three—sacks of gold. She stop!" The narrator spread his hands palms down. "She sniff!" The Frenchman sniffed with a large brown nose. He made rending gestures with his hands. "She comes faster!" The hands paddled.

The storyteller was throwing sacks of gold with both hands when Old Malcolm, his face as sour as the smell of whiskey in the room, made passage with his shoulder and headed for the door. He shook his head at Romig and threw the Frenchman a look to freeze gun grease.

Romig heard the story out, grinning. And then the Frenchman had a serious interval, during which he described placer ground on the Blue to make the vanished gold of California Gulch forgotten bagatelle.

It was not until the next day, after the Kentuckian had been buried and men were thawing ground for two more graves, that Romig began to realize just what the Frenchman had started. The man was gone by that time, having headed toward Mosquito Pass on webs, half drunk, singing, swinging his feet to the rhythm of the tassel on his cap.

Romig, Ruthven, Muchow and Arnold shared a small cabin. They were eating fried corn-meal mush from messkits on their bunks when Muchow asked

Ruthven, "Day after tomorrow?"

"If the Rebs don't start sooner," Ruthven said. He looked quickly at Romig. "We're going to the Blue. Oh, I know the Frog was lying even when he tried to be serious, but the people around here say there was gold found on the Blue before the war, at a place called Fort Marabee."

"I was there," Arnold said. "There was some gold." He smiled. "But not to throw at bears."

Muchow's green eyes were glowing. "At least, it isn't all worked out—like this place. The first bunch over the hill—"

"Hill," Arnold mused.

"—will get the pick of the ground." Muchow forked his mush.

Romig looked around the draughty cabin. It was gloomy in here, even with the door propped half open. The place smelled of deadness. He never had cared much for walls of any kind around him. "I'm for moving on," he said.

Arnold wiped grease from his beard with a white handkerchief. He was the only man west of the Missouri Romig had seen with a clean handkerchief, one of the few he had seen with any kind. "We'll have to go down the river about forty miles, skirt the Mosquito Range, and then turn west in South Park," the Mormon said.

"Too far that way," Ruthven said. "The Rebs will go straight through from here."

"There's a pass, yes," Arnold said. "But I wouldn't advise trying it—at this time of year—without webs."

"According to what the natives say, we can't take the mules," Romig said. "That means we won't have enough tools to do any good when we get there."

"The Rebs are taking theirs," Muchow said stubbornly.

It came to Romig then how deep the old war infection was, for Muchow, like Ruthven, had proved himself steady and cool on the long haul from Independence; but now his sharp features were set defiantly. "We can take mules where they can," he said.

Arnold nodded. "The animals belong to you and Ruthven, but I would not like to see them dead in the snow."

Ruthven rose and put his messkit by the fire. His head almost touched the ridge log when he straightened. Poor light gave his skin a swarthy cast, put sullenness around his mouth and along the heavy markings of his brows. "I'm going to the Blue," he said. "I'll take my mules. Let Malcolm Alexander do what he pleases."

"You *know* the Southerners are going?" Romig asked.

Muchow grunted. "They're not squaring away their gear for nothing."

Arnold nodded. "They are going. They intend to use a pass that Fremont crossed years ago, but my advice is still to go the long way and try Hoosier Pass—and that will be more than enough trouble. Once you're over Hoosier, you're right at the headwaters of the Blue, and—"

"Too far that way," Muchow said. He and Ruthven

looked at each other in complete agreement.

Arnold kicked a pitch limb toward the fire. He watched it for a moment, then looked at Romig with a faint smile, and lay back on his bunk.

That day the North and South made work of ignoring each other. Shrewd looks of calculation replaced hostility. Men met in little groups. They raised their heads frequently to appraise the peaks. They sorted packs, checked the mules, redivided gear. In the saloon, Romig listened to the Frenchman damned by everyone as a liar. All agreed on that: Frenchy had not spoken one single word of truth about anything.

Wind fretted at the corners of the building. It threw smoke back down the chimney, and then went keening to the snow flats beside the frozen Arkansas. Cold rolled under the door and gnawed through worn boots.

There were men who felt the cold and heard the wind, Romig observed; but the wind was carrying also a song of gold waiting on the Blue—and that was not so far away.

Romig had no need of gold and only faint desire for it, but he was going. He might be able, he thought, to help bring two bitter groups to understanding of each other. It was a small step, but it also might prove a step toward the understanding Jonathan Romig wanted of himself and God. There was that—and there was, too, the bright beckoning of motion and adventure.

The Blue. The Valley of the Blue. It must be a beautiful place. All places lying just out of sight were beautiful in Romig's mind.

CHAPTER 2

Y OU'RE GOING UP THE PASS and get your belly wet?" Romig asked Arnold the day before departure, when neither party pretended secrecy.

Arnold nodded. He was squatted by the fireplace, trimming a broken fingernail. Muchow and Ruthven were somewhere in the gulch storing their minds with details of sluice construction.

"Why?" Romig asked.

"It's a little closer to Zion."

Sprawled on a pole bunk built for a man a foot shorter, Romig raised on his elbow to see the Mormon's face. "You've been a long time returning to Salt Lake."

"I have. But now I'm going, by degrees."

"You'll practice medicine out there?"

Arnold put his knife away. "The Saints have no use for doctors—not that I consider myself one."

"Why not?"

Arnold hesitated, looking at his jacket on a wooden peg. "I studied about two and a half years. I worked seven months with a physician-preceptor in Philadelphia. I was learning. I had hopes of going to Vienna. The war came, and I went south. You'll never know, Romig, what they lacked. From First Manassas on I was a surgeon." He took his jacket down. "That is, I was called a surgeon."

Quacks became doctors overnight. In some of the

states men leaped from pharmacy to medicine by changing residence. Integrity was deep in Arnold, and yet, Romig thought, there must be more than that behind the Mormon's disavowal.

"Suppose we find gold," Romig said. "Why couldn't you resume your studies?"

Arnold donned his jacket with quick movements. "You could return to the ministry. You don't need gold for that."

"My case is diff—"

"You jumped the traces to look for something wise men never found." Arnold moved toward the door. "You left a creed. I don't know why, but I do know that, unless a man has a creed to follow, he has nothing to believe except what suits his wilfulness. Then he's lost his way and knows it, and tries to cover up by thinking that he's seeking God—or following God— unhampered by narrow restrictions."

"Am I like that?" Assurance that had been strong as a weight inside Romig was washed with chilling uncertainty.

The Mormon paused at the door. "No," he said slowly, "I don't believe you are. I'd say you had the strength to rise above wilfulness and find a compromise between what you can know and what you would like to know."

"I want no compromise."

Arnold nodded, smiling gently. "You believe that now, but time generally straightens the ranks." He thinned mobile lips and cocked his head. "You and Brigham Young have the same sort of power inside. He has used his as God directed. Be careful, Romig, what you do with yours."

Arnold went out and closed the door before Romig could hold him with a question; he left behind a puzzled man who could feel within himself none of the power Arnold had described, but only uncertainty born of not knowing whether he was seeking something or being pushed by urges that would not bear examination.

The cabin was narrow, rank with the odor of dead time. Romig went outside. He breathed deeply of the thin needles of the air and looked at mountains pushing into a bright sky. Looking was enough. Romig knew he was not wrong in going on. He had to.

Old Malcolm Alexander, a stout pipe in his teeth, a belligerent thrust to his short sandy whiskers, beckoned Romig to join him on the lee side of the saloon.

"Ye're going?" Old Malcolm asked.

"Uh-huh."

The Scot scowled at snow pennants on the crags, and his face said the world was full of idiots. "The twa packs will like be gray as rats befoor finding gold where a heathen, runagate Frenchmon says."

"Aye," Romig said, and grinned.

"Aye!" Old Malcolm shot him a hard glance and then looked back at the peaks. "Fine curling weather oop there, the noo." He cleared his throat. "This bairn of mine . . ." he said gruffly. He scowled and made gurgling sounds with his pipe. "This bairn of mine . . ." He grunted.

"A strapping lad who can play the pipes to make

your blood dance, that Young Malcolm."

"With a head like a piece of oak," Old Malcolm said, his way to criticism cleared. "Sensible trade? No! Oop the mountain he must go—like a wild bear wallowing in the snow." He took the pipe from his teeth. "And Bruce Ruthven—a fine lad, Chaplain, but stubborn like Young Malcolm. Mony's the time I've had business with Bruce Ruthven's ain father in Philadelphia, and a fine mon." Old Malcolm shook his head. "They're headstrong lads, ye ken, Romig—like two young stallions." The Scot scowled. "The Young Malcolm is hiring a guide, a little mon named Bull. A hundred dollars. Foolish." He spat. "Trooble, Romig."

Trouble was right. The Unions could bide their time, follow in a broken trail, and have the services of a guide—all for nothing; and that, Romig knew, was just what Ruthven would do.

"Another thing," Old Malcolm said. "This Virginian that the bairn thinks so well aboot—Joel Roberts. He's a bad one. He'll make trooble."

Romig did not know the man.

Old Malcolm pointed with his pipe at the mountains. "If they last to get over the likes of those, the twa bunches will be together. Then watch for trooble, Romig. Keep your eye on, Roberts; and when the Young Malcolm and Ruthven start at each other's throats, cool them with a club."

"Why me?" Romig asked.

"I've watched ye. Whatever ye thought aboot the war, ye're not thinking of it the noo. Anybody but a bellowing heathen—like that Frenchmon—will listen to a preacher. Ye've got the legs and arms of a hammer thrower, Romig, and a voice more suited for the crags than a kirk. Use it! Blast them with your voice! Smite them with your hands, a club, a rifle barrel! We want no fools murdering each other."

Old Malcolm put his pipe between his teeth and burbled tar in the stem until he realized he had no fire. When he spoke again, it was in a normal voice. "Trade's the thing." He jerked his thumb toward the logs behind him. "Mind this, that robber Dill will make eight hundred dollars on one barrel of bad whiskey. Ye can drown in a river a-looking for gold befoor ye find eight hundred dollars—not that I will deal in whiskey."

As Romig went up the street a few minutes later, he saw a figure in a white *capote* standing on the hill where he had climbed the day before. As he passed Sull's cabin, the door opened and the Irishman stood there with Timmy peering around his legs. Sull nodded, and watched Romig start up the hill.

The wind was whipping at Charity Megill's woolen skirts, pushing her heavy clothes against her. Long-limbed, Romig observed, unbraced with stiff fabric, whalebone and a million laces. The hood of her *capote* was back, and her rich brown hair shone against the snow. There was a clean firmness of chin and mouth that made him remember what he had said to Arnold about her ploughing fields. Yes, she had the look of one who could plough if she chose; and behind the appraisal of her eyes he sensed a depth of fire that could lead a man to hell, if she set her mind on taking him there.

She smiled as he approached. "You walk as if you were going all the way today, Mr. Romig."

That had been a favorite expression of his father's, pleasing to hear again. "I was just coming up for my usual view." Romig smiled. "And a greatly improved one, too."

"I see you haven't spent all your time in the pulpit, Mr. Romig. Or did you learn that sort of thing bowing to the women when your congregation was going out?"

"I didn't bow enough." Romig turned to look across the valley. A storm was blowing along the great triangular planes. Clouds were rolling like battle smoke in the troughs of the wooded V's that ran to white slopes. For a moment, on one of the highest wedges, the wind ripped snow aside and exposed the gleaming point. And then the storm raged back.

Perhaps, Romig mused, he did have a little of the strength Arnold had mentioned: courage to go on until somewhere beyond the ranges of what was easy to accept he should catch a glimpse of certainty as solid as the height he had seen for just an instant.

Eyes blank with musing, he kept looking at the storm.

CHAPTER 3

NOT EVERYONE was going to the Blue. Some remembered the snow they had fought to reach Oro City. They liked the feel of cabin walls around them, and they looked four thousand feet above them and shook their heads. They would make other plans.

But some looked at the peaks and laughed. A mountain was just a lot of land tipped up. They had walked over plenty of land, at least a thousand miles during the war, not to mention the trip out here. So said Young Malcolm Alexander in the saloon, for all to hear. He had been in the cavalry, but he said it just the same.

Romig found him later with another man checking packsaddles at one of the corrals.

"Hi, Parson. How's sin?" was Malcolm's greeting. The second man said nothing.

Sin was doing well, Romig said, and eyed the mules. "You're taking them, of course?"

"Damned right!" Young Malcolm said. "Ruthven would be tickled to death to get over there with tools to spare—while we had none."

A man to anger in a flash and cool off the same way, Romig thought. There was nothing personal in Young Alexander's attitude, just the undisciplined flaring of a mind that readily reached out to challenge. He was a powerful youngster, with a cavalryman's back. He had his father's blunt-jawed face and a suggestion of its steadiness, but the expression was merely hovering as if unsure of a place to light.

"Ruthven is another hardhead," Romig said. "Maybe both of you will get some comfort when neither of you get the mules across."

"They're *our* mules, Yankee Man of God." The insolence of that voice was studied, brutal.

Romig looked closely at the second man. This would

be Joel Roberts, the Virginian Old Malcolm had mentioned, for if ever a man's tone asked for trouble, Roberts's did. He was a slender man, with cold blue eyes. His face was finely molded, dark and narrow . . . clean from recent shaving.

"They are your mules," Romig agreed, and looked back at Malcolm. "I came here mainly to talk about the guide you've hired."

"What about him?" Roberts asked.

"Let the man talk, Roberts!" Young Malcolm said.

"It would be fair if both parties shared the guide's expenses," Romig suggested.

Roberts spat a short word. "Keep your Yankee money!"

"We don't need it," Young Malcolm said. He grinned. "Who commissioned you to bind up the wounds of brotherhood?"

Romig smiled. "Two bunches of roosters." He could not keep the smile when he looked at Roberts. "You know Heber Arnold, don't you?"

Roberts did not answer.

"The Mormon? Sure," Malcolm said.

"He was a surgeon in the Confederate army, there from First Manassas. Do you like him, Roberts?"

"Those surgeons," Roberts said, "took care of Yanks along with anybody else. To hell with your Doctor Arnold—and his forty wives."

Romig felt his temper surging, but he held his voice even. "You're just about to hell with everything, aren't you, Roberts?"

"Everything Yankee, particularly mealy-mouthed

preachers that gallop up a hill like a studhorse at sight of a mare."

Malcolm laughed.

Romig walked away with his face white. An instant longer and he would have smashed Roberts's curling lips and ruined everything he was trying to do. His mother had always said that temper was a Romig curse. The man striding up the street did not know the truth of that, but he did know that he had turned from Roberts just in time.

Hans Leibee stopped him near the saloon. The keg-chested German leaned close, poking with a mittened finger. "I haf found something out, Vromig." His eyes moved sidewise with his flaxen beard. "Two of dese Rebels vas in the Fifty-fifth Georgia!"

Finding no significance in that, Romig said, "So?"

"Dere!" Leibee nodded toward the saloon.

Two stringy lads in fur caps had come out. Brothers, perhaps twins, Romig thought, loose-jointed, long-haired lads whose faces did not take well to snow glare. They stood on the porch blowing their breath to watch the vapor.

"Guards at Andersonville!" Leibee whispered.

"Those two? How do you know?"

"Dey was in the Fifty-fifth Georgia. I heard dem say it!"

The two lads began to wrestle, trying to shove each other into a pile of deep snow. They both fell off the porch. They came up laughing and ran down the street throwing snow crusts at each other.

Leibee shook his head. "Dem poys! Shooting hungry

31

people dot crawled in the sand!" All the old misery was on the German's face, and hatred, too.

Romig clapped him on the shoulder. "We're going after gold, Hans. Given a little luck, you'll wind up with a stretch of Iowa bottomland you can't see across!"

Leibee's face began to relax. "I get dot land, Vromig! I haf seen it." He raised his arms chest high and made crumbling gestures with plaid mittens.

He was nodding to himself and smiling when Romig went into the saloon.

Both parties had planned to start at dawn. Dawn came, full sunlight followed and found disorganization and foul tempers. Many had celebrated their going the night before, drinking by flatland standards. Now they were hard to move. Others, red-hot for the trip the day before, shivered in the cold and went back inside their cabins, minds changed. There were new divisions of packs and gear. Two Union men, one going, the other staying, fought over ownership of a frying pan. Romig heard South Carolinians cursing Georgians and Georgia's puny efforts in the war. The mules were packed and unpacked. Tempers ran and reason fled. Those whose purpose withered at the last moment were called cowards by their comrades, and in turn called their comrades damned fools.

One party had no more trouble than the other. Romig heard Young Malcolm raging when a mule had to be unpacked a second time to take off a side of bacon belonging to a Kentuckian who had changed his mind. "There'll be Yanks with grandchildren over there before we get started!" Malcolm yelled. He threatened to go on alone, and hotheads told him to take his mules and himself and go to hell.

Ruthven did not rage at the Unions, but he was nettled by delays and arguments, and the black bars of his brows were darker from his scowling. "Muchow and I are willing to risk our mules to pack tools and food for the rest, and they can't make up their minds to move— the lead-butts!" he told Romig.

Romig grinned. "We'll get started soon enough. Two months early, I think."

Ready to go, Arnold sat for hours beside the fire and read scraps of a four-year-old Chicago newspaper he had dug from pine needles under one of the bunks. "When the great moment arrives, let me know." He smiled and tried to fit two stained fragments of print together.

It was midmorning before order leveled out of confusion. Led by a little mountaineer named Ephraim Bull, the Southerners went first, swinging out with a chorus of yells. A few fired rifles. Some carried jugs. The Unions gave them a quarter of a mile start and then moved out on the broken trail.

Shrouded with blowing snow, the mountains lay ahead. Behind were the careful and afraid, Oro City with its look of death and its dead upon the slopes in shallow graves. The gulch wound on. There came the sound of bagpipes, wild as the land ahead.

"Young Malcolm has wind to spare," Arnold said.

Before timber cut from view the last of Oro City, Romig saw a figure standing on the hill where he had talked to Charity Megill. He kept looking back until he stumbled.

"Try this." Muchow thrust a short round case against Romig's arm.

Romig stepped from the trail and ran out the telescope, feeling polished brass warm from Muchow's body. It was an honest glass that brought the woman's face close. She was standing with her hood thrown back, tall against the white slope, looking straight at Romig.

He ran the tubes together and hurried to regain his place. Even the mules had passed by that time. For a while Romig was oddly disturbed; then the wailing of the pipes came down the wind, and far ahead he caught a glimpse of Shining Mountains through the storm.

CHAPTER 4

BY EARLY AFTERNOON they had crossed timbered flats and gone downhill to reach a little valley. The way was not steep. The mountains on either hand did not look high; then suddenly a pyramid of granite peered from the V-notch of lesser mountains.

The going had been comparatively easy for the Northern party, and they knew it, for three times they had slowed down to keep their distance while the Confederates fought stubborn drifts ahead.

Romig said to Ruthven, "What if I go up and pay their guide half his fee?"

From under the heavy arches of his brows Ruthven sent a steady look. "Will a simple thing like money help get what you're after, Chaplain?"

"It might."

"If Malcolm Alexander had suggested in Oro City that we share the cost of the guide, I would have agreed," Ruthven said. "Although from what the natives said of this pass, any fool can find his way across."

There was probity in Ruthven that was reassuring.

"You hold no bitterness from the war?" Romig asked.

"Not like that slim Virginian with Alexander."

Muchow laughed. "*You* didn't lose, Ruthven."

"I lost two brothers," Ruthven said.

Romig forged ahead. He passed the Confederate mules, where Roberts seemed to be in charge. There was surliness among all the Southerners, springing no doubt from the realization that they were doing most of the work for both parties. They were walking as Romig had seen men walk on battlefields, relaxed, seemingly careless with their rifles. Fourteen, he counted, including Young Malcolm up ahead with the guide.

One man spoke to Romig as he passed, Rutledge, the dark-faced Kentuckian who had stood with a jug of whiskey beside a dead companion. "Hi, Parson," he drawled, and watched curiously as Romig went on toward the leaders.

Clad in buckskin and beaver fur, Ephraim Bull, the guide, was a chunky little man with coal-black whiskers who looked as tough as the trunk of a dead pinion tree. A fur cap, worn and shiny around the edges, rested well below his ears. He carried web snowshoes on his back.

Bull looked at Romig sharply and spat tobacco juice. The guide's nose, Romig observed, was curiously crumpled.

Without slacking his fight against the snow, Malcolm glanced around. "Hi, Chaplain."

The guide gave Romig another glance of incisive appraisal.

"What are you going to say, Alexander, if I pay the guide half his fee right now?"

Malcolm kept thrusting at the snow. "Keep your money."

Romig looked at Bull and saw at a glance that the whiskered man had grasped the situation. "Been paid?" Romig asked.

Bull sent a shrewd look back toward the Union party. He shook his head. "Alexander hired me, but if someone insists on paying half the money, and then the lad here wants to pay me in full when we reach the pass, I'll take—"

"The hell!" Malcolm said. "If Romig pays half—" His anger faded when he saw Bull and Romig grinning at each other. He watched greenbacks from Romig's hand disappear somewhere under the rat's nest of the guide's knee-length furs. "That's half your fee, remember," Malcolm said. He looked at Romig. "You paid it, Chaplain. Don't expect me to say it came from Ruthven or from any of the rest behind!"

"No need to say anything, is there?" Bull asked. "If it just happens to be known that half my money is already—"

"I'll take pains to explain that a meddling preacher

paid the shot." Roberts had come up behind them. There was challenge in his voice, a press of coldness behind his narrow features. "Why don't you stay where you belong, Preacher?"

Ephraim Bull rolled his cud and spat. His eyes were like sharp points. "The land out this way is pretty free, Son."

He stepped up beside Malcolm, and Romig took the other side. For a time they broke trail three-men wide, a waste of energy, but a rebuke to Roberts.

"What part of the South are you from?" Bull asked the Scot.

"Illinois," Malcolm said.

"By Ned! I knew that war was going to be a crazy thing—even before 'fifty-seven when the panic busted me and run me west."

"You stayed here, huh?" Malcolm's tone carried disparagement of such a weak-kneed act as avoiding war.

"Yep! I sure did." Ephraim was undisturbed. "How much you got in the mules, Alexander?"

This weathered little man was wise, Romig thought. His value in keeping peace would be great; but Romig wanted more than peace. He wanted unity.

"I got plenty in those brutes," Malcolm said. He adjusted the position of an odd-looking rifle slung on his back, and pushed his leather bagpipe carrier around to the side. "They're better mules than Ruthven's."

Ephraim sprayed the snow. "They'll be the same value dead."

"We heard you the last time you said that," Roberts sneered.

"You'll see it happen." Ephraim whipped off his fur cap. The shine of near-baldness in contrast to coal-black whiskers was startling.

Romig stared at indecent-looking twists of red flesh where ears should have been. "Remember what you see," Ephraim said. He slapped the cap back on, low across his forehead. "In the middle of June I froze those ears on Argentine Pass. When they started to slough I did the job with a knife. Froze my nose too, but I didn't have the guts to tackle that, and it got well—in a way. Sometimes when the cold hits it, I wish I'd sliced it off—right across my throat."

Someone in the Rebel column began to sing *The Bonny Blue Flag*, and slowly others joined in.

"Before you lads get through with this deal, you'll have some respect for the mountains," Ephraim said. "Not much higher than this you'll be picking flowers one minute, and the next a blizzard will be biting at your marrow."

"Now tell us about grizzly bears and Indians, Grandpa," Roberts said.

"You'll thaw a lot of ice between your fine Virginia toes before you ever see either—Son," Ephraim answered.

Malcolm laughed. He took the bagpipe from its carrier, inflated it, and began to play the fierce old Jacobite melody the Southerners were singing.

The piercing notes ran up and down Romig's spine in hot tingles. He knew why the piper was called the most dangerous man in battle. Malcolm's tune had caused fat Brunswick kings to stir uneasily; it was potent enough to challenge this wilderness of snow.

Romig stepped off the trail when the last note died. No one was singing now, but the song had left a flush, a remembrance of bitterness. Hostile eyes looked at the man standing beside the trail that others had broken. Only Rutledge nodded as he slouched past.

The Rebels' mules went by with steaming breaths. Wounds on their legs, cut by crusted snow on the way to Oro City, were bleeding again.

The Unions came up strongly in the broken trail.

"You paid the man, no doubt?" Ruthven said. "And you suggested we take turns breaking trail?"

Romig grinned. "One thing at a time. We may come to breaking trail together with no help of mine."

Arnold looked at the wrinkled mountains. "We'll come to it—one way or another."

Camped among lodgepole pines that night, on a southern slope where the snow was only two feet deep, the Confederates built their fires a few hundred yards closer to the pass than the Northern men.

After supper Romig said, "I think I'll put my big nose into the Southern camp again."

Muchow was sloshing snow water in a messkit. "Why don't you join 'em?" He was almost serious, but he broke the temper of his words with a grin.

"All right," Romig said. "What's your biggest complaint about the war?"

Muchow dumped the snow water and looked with distaste at a scum of grease still in the utensil. "I have nothing personal against this bunch, but . . . It's hard to forget some things. I was captured when an idiot decided we ought to retake the ruins of Fort Sumter. I wound up at Libby Prison. Three of pig-faced Dick Turner's guards beat hell out of me when I refused to give up my peacoat and sixty dollars I had in the lining." He refilled the messkit with snow and held it over the fire. "They got the coat and the money, of course. I got three cracked ribs and a broken wrist. What hurt me most, later on, was the swill we had to eat. Before they moved me to Belle Island, I got away."

"They didn't have much to eat themselves," Romig said.

"That wasn't my fault."

"Men got worse treatment than you—from both sides. At our own prison in Elmira—"

"I only know what happened to me," Muchow said. "And that's what you asked about."

It was an honest reply, Romig had to admit.

Arnold came up from doctoring the legs of mules.

"There's one of your Rebels," Romig said. "What do you think of him?"

"He really didn't belong with the Johnnies," Ruthven said. He was sitting on a log, feeding a tube of cartridges into the magazine of a Spencer rifle he had just finished oiling. "I don't know why Heber went South, but you can tell at a glance that it wasn't to play at war—like Malcolm Alexander, who probably thought he was going off to a Crusade."

"I went where help was needed most." Arnold stared at the fire. "Is the war going on forever?"

"Ask these young cockies." Romig started toward the Confederate camp.

Ruthven called after him, "I'll not share breaking trail with Malcolm Alexander! He went out of Oro City like he owned the mountains. Let's see how far that flourish of pipes will take him."

Ruthven and Malcolm had seen each other for the first time in Oro City, Romig knew, and they had disliked each other on sight. Even if they had not been on different sides in the war, they still would not have had any use for each other.

Romig's boots made swishing sounds against the snow. The wind was stilled now. Ahead, the heights looked bluish in the gloom.

From somewhere outside his conscious mind Charity Megill's face leaped up as he had last seen it through Muchow's glass. Only twice had he talked to her, but something in her bearing had left an indelible impression. It was well, perhaps, that he would never see her again, for a woman like her could be the instrument to bring him to the compromise Arnold had talked about. But she had been strong and beautiful to look upon . . .

He came into the light of the Confederate fires.

Like the Unions, the Southerners had brought one large tent where everyone would sleep; and like the other party, they had scattered their fires according to the habits of war bivouac. Beside the first one Romig saw Rutledge and the two boys who, according to Leibee, had been guards at Andersonville.

His hat on the back of his head, Indian-straight hair slanting across his forehead, Rutledge held a jug high in the crotch of his thumb and hailed Romig. "Have a swig of panther piss, Parson?"

Romig refused the drink, and Rutledge took no offense. He introduced the lads beside him. "The Greene twins from down Georgia way. Good boys for swamp hogs, but they're more used to rain water than whiskey." He scowled at the twins. "This is the fellow come up to help me with Jim when the rest run off to hear that foreigner tell bear stories."

Romig said he was glad to know the Georgians, and asked their first names and ages. Sampson and Will, they said, twenty years old. They might be seventeen, Romig estimated.

"Were you men with the Fifty-fifth Georgia at Andersonville?" he asked.

One said, "Samp was. I fit before Atlanta. Didn't I, Art?" he asked Rutledge.

Art Rutledge was staring at the fire. "I fit from hell to breakfast," he mused. He had another drink before Romig left to find Ephraim Bull.

The little mountaineer was sitting with Malcolm and Roberts on logs resting on crossbars lashed to trees. Their fire was backed by a heat reflector of green poles, an arrangement Romig noted for future use. Ephraim was greasing boots with tallow. Malcolm was polishing the odd-looking rifle Romig had seen that day. Roberts was merely sitting, looking at the flames. He raised his head quickly when Romig approached. "The great plenipotentiary comes!"

Romig included Roberts in his greeting and watched civility break against the Virginian's arrogance.

"Find any gold we missed along the trail, Chaplain?" Ephraim asked.

Romig spread his hands to the fire. "Only a small basketful or so. Little nuggets, not well shaped."

Malcolm smiled at his rifle. From the attention he was giving the stock—curly maple with a raised cheek rest—it was evident that the piece meant more to him than something to shoot.

"That's a beautiful rifle, Malcolm," Romig said. "I don't recall ever seeing one like that before."

"You won't either!" Malcolm's face took on a boyish look. He handed the piece to Romig. "Ruthven and that damned Spencer of his! I could shoot rings around him—and this rifle is almost a hundred years old."

"A beautiful gun," Romig said. At first he thought it was a flintlock, and then he saw that it had been altered to percussion. He turned the browned barrel toward the fire to read the Crown marks.

"My father's great-grandfather wrestled a British soldier for it at King's Mountain," Malcolm said. "It's a Ferguson. That's a rising-screw breech lock. . . . Push the trigger guard forward." Malcolm watched as Romig dropped the breech. "It was the first breech-loading flintlock ever used in America. I had it changed to percussion, but the rest—that stocking to the muzzle and everything else—is just like it was made, and the bore is clean as glass."

Scotch rebels wrestling rifles from duly constituted authority a hundred years before, Romig thought. They had won, and consequently were no longer rebels but patriots. "That's certainly a beautiful piece, Alexander," Romig said. He returned the rifle.

Roberts thrust out one boot. "See that, Yankee? The

first boot made in America with a hole in the top and bottom. Praise it, Yankee; lick it if you want to." He laughed. "A beautiful gun, Malcolm!"

"For Christ's sake, Roberts!" Malcolm said.

Ephraim gave the Virginian a pitying look.

"You don't like my boots?" Roberts made soft sounds with his lips. "But you like the rifle, and Malcolm is a fool about it, so having worked on that weak spot, you may now get on with your talk of the brotherhood that must be rebuilt, now that the frightful war is over. Shall we start with a little prayer, Chaplain?"

Romig beat down his anger, and when he knew that he had won, it came to him that anger or violence would never work with Roberts. There was calculated invitation to violence on the Virginian's face all the time.

Romig let the challenge pass. He looked at Ephraim. "Will the snow be like this all the way?"

Ephraim spat. His eyes saluted Romig's control. "Worse. Trail breaking will be hell by tomorrow afternoon." He sent another sizzling discharge against a log where the flames were curling. "But—nobody ever learned anything from being told." He touched his cap near one ear.

Young Malcolm's face was sober for the first time since Romig had known him.

"Praise the little man's ears and nose, Brother Romig," Roberts mocked. "Be mealy-mouthed and gentle."

Without anger, Romig said, "I wonder if breaking you in two would make you whole, Roberts?"

"Trying to find out would make a hole in one more Yankee." Roberts's words fell softly, burnished with deadly sincerity.

Romig glanced at Ephraim and walked away. His words had been a thought spoken aloud and had not been intended as a challenge to the Virginian, but they had emerged like childish prattle. There was no help for men like Roberts. They were the core of things that might forever block the way to Shining Mountains for all men. But the thought could not last long. Before Romig passed the first fire, where South Carolinians held silence as he walked by, he had thrown away the easily accepted conviction concerning Joel Roberts.

There was help for any man—not qualified by if, if, if. For every creature created in His image there were Shining Mountains standing pure and clear, summits that had been waiting for an eternity. Men would climb them someday, helping those who faltered on the way. But *someday* was too remote for Romig. There ought to be a way, for him to help a few men now.

Somewhere behind him Young Malcolm's voice rose angrily. "Sometimes you act like a damned idiot, Roberts!"

Roberts's laugh was clear. "What a perfectly lovely rifle you have, Mr. Alexander. Will you bring it to my Sunday School to show the little Federal bastards?"

Art Rutledge was weaving drunk when Romig neared the last fire. The Greene twins were gone, and Rutledge was standing with a blocky man whose curly whiskers looked as if they might snap and crackle in the frosty air if rubbed. The fellow wore a bedraggled Confederate officer's hat.

"Rough day tomorrow, Art," the chunky man said. He tapped his boot against a jug at his feet. "Forget that and get a bed with me in the tent before the best places are full of lousy South Carolinians."

"Hell, Jake!" Rutledge waved his hand at the world. "Do I want to, I'll stay right here and drink all night!"

"Let me keep that jug for you tonight, Rutledge," Romig said.

Rutledge gave Romig confused but savage attention. "Tech it, Mister, and I'll stick this in to the hilt and walk clean around you!" He fumbled with a bone-handled knife in his belt.

"And ruin my supper?" Romig laughed. He stooped, caught the jug by the neck and backed away with it. "Now forget that knife," he said in a conversational tone, and never knew just why he was sure that Rutledge would obey.

The Kentuckian stood with his mouth hanging open, teeth gleaming in the firelight. He slipped the half-drawn blade back into its sheath. "By God, Jake!" he said. "It's the Yankee preacher. He come to the cabin—"

"There goes your whiskey. I'll slit the thievin' bastard's throat!"

"Shet up, Jake Rutledge!" the drunken man shouted. "You shet up about that preacher, you hear me! You get to hell to bed. Where at is that goddamn tent anyway? Cousin Jake, let me tell you something about your big mouth . . ."

Romig went toward his camp with the whiskey sloshing in time to his stride. If poison could be taken from men's minds as easily as he had snatched the whiskey, the tiny step he was trying to make would be simple indeed. He wondered again why he had ever thought that Rutledge, drunk as he was, would put his knife away. If he had not—well, he had.

Union men getting ready to bed down in their tent stared curiously when Romig entered with the jug.

"You must have licked the whole Rebel camp to get away with that," Ruthven said.

Red-bearded Ezekiel Davis, an East Tennesseean, licked his lips. "I could stand a gurgle of that, Chaplain. Feels like a fearful cold night a-coming."

Romig shook his head. "This isn't mine, Zeke, but if you have to have a drink I've got a pint bottle in my pack."

Slope-shouldered Job Davis, Zeke's brother, spoke quickly through broken teeth and lips that had been mangled by a Confederate carbine butt at Seven Pines. "Zeke don't need no whiskey, and he knows it."

"I guess I don't," Zeke said. "But happen I see a jug, it reminds me of setting in the yard at home, with the fire bugs flying around and some old hound mourning at the moon, and Ma rocking steady and easy on the porch. . . . But I guess I don't need no drink." He began to spread blankets.

With only boots and jacket off and lumpy objects removed from his pockets, Romig stretched out in a bulky buffalo-robe sleeping bag his father had owned. The raw sides of the skins were covered with waterproof canvas. The hair sides were rare "silks."

Firelight began to die against the front of the tent. Cold became a creeping, powerful force. The last American frontier was deathly hushed.

Snug in the long silky hairs, his nose warmed by his own breath, Romig dozed, and just before he fell asleep he was standing in the snow talking to Charity Megill.

Cold unknown to Cumberland hillsides or Southern swamps walked through the canvas walls. Men hugged their arms against their chests. They dozed and groaned and fought the snow again. Hans Leibee whimpered in his sleep. In a shelter under spare canvas the blanketed mules stamped restlessly, shaking their heads to warm their ears.

Several times during the night Romig half roused and heard shivering men rebuilding the fires and cursing the cold.

Thick slices of bacon and bitter coffee brought new life at breakfast. The sky was bright above the reaching tips of lodgepole pines. Far ahead the peaks cut the sky so sharply it seemed to Romig that the summits must be razor thin.

After breakfast Ruthven said to Romig, "Last night while you were gone we decided to rest here a day. Everybody but Arnold voted for it."

Muchow grinned.

"I see," Romig said. "We rest. They break trail. Then in a few hours we can cover the ground it took them all day to make."

Ruthven nodded. "We'll see how Malcolm

Alexander likes that."

They heard the Southerners pull out with yells, and soon the sound of Malcolm's pipes came shrilling back.

Heber Arnold looked at Romig and shrugged.

CHAPTER 5

MEN RESTED WELL in the Union camp that night. Following Arnold's suggestion, they split seams near the peak of the tent, propped the canvas open with forked sticks, and set one-hour watches to keep a small fire going inside.

They took the trail at sunrise with energy to spare; some were grumbling that the delay might have given the other party a lead that could not be overcome.

It was a warm day, almost windless. In fifteen minutes men were shedding coats and extra shirts. They sweated. They squinted fiercely against snow glare. Even in a broken trail the drag of snow began to tell. In places the bellies of the mules were covered.

Romig had worked warm tallow into his boots until the leather had been like wilted lettuce, but even so his feet were wet.

To the left there lay the promise of a pass.

Arnold lifted a piece of crust from the edge of the trail. "Four inches thick, but rotten. Those boys ahead must be just about all in by now."

Before noon they came up to the Southerners. For a long time the leading party had been in sight, appearing to Romig to be stopped dead, but when he got closer he saw the column was moving slowly. He was beside Ruthven when they caught up with the Confederate mules, which looked around wearily as if for help.

"What now, great strategist?" Arnold asked Ruthven.

"We go around them," Ruthven said.

He started. The crust broke under him. He wallowed helplessly for a few moments. He lunged and broke the snow ahead with his arms and fought on for a short distance. No one followed. They looked ahead at the rumps of tired mules, at snow-soaked Confederates with bloodshot eyes.

"That's quite a waste of effort, Ruthven," Romig said. He looked at those behind. "You fellows want to tackle that—or share the trail breaking with the South?"

"I don't care much about any part of the whole mess right now," someone said wryly, and brought a laugh.

"Two trails is foolish!" Leibee said. "I vill break the snow with anyone to get out of this!"

Muchow leaned out on the crust to see what was going on ahead. He pushed out his lower lip dubiously. "If we're to get anywhere before summer, I guess we'll have to help. Ruthven!"

Ruthven stood where he was for several moments, one leg up, the other down. He turned and wallowed back, not looking at Romig. Ahead, Confederates jeered. Stubbornness died slowly on Ruthven's heavy face.

"I underestimated things a little, I guess." He looked at Romig then. "Let's go up and talk to them."

Romig, Leibee, Muchow and Ruthven pushed on ahead past sullen men standing hip-deep in a narrow trench. If the broken trail had been bad, one glance at drooping shoulders and sweating faces showed what the first attack had been. They passed Art Rutledge, rubbing reddened hands together, wet leather mittens balanced on his shoulder. He grinned at Romig. "Got my whiskey, Chaplain?"

Romig nodded. "You want to come up with us and talk to Malcolm about both parties sharing the heavy work?"

"By God, yes!" Rutledge fell in behind Muchow. "There ought to be some way we could plow this stuff out'n—"

"Yes! Ve should haf a steam locomotive!" Leibee said with an attempt at sarcasm that turned to humor.

Roberts was coming toward them, making no attempt to share the trail. Romig turned sidewise and leaned back to let him pass. The Virginian bumped against Ruthven and started to plough past Muchow in like manner, but the sailor threw his left hip out and sent Roberts staggering, clawing at the edge of the trench for support. The Union men went on.

Romig glanced back. The Virginian had pulled his jacket aside and had one hand on the grips of a Navy Colt. His eyes were burning. Then, slowly, Roberts's hand left the gun. He buttoned his jacket again.

Malcolm and Jake Rutledge, the wiry-bearded man who had threatened to cut Romig's throat, were in the lead. They were flailing the crust with shovels, inching on to whack some more. They were wet and tired, with temper stretched thin across their faces. Ephraim Bull stood on snowshoes above, dry and warm. Malcolm's rifle was on his back.

"Make your own trail if you want to pass!" Malcolm said.

"We'd rather work together," Romig said.

Malcolm glared. "Like today, huh?"

"Common sense says we'll have to work together." It was a hard admission for Ruthven. He looked sidewise at Romig.

"You're not just vaporing," little Ephraim said.

Art Rutledge spat. "Fighting is fine—on ground; but fighting and freezing—to hell with that, Malcolm!"

Jake Rutledge rubbed his nose on his sleeve. His gray officer's hat was drooping sadly. He said flatly, "I favor taking turns."

Someone behind yelled, "Let the damned Yankees pound snow, Alexander! They was all born in it!"

"Keep scrapping, and you'll all have a chance to freeze in it," the guide said calmly.

And so it was the snow that won a compromise. Romig felt that he had done nothing, but he was satisfied, knowing that men who have to work together must share their present relationship instead of viewing each other through the past.

The mules were put together. They had no bitterness, Romig thought; only suffering to share.

"I misdoubt the mules will be with us tomorrow." Little Ephraim spat and looked at the sky. "Nice today. Colder than old Billy Hell tonight."

The Union men went ahead to break trail, swaggering as they passed the Confederates. One hour periods was the agreed time; before the first hour was out, there was no swagger left in the North. The snow was getting deeper. The air seemed thinner. The faces of the mountains expanded, rising in great sheets of sparkling white that stabbed the eyes. The way grew steeper.

Hard and dry, loose to hold in the hand, coarse in the mouth before melting, the snow soaked into everything it touched. It softened skin and made legs and feet gall and blister inside wet boots. It gave way to one leg with disarming readiness, then fouled the second leg; and gradually it deepened until men were wallowing belt-deep.

Above the trench Ephraim walked back and forth along the column, spraying tobacco juice and waiting, always waiting for those who wrenched and thrust their way below. He took Malcolm's rifle from his shoulder and sighted at objects far ahead. His weathered face was calm.

Men tripped over logs and rocks. They fell chest-deep into sudden pockets. To get the mules over such places they spread canvas. Even so, the mules frequently fell helpless on their sides.

Roberts directed work with the animals. He had a way of giving courage to the mules, sometimes getting a frantic animal on its feet after others had pulled and tugged and cursed in vain. Bleeding, trembling, bellies soaked, the mules went up the slowly growing trench.

They were becoming a burden.

Men's tempers burst sharply over little things. They cursed themselves, the wallowing animals and the universe of snow all in the same breath. An exhausted man, half sobbing with anger and fatigue, raised a rifle barrel to strike a mule that had fallen three times in the same place.

Roberts broke the fellow's arm with his pistol butt.

Word went forward. The column halted. Heber Arnold struggled back, rubbing his hands as he went. The guide was giving orders in a quiet voice. Arnold's face was weary when he returned to where Romig was sitting on a shovel.

"Kansas boy, nice-looking lad," the Mormon said. "Worn out. Roberts warned him once about sticking a knife in the mule's rump to make it get up." He leaned against the snow wall and smiled faintly. "What are you going to buy with your gold, Romig?"

Ephraim stopped midway along the column. "Listen," he said.

Men looked at him, some enviously, some as though he were responsible for their miserable, sodden condition. But he was dry and untired, so he must be a wise man. They waited for him to speak. He put one finger against his nose and blew downwind, then shifted to the other side with grave impartiality. He rolled his quid and spat. Wet men with bloodshot eyes looked up as if the simple actions were the esoteric preliminaries of an oracle.

"The pass," Ephraim said, "is just behind that." He pointed to a ridge where the twisted arms of trees raised above the snow as if the parent trunks were being tortured by fiends below. "Still want to go on?"

"*Ja!*" Leibee shouted instantly. He was waist-deep in snow, his cheeks blazing red above his flaxen beard. He stood obdurate, eyes squinted fiercely.

"The pass isn't so far," Ruthven said.

"Sure we're going on!" Malcolm cried.

"There's nothing up there but more snow," Ephraim said. "And we won't reach the pass tonight."

"So what!" Malcolm shouted. "We know that. We're wasting time. Let's go!"

Men would have followed that shout into battle, Romig thought. It shattered reason and appealed to emotion; but this was another kind of battle, lacking rapid movement to numb the thought of consequences. The snow was fact, apparent to an idiot. Romig placed two shovels on the crust and stood on them to see how men reacted.

"I got plenty!" someone shouted.

"We can't quit now!" another said.

Ephraim spat and waited for five or six heated discussions to subside. When men were looking at him in silence again, he said, "About a half mile ahead is a little cabin in the timber, a mighty little cabin. I misdoubt the mules can make it—and some of the rest of you, too." He paused and worked his jaws. "The back trail is broken, and downhill to boot. You can get back to Oro in half the time it took to come."

"No!" Leibee shouted.

Little groups began to gather in the trench. The Kansan with the broken arm seemed to be alone, Romig observed. His arm was in a canvas sling. Pack still on his back, he leaned against the side of the trench and waited.

Roberts came up to Malcolm and said, "Christ's sake! I hope the deadwood clears out fast so we can move."

Romig signaled the guide. "See if you can get them to send the mules back."

Ephraim tried, but distrust leaped quickly between Malcolm and Ruthven. They watched each other while supervising the shifting of gear, and in the end took one mule each, sent back the heavy tents, and loaded up with as many tools as possible.

"Take a little grub too," Ephraim said dryly. "It's handy to eat—and tools ain't."

Thirty-one men had left Oro City. Twelve now turned back, stumbling away as soon as packs were shifted on the mules. There were few words of parting. Leo Gorham, the Kansan with the broken arm, said he was going on, although Romig and Arnold tried to persuade him to retreat.

"A busted arm heals as fast in one place as another," Gorham said. He was a handsome youth, clear-skinned, with just a trace of down upon his jowls.

Nineteen men pushed on.

When the sky was dead above the peaks, they came to the cabin. Half buried on three sides, it sat upon a ledge that overlooked a frozen beaver pond. Strange play of wind had made a bare spot on the lee side of the logs. There Roberts led the mules, breaking a way through terraced crust. Without speaking, he and Ruthven covered them with blankets, gave them grain, and built a sloping canvas shelter from the cabin roof to trees at the edge of the drift.

As Ephraim had said, the cabin was small; low-roofed so that tall men had to stoop to miss the ridge log, windowless, with a small fireplace and a double bunk. There was wood inside, and more was handy in dead, leaning timber.

"Who built this?" Romig asked Ephraim.

The guide and Arnold were examining faces for white spots. "Couple of fellows that prospect here summers," Ephraim answered. To the man he was examining he said, "Rub the very devil out of those ears with snow."

The room grew hot. Clothes began to steam, and men began to nod with drowsiness. Art Rutledge had recovered his jug from Romig. He passed it around to all, and it was emptied quickly. He started to heave it out the door, but Ephraim stopped him. "Leave it," he said. "Never throw away anything that might come in handy."

"That's what I allus say." Rutledge laughed and took two quarts of whiskey from his pack. "Tonight I'm getting shet of these, because tomorrow I may fall down and bust 'em!"

The whiskey bridged one gap. It made Art Rutledge and Zeke Davis, formerly of the Federal army, quick drinking friends. They sat against the wall arguing amiably about the relative merits of Tennessee and Kentucky.

"We're jammed in like pebbles in a crick," Ephraim said, "so let's work out some system about the cooking."

Muchow suggested that pairs or groups who shared each other's packs delegate one man to do their cooking, all others to stay clear of the fire until the cook had finished his job. The plan worked well. While one man cooked, the others sat against the wall, poked into their packs, changed socks, hung boots to dry, or merely drowsed. The odor of wet leather and drying wool, smoke and man smell mingled with the aroma of cooking.

Romig scowled as he watched Art Rutledge and Zeke Davis drink. They were going much too fast for men with empty stomachs. Finally he said, "You boys will have heads like candy buckets in the morning if you don't slow down."

Job Davis turned from his cooking at the fireplace. "May as well let Zeke get it over with, Chaplain. When the whiskey's gone, it won't bother him none about where's a drink, who's got a jug. He's like that in streaks. Ma made me promise when we left to keep him from fighting and drinking too much, but—"

"Don't gab so much, and get to hell done with that fire!" Roberts was standing with a pan in his hand.

Job Davis put his cooking aside. He stood up and spoke so fast the words hissed a little in his broken mouth. "You ain't a-talking to no niggees now, you goddamned, Secesh bastardly Virginian!"

Ruthven and Romig collided as they moved to block trouble. Malcolm leaped from the bunk where he was sitting beside Gorham. It seemed to Romig that the Scot intended to shout at Roberts, but when he cracked his head against the ridge log, Malcolm turned angrily toward Davis.

"I'll knock the rest of your teeth out, if Roberts doesn't!" Malcolm said.

"You'll try." Muchow was holding a piece of fire-wood.

Men were bumping against each other as they tried to rise.

Romig tried the first part of Old Malcolm's advice. "Shut up, the lot of you!" He hurled his voice with all his power. "Shut up! Sit down!"

He was surprised at the silence.

"My God!" Art Rutledge said. "You like to busted my eardrums." Neither he nor Zeke Davis had tried to stand.

"There will be no war re-fought in here." Ephraim's voice was soft but even after it was gone, its authority still lay on those who had heard.

"No soft-handed Virginia officer is a-going—" Job Davis stopped when Ephraim pointed at the Tennesseean's frying pan. "To hell with him, just the same," Davis said before he knelt again beside the fire.

Art Rutledge and Zeke were smoking broken cigars that Zeke had carried in his hat from Oro City. They were both so drunk that Romig knew they had actually missed the incident. Except for them there was little talking in the room during the rest of supper preparations. An ugly feeling seemed to swell and pulse against the walls. Faces showed that tempers lay just beneath the skin. Conditions would have been bad enough if all had been on one side, Romig thought, for they were so pack-jammed in the place that no man could move an arm without disturbing his neighbor.

They ate in silence, some drowsing over their messkits, but any quick movement or sudden noise brought rapid lifting of heads.

Romig studied Roberts frankly. He got an insolent stare and a thin twisted smile in return. If Joel Roberts had turned back, it would have been a blessing; but no—there were men like Roberts everywhere. They did not bar the way to Shining Mountains; they only made the path more difficult.

Ephraim foresaw another problem that might have grown to unreasonable proportions: the bunk. Dried poles and brittle boughs all rat-befouled, it was no better than the floor, but it was a symbol of privilege. "Me and the injured boy will use the bunk," Ephraim said, and that settled the matter.

Gorham was already on the bunk. He had eaten food prepared by Arnold, who now leaned over to feel his brow. "You'll have more fever soon. Arm thumping bad?"

"Not bad." Gorham's eyes strayed to Roberts.

"Shall we set watches, men?" Romig asked.

No one wanted to answer. Then Roberts smiled and asked, "What for?"

"For one thing," Ephraim said, "we wouldn't want to burn the cabin down. I'll guarantee this night would freeze us all if we had to stay outside."

"Too hot already." A dead cigar was hanging from Rutledge's lips. Zeke Davis was asleep at his side, head sunk on chest. Neither had eaten.

"Shall we have watches?" Romig asked.

Roberts laughed. "What for? I'm not afraid to sleep. Are you?"

There was no watch.

Men settled against each other on the dirt floor. Outside the banshee wind slashed snow against the logs. Tight seal of drifts and animal heat kept the cabin stuffy. Romig got inside his bag and then got out again when he found it too hot after a half hour. Beside him Ruthven grunted sleepily, "Light somewhere, will you?"

Romig watched firelight die against the dark roof logs. He heard the roar of growing wind, the hiss of snow skidding off the roof. Ephraim began to snore with a mighty rasping sound. Gorham groaned in his sleep.

Sometime during the night Romig woke up chilled and got inside the bag again. He heard an odd clacking sound outside and wondered what it was; then he knew: the mules were shaking their ears, and their ears were frozen.

He began to drowse. He was pushing his legs through the snow, stumbling, falling. Great gleaming mountains stood before him. He was struggling painfully toward them when he fell asleep.

CHAPTER 6

EPHRAIM WAS BUILDING a fire when Romig awoke. It was near dawn, the guide said, referring to nothing but a sense of time. Gorham was sitting on the edge of the bunk, fever flushed. Romig was dressing when he saw Roberts sit up. For an instant the Virginian's face was calm; then he looked around the room, saw Romig, and the clothing of his arrogance fell into place.

Romig finished dressing and started outside to relieve himself. The leather strap that held the door was not hooked on its peg, but the door was so tightly jammed from rime that furred the sill and framing that Romig had to use his shoulder to thrust it open.

Cold seared his lungs and made him gasp. During the night, winter had walked with heavy steps. The trees were sparkling. Fine frost was drifting from the cabin roof. The mountains were solid in a crackling sky.

Romig turned and saw the man sitting against the cabin wall, head resting on arms that bridged the knees of doubled-up legs. It was Zeke Davis. There was hoarfrost on his red beard; snow across his legs, in the wrinkles of his clothing and in the open collar of his linsey shirt. He was frozen.

Romig pulled the door open and called, "Arnold!"

The tone caused Ephraim's eyes to train and fix like the muzzle of a gun. Before he started toward the door, the guide shook Arnold, who was still asleep.

Everyone was awake moments later.

Job Davis knelt and felt his brother's arm, then pulled his hand away in astonishment. "He's cold!"

"He's dead," Roberts said.

They carried Zeke inside and laid him on his side upon the bed. Frost vanished from his beard, and the red whiskers looked alive. He lay like a fallen statue, and they couldn't change him.

"Is he really dead, Arnold? Is he really dead?" Job Davis asked.

The Mormon nodded and led Davis toward the fire.

"Put on the rest of your clothes," he said.

Romig went outside again. He looked at logs where frozen vomit clung, then looked at Ephraim, who said, "Got sick. Sat down out here and never felt the cold at all."

From around the corner of the cabin Sampson Greene shouted. Ephraim and Romig and others went to where the Georgian stood looking down at the beaver pond. One of the mules was in it, hind quarters under the ice, long neck extended toward the trail to Oro City. Wind was stirring the hairs on its back. It was dead.

"That's your mule, Ruthven," Malcolm said.

"Small difference." Ephraim spoke with quiet anger. "Look there."

The second mule was down. The canvas shelter had blown away and was wrapped around a tree. Men leaped at Roberts's orders to help get the animal on its feet. They were glad of anything that would help cover the sounds Job Davis was making in the cabin. But it was useless. The mule was alive, and that was all.

Roberts bit his underlip and felt for a gun he had left inside. "Shoot it quick!"

Jake Rutledge drew a Butterfield revolver and looked at the caps. The first one missed fire. He tried again, shooting hurriedly. The ball tore away bone from the mule's nose and broke its jaw. The animal jerked its head and looked reproachfully at its tormentors, soundless, blood running from icicles on its nose and underlip. Rutledge's next cap missed fire. "Goddamn!" he cried and almost hurled the gun away.

The Starr in Ephraim's knotty fist spoke louder because no one was looking at him. He shot the mule between the eyes, and whisked the gun somewhere under his furs. He strode away, softly speaking the only blasphemy Romig had ever heard him utter.

Breakfast was a silent chore. They cooked and ate while the dead man lay under a blanket on the bunk. Job Davis had protested savagely about taking him outside in the cold, and Arnold had sustained him, saying, "Leave him here for the time. There's no one in this cabin who hasn't wallowed in death."

Gorham was sitting on a block of wood beside the fire, his clear skin bright with fever. He wasn't going on, he said. He would return to Oro City with four others who had decided this was deep enough. It was the Kansan's eyes that brought Romig's attention to the bunk. Gorham had been glancing around restlessly, watching Roberts from time to time, but now he was looking at the bunk, and his eyes were filled with terror.

The blanket over Zeke Davis was moving. One hand came from under the shroud and tapped the bunk poles.

"Jesus Christ!" Art Rutledge yelled.

"He's alive!" Job Davis sprang up.

"No!" Heber Arnold pushed the Tennesseean back. "The heat, Davis, the heat!"

Romig and Ephraim straightened out the thawing form and covered it again. Job Davis looked as sick as if he had seen his brother die a second time.

There was little eating after that. One of those who was going back dumped his salt pork and pan bread in the fire and cursed in a shaking voice. "The dirty, damned Yankee ruint my breakfast!"

"Too bad," Arnold said. "However, my delicate friend, the dead know no uniform or flag. He's not a Yankee or a Rebel now."

Sweeping wind blasted thirteen men going toward the pass. The crust was hard now, and they walked upon it easily, but Ephraim had his webs strapped to his back just the same.

Of the original Union group there were left only Ruthven, Muchow, Leibee, Davis and Romig. In the other party were Malcolm, Roberts, the Greene twins and the Rutledge cousins. Arnold belonged to neither party and to both.

Muchow was carrying a long rope that he had started to cut several times before he finally threw it all into a coil. "Never cut a line at sea," he had said, "and I guess that goes for the mountains too." Davis had a five-foot whipsaw across his shoulder, the blade stiffened with shovel handles, the whole burden wrapped in canvas. The rest were carrying at least one tool apiece, their blankets and all the food their packs would hold.

Ephraim had bargained with Ruthven and Muchow for their packsaddle and other equipment left at the cabin. The guide had talked, too, to Malcolm and Roberts about buying their abandoned gear, but they had not yet reached agreement.

To the last the wind defended the pass, sending steady billows of powdery snow, ripping at the remnants of war-contract uniforms. Some men had wrapped their legs with canvas and had tied canvas over their heads to press their hatbrims closer to their ears. Will Greene had a meal sack around his neck. The Rolla Mills, it read.

They came at last to the saddle of the pass, a wide place that did not fit Romig's idea of a pass. On their right a rounded mountain curved up, sheer white except near the crest. At their backs were the wrinkled peaks.

This was as far as Ephraim was going. He stopped and put his back to the wind. His spittle went flying and was lost in a powdery white swirl.

"Twenty-five miles to the Blue, huh?" Ruthven asked.

Ephraim nodded. "About."

Sampson Greene rubbed ragged mittens together. "How far we come already?"

"From Oro?" Ephraim spat. "Ten, 'leven miles."

Malcolm scowled. "Twenty-five miles more. What if the crust doesn't hold out like this?"

"Bad," Ephraim said. "Stay in the trough of the mountains down the Tenmile. You'll come out on the Blue below the canyon. Don't try no short cuts, no matter what looks good and handy."

Malcolm squinted up at the rounded mountain. "The Blue lays just across there, eh?"

"Just across that," Ephraim said dryly, "and about three ranges of mountains that tried to get in the same place while the Creator wasn't looking."

Lawless glints were high in Malcolm's eyes. He shook moisture from his nose and grinned. "The snow looks like it was all blown off up there. How far that way?"

The guide looked at Romig in alarm. "Not far, I'd say—just like it ain't far from the top of the ocean to the bottom."

Muchow stamped the crust. "This is better than dry ground. It's probably the same up there."

"Up there," Ephraim said, shouting above an increasing blast of wind, "it probably never thawed to make crust." He looked at Romig and Arnold for help, and then he looked at the faces of the others lifted toward the mountain. He told of icy rocks, of wind that set the teeth on edge, of powdery snow two hundred feet deep in crevices, of snowslides on southern slopes.

"You've been that way, have you?" Malcolm asked.

The guide rubbed his misshapen nose. "No, I have never been that way, and I never intend to go that way in winter."

"I think I will," Malcolm said. "I think I'll go straight over the mountains instead of stumbling twenty-five miles down a valley belly-deep with snow."

"Don't try it." Ephraim shook his head.

"Straight over the hill for me," Malcolm said.

"You might let the others say something," Romig suggested. "Myself—I'd say Ephraim knows what he's talking about." Ruthven looked steadily at Romig, who added, "I stand with Eph."

Roberts looked at Malcolm and smiled. "Let's go."

"Who gets dere first gets de best ground!" Leibee said.

Men shrugged at their packs and studied the mountain. Some faces showed doubt, some fear. "What do you think, Jake?" Art Rutledge asked his cousin, who wiped moisture from his eyes and looked at Northern expressions without answering.

"Fifty dollars for the junk I left behind," Malcolm said to Ephraim.

The guide nodded. "That makes us even."

"If you ever get back to Oro City, tell my father I went down fighting." Malcolm grinned at Ephraim, tightened a whipping plaid scarf around his neck, swung a pack and two shovels on his shoulder and strode away—straight for the mountain. Roberts was at his side. The Southerners began to follow.

The Unions hesitated, and then, when Ruthven and Leibee started, went the same way. Arnold and Romig were left with Ephraim Bull, who shook his head, but smiled as he watched the party move away. "Well," the guide said, "you two look like you had good sense, but . . ." He dug under his furs and gave Romig a salt sack full of tea. "Make a hundred cups, where that much coffee wouldn't last one camp." He mined out a flat pint bottle of brownish fluid and gave it to Arnold. "The juice of boiled Oregon grape roots, with some aspen bark and other stuff. It helps some kind of fevers—sometimes."

He produced two pairs of woolen socks, four fish hooks stuck in a cork wound with line, two candle stubs, a waterproof tube of matches, a half-pint bottle of whiskey, two face masks made from the legs of red flannel underwear, and a stick of charcoal wrapped in canvas. He divided the articles between Romig and

Arnold. "Use the candles when you can't get a fire any other way. Bear east until you can see the Blue Valley, and be sure you hold that way instead of dropping back into the Tenmile, because if you do you'll be so pooped out by then you'll never make it." Ephraim looked at the sky. "There'll be a hell of a thaw in a few days. It's long overdue."

He spat and looked at Arnold. "You know about a poultice of balsam bark for feet and hands that get froze and look like they might get well?"

Arnold nodded gravely.

"For chilblains afterward, put gunpowder on the foot and light it."

"I'll remember that," Arnold said.

Ephraim nodded. "I'll see that the boy in the cabin gets the best we can do for him."

They watched him go, a tiny figure in sooty, grease-stained furs. He moved swiftly, not looking back. From off the curving slopes a blinding gust of scud enveloped him and merged him with its whiteness. When the snow dust cleared, Romig was still watching. Little Ephraim seemed very far away then. And he did not look back.

"Well . . ." Arnold smiled. "Excelsior, my Alpine friend."

They laughed and went together toward the mountain.

Long before they caught up with the others they saw discarded tools. The wind came slashing with its cargo of dry snow, hurling from their mouths the very air they tried to gasp. Snow went by in sheets of blinding white. Eyes streamed. Lungs burned and muscles dragged. High above, the snow cornice hung like the curl of a tremendous breaker. The little valley that they had followed seemed right at their feet, brought close by pitiless rarefaction. More tools lay behind when they followed Young Malcolm around the shoulder of the mountain where the snow was glassy smooth and hard-crusted.

And then they saw they had not yet begun to climb. Ahead lay granite wedges so sheer that snow was lying only in the crevices.

They went on, using the rope sometimes, using picks and shovels to help claw their way. Broken summits lay all around them, mighty basins filled with snow, and always the bulleting wind that tried to rip garments from their shaking bodies. Romig cupped his hands before his mouth to breathe. Ephraim was right. God had been busy elsewhere when this was made. He wondered how the snarling atmosphere could ever tolerate the penetration of warming sun, or if it ever had.

As much as possible they clung to the rocks. Pale from the dizzy altitude, they came to the top of a serrated spear of granite. Romig's stomach turned when he looked from the knife-edged summit. The mountain leaned back under their feet. They retreated and went along the side until they found a place where the wedges were more blunt, where it seemed they might be able to descend. More mountains lay beyond. This was only the first crest.

Sometime in the afternoon they reached a place where there were points of granite all around them.

They huddled in the wind and argued about directions. Muchow had his way; it was not the way his compass said but was based on the single glimpse they had had of the sun during the last four hours. They crossed another granite wedge. Mountains still lay in all directions. They were on the crest of the world where winter was playing its own symphony.

Romig squinted at vastness all around, feeling the stiffness of his cheek muscles. He wished now that he had let his beard grow from the day he left Independence. For some moments all the crests seemed to weave, but he shook the dizzy feeling off and anchored the rope while the others inched down a frozen face of rock. They stood together in the shelter of a granite buttress that ripped glazed white. Romig took out the face masks. One he gave to Davis and the other to Will Greene. The scars on Davis's upper lip were bright orange. His mouth was twisted sideways so he could breathe without opening it directly to the wind.

Arnold got out the charcoal. With stiff fingers they smeared it on their cheekbones, and the blackness accentuated the tallow color of their faces. Arnold got none under his eyes, for when Jake Rutledge started to return the charcoal, the wind tore it from his mittened fingers and carried it away.

They staggered on, shoulders to the wind, pygmies moving slowly in a world of whistling fury. This Shining Mountain that had symbolized Romig's search for values and belief, had given nothing, he thought; nothing but a test of brute strength. But he knew that he would forever look at gleaming summits and want to stand on them, and want to search beyond them.

They tried to bear east by Muchow's calculations, but basins filled with velvety snow forced them northeast. Their beards were pale with frost. Their eyes were red and streaming; charcoal smears washed downward on numb cheekbones.

Trembling, they all gathered under an overhanging ledge and agreed that they had to get down quickly.

Where a jutting crest ran in a semicircle above an abyss, they stopped to search a way. Spinning snow far below gave the chasm the appearance of a bottomless whirlpool that sucked in scud, then spewed it forth in streamers. They inched down a chimney to reach a ledge of broken rock beneath iced capping. The first few hundred feet along the shelf was easy, and then they came to a wide fissure where snow and ice ran like a toboggan slide to hell.

Malcolm tied the line around his waist. He edged out cautiously, using a shovel as a staff on the lower side. His pack and blankets and Ferguson rifle moved gently as he felt his way. He gained the opposite side and tried to grin back at the others, but the stiffness of his face made the attempt resemble the silent warning of a dog about to leap. He took two turns with the line around a rock and waved for the rest to follow him.

One by one they crossed, sliding one hand along the rope, until Leibee, Roberts and Romig were left on the near side, holding the line while Muchow made his way over the glassy swoop. Muchow slipped. He made a twisting turn and grabbed the rope with both hands. Feet foremost he slid with his face to the sky. He was a helpless weight on the V of the line.

Those holding on the near side were thrown forward by the jerk. Roberts was in the lead, then Romig, with Leibee at their backs, and only Leibee now had stable footing. Short animal grunts came from him as he strove to hold all strain. Romig was slipping, and Roberts was nearly gone.

The V in the line grew sharper.

"Back up!" Roberts cried.

Muchow's face was twisted toward them now. He made no outcry. He held to the line and looked back, and Romig never was to forget his face.

Those on the far side of the chute were helpless. If they tried to draw Muchow up, the act would put more strain on the three who could not hold what they already had.

"Holt! Holt!" Leibee grunted.

Romig felt his boots grate against a rock and stop sliding. He tried to lean back, pulling with numbed hands that were going to lose all power in a few moments. Muchow's gray face stared at him.

Leibee shouted triumphantly. "Back up, Vromig! I got dem!"

Leibee had driven a pick to the eye into a crack and taken two turns around it with the rope. Romig and Roberts fell back to stable footing. Those across the chute pulled Muchow up to them.

The German was the last to cross. He carried two shovels and a pick along with his pack.

Against the whiteness of his face, Muchow's eyes were as green as the stormy Atlantic. He reached out to thump Leibee on the shoulder. The German shrugged away and said, "Go!"

Excitement had poured new warmth into everyone's blood. They all went on along the ledge, which took them east around the chasm. Far below they saw the flatness of a frozen lake, and now and then through a world of racing snow and wind they saw the Valley of the Blue. It was close, and yet it was fearfully far away. They reached the lake, using the rope to slide down through snow that was fine enough to smother. Ice groaned as they passed the upper end of the lake. Beyond was a ridge where snow had cleared dark granite. The old, old voices of the mountains roared at them as they gasped and cursed and stumbled upward once again.

On top, where quartz-spotted rock lay bare, they paused to look below. The drop was sheer. Ruthven's brows were white with frost as he pointed north along the spine. It was the way. There was no other.

Gradually the top began to widen until a hundred feet of snow lay between them and the edge of an ever-increasing gorge on their left. Sometimes they made a hundred yards or more on wind-cleaned rock before being forced into the snow. It was crusted underneath five or six inches of fluff, but the crust did not always hold. Art Rutledge plunged through in one place until he was only a dark spot of frantic face with hair spilled slantwise across his forehead.

They got him out and went on, humped against the wind. Job Davis still had the whipsaw and would not let anyone else carry it.

From the gorge on their left, snow dust boiled up in spirals, until the wind bent them and sent them streaking down the back trail. Sometimes the wind shifted suddenly, leaving their faces so quickly they staggered and felt sudden warmness in their flesh; and then the wind, exploding with vindictive fury, would strike them in the back and send them stumbling forward.

Light was getting dimmer.

They were crossing slanting snow when a loud thump sounded and their footing jarred beneath them.

"Get off the snow!" Heber Arnold shouted.

Men scrambled upward toward the serrations of ice-coated granite, while behind them a broken mass of snow moved away, slowly at first and then with gathering power.

Sampson Greene was on it, staring at his feet.

"Run, Samp! Get off it!" Will Greene screamed.

Sampson's bewilderment gave way to terror when he saw where he was going. He tried to run. He fell. The surface around him heaved. Snow crust popped and turned on edge to ride the heaving mass like giant fins that slanted, broke and disappeared. Under Greene the section held firm, although tilted. Then something stopped it, and Greene was motionless on hands and knees, staring at men who clung to solid rock.

"The rope!" Ruthven yelled.

Muchow already had it off his shoulder. He ran into the snow and tried to throw the rope as a heaving line, but the coils were stiff and clung together. Leibee whipped one end around his waist and Muchow deftly bent a bowline. Help did not reach the anchor end too soon, for Leibee plunged away recklessly, his short arms pumping, snow eddying around his legs.

He went to the end of the rope, and it was not far enough. Greene tried to leap to catch the German's outstretched hand. The crust beneath him broke, parting around the rock that had impeded it. They gave Leibee sudden slack then by moving downhill. He flung himself full length, one arm reaching. The slide was running slower now, just fragments following what had broken loose before; but it was enough to turn Sampson Greene under, thrust him up again, and carry him clawing wildly with just his head and arms above the snow.

He was that way when he went over the edge.

A scream that chilled Romig's very being rose above the wind. Snow poured slowly into the gorge— stopped. The wind howled with a new triumphant roar.

"I'm a-going down there after him," Will Greene said, and tore off his face mask. He began to run.

Romig lunged full length and tripped him. Jake Rutledge and Malcolm held him until sanity came back; then they let him go to the edge on the rope. He was a long time there, lying on his stomach while cold soaked into those who held the line. He would not signal for them to haul him back, so they pulled him away against his will.

He stood shivering, staring at gusts of snow rising from the gorge. "Maybe he's alive down there. Hurt. Maybe—"

"No, Will," Malcolm said with gentleness in his voice. "It's hundreds of feet to the bottom."

"The snow is soft!" Greene cried.

And smothering, Romig thought. He looked at Arnold. "Suppose you go to the edge and have a look?"

The Mormon went down on the line and walked along the edge with his brown beard whipping. The others waited, stamped their freezing feet and looked anxiously at the sky. They were nowhere yet. No trees were close. Just the wind and snow and mountains running wild with winter.

Heber Arnold shook his head when he returned. His patient eyes were sad and bloodshot. He blinked wearily.

Romig took Will Greene's arm. "When summer comes—"

"Summer!" the Georgian cried savagely. "Summer! Goddamn this dirty country!" He began to sob.

They gathered up the tools they still had and went on, straight up the spine of rock and snow that had no breaks to let them go down either side. Ruthven was leading now, sticking to the rocks even when the route meant loss of time and jars and bumps against knees and legs that went sick with pain at every blow.

Behind him walked Job Davis, head bowed, the five-foot whipsaw still on his shoulder. He saw his mother standing on the porch of a cabin in Tennessee, with the haze of the Great Smokies warm in the distance. She compressed her lips and forced anger into her voice the way she always did when she was feeling soft inside. "The fighting scarcely over, and now you brats a-skeetin' off to Californy—"

77

"Colorado, Ma," Zeke said. He had his rifle across his shoulder and was standing by a trembling hound that had been almost too blind to see them when they came home from the fighting.

Job's mother twisted angrily, one hand clutching at her faded dress. "Don't sass me, you Zeke! Californy or Colorady! Varmints and murderers is all there are out there!"

"Don't worry, Ma." Zeke laughed. "We seen a few of them things in the war."

"Mind you, Job Davis"—the lips were quivering now—"you take keer of Zeke. Don't you let him drink away what brains he has, like his Pa done. You got a few licks of sense, Job Davis. You promise me to keep Zeke from fightin' and drinkin' too much."

"I'll do it, Ma. I promise I will."

Job Davis staggered on into a wind that flattened the face mask against his brow. Snow flowed inside the eye holes, melted on his cheeks. The breathing slit was stiff with ice. "You take keer of Zeke," his mother said. "I'll do it, Ma," he answered—or was it the wind that mocked him hideously? He saw Zeke sitting by a cabin wall, snow gathered in his ears, thick rime in red whiskers, flesh metallic cold.

Wind twisted at the whipsaw and tried to take it from him. It was a cross, something like what the preacher used to moan about in Tennessee; not exactly like the one Christ carried up a hill, but something a man had to bear because of that. He would carry it to hell and back, and no one else was going to help. They did not know what it was.

The wind tore at his mask and jeered, "I promise, Ma."

He raised one hand and used the bent wrist to drag down on the mask. He was seeing the inside of the thing, and yet he could still see snow and Ruthven's boots lifting, moving, loosening more snow to trail behind them. But still there was something wrong. Davis was seeing the inside of the red mask.

Jake Rutledge was following Malcolm's broad back, stepping where the big Scot stepped, stumbling where Malcolm stumbled. By God, this was awful! There was no use now. They were going to freeze to death or all go bellowing over the edge into that hole where the Georgia kid had gone. The mountains had trapped them. There were spirits up here, evil things that Jake's grandmother had told him about long ago. They stayed on mountains and couldn't come down, but if you went up, they had you. That sharp-faced Yankee sailor . . . the spirits almost got him, but the crazy German fellow saved him; that had made the spirits mad, so they just took another man when they damned pleased.

Rutledge sagged when he jammed his knee against an edge of rock. They were going to freeze . . . even that big Yankee preacher, who didn't act like a preacher and didn't seem afraid of anything. But before Jake Rutledge got like that red-whiskered fellow who had drunk Art's whiskey, he was going to pray. He was going to pray, even if lots of times he got a sneaking satisfaction out of hearing Cousin Art curse about there being no God at all, just a lot of liar talk to keep poor people from wanting things they couldn't have. He wasn't going to yell for no help either. All he wanted was for God to chase that scary feeling about spirits clear away, and forgive him for some things. Little meanness and his meanness—you had to tell about it all. God knew all right, but if you didn't mention everything you could remember, He might think you were trying to hide something.

That about the men was worst of all.

Seven of them that he'd seen real close. Six he couldn't help; all he could remember was the menace of their blue jackets. God knew about war and what a man had to do. God had a lot of forgiving to do about the war. Only that one was real bad, the tall boy with staring blue eyes and black marks on his mouth from biting cartridges. He'd dropped his Springfield and was turning to run away when Jake Rutledge's bayonet took him sidewise through the stomach. "No! No!" he screamed and tried to hold his guts inside. "No! No!" he kept screaming even after Rutledge had gone on. That was the bad one. That was the face that Jake Rutledge saw before him now. *Jesus Christ, I should have let him run, but someone would have got him anyway.*

Why didn't his face go away now?

Maybe it was the yell that Georgia kid in the fur cap had given that had started it all again. Clawing at the snow like a man trying to get on a raft, with the water sucking his legs against the bottom of it; way down there now where you couldn't even guess the bottom. Jesus Christ and God Almighty! This was an awful country. There were devil demons in the wind, hiding behind cold rocks with caps of ice. What if all the snow melted suddenly and turned to muddy water? When Jake was a little shaver he'd tumbled into the flooding run and been carried under, tossed over and over, trying to scream for his mother, with muddy water choking him and a terrible whining sound in his ears. If only God . . .

Rutledge stared at Malcolm's footprints. He stared and horror choked him. Dirty, stinking horned Satan was working magic, getting ready to pitchfork all of them, but first he was going to drive them crazy. Why didn't somebody say something? Why didn't they know Jake Rutledge was going crazy?

Malcolm's boots went down and up and each step left behind the same fluid that had been on a bayonet Jake Rutledge had thrown away in the middle of a battle.

"No! No!" the wind howled. "No-o-o-o!"

Jake Rutledge's shout was hoarse and terrible. "Malcolm, your feet are bleeding in the snow!"

The cry halted the column. Malcolm did not look at his feet. "They're all right," he said in an odd voice, and looked at Romig.

Romig had been seeing red flashes before his eyes for some time, but he had told himself they came from moisture and the burn of snow he had faced. He looked at Arnold's tracks and then glanced quickly at Malcolm. It wasn't all from tortured vision. Great God! What *was* it then? He looked behind and saw a trail as palely red as if warm blood had spilled and been diluted by the snow.

"It's blood!" Job Davis screamed, tearing the mask from his face. "We're dying!"

They were jarred and scared, and Romig with them. Leibee grunted and stamped his feet and muttered in German.

"Oh, Lord, I ask of thee . . ." Jake Rutledge started, but he could not go on.

Ruthven recovered first. "All the snow is red," he said. His reasoning broke against primitive fear and scattered to the wind like powder.

It was so, Romig saw; all the snow was red, but for a few moments the rational was lost, and he stood like the others in the dawn age of man, with superstition of the unknown and strange throttling his mind. At last he said, "It's just red snow." He raised his voice and roared, "That's all it is!" Afterward he was to laugh about his trying to dispel fear with bellowing when he was as afraid and ignorant as the rest.

Arnold seemed confused. He held a handful of snow close to his face and peered at it. "I've heard of it," he said, "But this is the first I ever saw. Sometimes it's green. Something in the air causes it, I think."

Leibee grunted, still distrustful. He was last in the column, where he had tried to pick up and carry every discarded tool. Now he had three shovels and three picks and a double-bitted ax. With a dry clatter of steel he swung his burdens on his shoulder. "Go!" he shouted.

Red snow was behind them when night caught them. Their refuge was an overhanging ledge where a great column of blue-white ice stood out from a fissure at one end. Huge cubes of fallen rocks lay all along the ledge. There was no tree or bush, just the ice and rocks and the wind raging above the ledge like a monster that had missed its prey.

Ruthven and Malcolm cut up two shovel handles while Leibee sulked and grumbled. Over a fire of splinters Romig used some of Ephraim's tea, lacing each cupful with a splash of whiskey. Every man had two lukewarm drinks, and then the fire was gone. There remained only the darkness and the wind and the hiss of ice crystals scouring the rocks above them. Romig began to feel that they were perched on the edge of some tremendous precipice.

"We shouldn't have come this way," Davis said.

"Don't whine about it," Roberts said. "We're here."

They pooled their blankets and Romig's heavy sleeping bag. That provided beds for four men, enough to keep them from freezing in their sleep. They decided to change at one-hour intervals. Malcolm took a silver watch from an oilskin case and checked it with Romig's watch. It was not yet eight o'clock.

About ten hours in which to try to keep alive, Romig thought.

Before midnight one hour seemed longer than those who had to stay awake could bear. They stamped their feet and beat their chests, rubbed fingers together, counted off at intervals. Once Jake Rutledge did not answer. His cousin brought him from stupor with brutal slaps, and before Jake realized where he was, he tried to draw a knife. His cursing was a warning. Romig fumbled in the dark to grab Jake's arms and shouted at him until he came to full awareness.

"I jest set down to pray a minute," he said. His words

went hollowly on the wind. "Couldn't *you* pray for us, Chaplain?"

"Sure! When we get out of this mess, I'll pray. I'll give thanks that we had brute strength enough to make it—and enough manhood to act together."

"You're not much of a preacher," Jake said. "But if you think we'll get out of this, that's a little something."

"We will!" Romig said. He struck Malcolm on the back hard enough to make him grunt. "What's a little cold?"

It seemed that eternal darkness had fallen. Romig strode along the ledge until he knew every rock and how to miss it. He kicked his feet against the wall. He beat his legs with his fists. Sometimes he sang, roaring with the wind itself. He had a voice for singing, he thought, if he could tell one note from another. He took one hour of warmth beneath the blankets and let the next one go to Will Greene. Not to be outdone, Malcolm skipped his hour and gave it to Job Davis. When Ruthven, who had been asleep at the time, found out what Malcolm had done, he gave his second turn to Jake Rutledge, who was moaning in his sleep.

After that Ruthven, Malcolm and Romig took only one more hour of rest.

"I can last as long as any other bullheaded Scot," Malcolm said, and laughed.

It was an honest laugh, Romig thought, and wished that he could have seen Ruthven's face.

The wind ripped at the ledge. It could not reach the men below, but the cold was there. To stay awake was torture. To drowse was death.

Toward morning the wind became irregular, now furious, then dying down to eerie stillness that left ears still ringing. During one of the quiet spells those who were stumbling back and forth along the ledge heard a distant roaring sound that was doubly ominous because of the dark.

"Snowslide somewhere behind us," Arnold said. "They don't usually run at night." He listened. "Big one."

The sound ran on for several minutes and Romig was glad to hear the wind come back.

When the gray pickets of dawn came into the sky, Christian Muchow said wearily from where he stood kicking against a rock, "That was the damn'dest night I ever hope to live through!"

It had been a night to shorten lives, but when full light came they were still alive. The wind was gone now. Behind them they could see heights that must have been impossible to cross; but they had crossed them. Far ahead where trees were showing they saw a wide saddle, and on beyond were mountains that must be rising from the north side of the Blue.

CHAPTER 7

I T WAS LATE AFTERNOON before they reached the saddle. Ruthven was breaking trail, thrusting slowly at hip-deep snow. His deep-set eyes seemed to have receded. His mouth was slack.

Behind him lay more tools, guns and food from their

packs. Davis was still clinging to the whipsaw. Art Rutledge had a poleax, and Muchow still had his rope, although he had thrown away a Jenks rifle, marking the place by two slender pines that rose almost together in a clump of lesser trees.

Hans Leibee's cheeks were pale now. He had two shovels left.

Arnold was snow-blind, and Romig was leading him. Romig knew now that the Mormon had been nearly blind the night before when he tried to see the red snow.

Jake Rutledge was breaking trail when they crossed the saddle and looked down into the valley of the Blue. Not far below them was dense timber, already collecting gloom. Wet to their waists, they wallowed down the slope, sprawling over snags and dead trees that tore flesh and clothing and sometimes tripped a feebly rising man a second time before he was fully on his feet. There was no cursing now. Men merely rose and fell and stumbled on.

"Let's stop and dig in soon!" Romig called ahead. His voice was hoarse with fatigue. He was tormented by a thirst that snow did not seem to quench.

"A little farther into the timber," Malcolm said. He took Rutledge's place in the lead.

Moments later Davis fell and did not rise. He struggled on his side, face half buried in the snow. Roberts reached down to help him. "Come on. Get up," he said dully.

Davis's battered lips twisted. "My leg—it's caught between two logs."

Muchow helped Roberts pull Davis to his feet. They both let go, and Davis fell again. "Hurt my ankle," he said.

"Drop that damned saw and let me have a look," Muchow said. "Get that damned saw out of the way!"

Lying on his back, Davis raised one leg, but he did not let go of the saw. Muchow felt the ankle with snow-reddened hands, then looked at Roberts. "Swelling in the boot already."

Davis was striking weakly at Muchow when Romig ploughed ahead and reached the scene. "He throwed the saw away!" the Tennesseean sobbed. "He throwed the saw away!"

Muchow looked in perplexity at Romig.

"Let me help him," Romig said. He looked back and saw that Leibee was leading Arnold.

"He throwed the saw away!" the injured man moaned. "I was carrying it for Zeke because I didn't take care of him like I promised Ma."

Romig realized that the saw had become a symbol of penitence. He sighed and lifted Davis in his arms.

In the gloom of timber, sometime later, the party stopped and went to work shoveling a pit to the needle mat. Some of them floundered away to break dead limbs or carry back the fuel Art Rutledge was cutting with their only ax. Fire changed the world. It was a wondrous thing, and the sodden men stared at it as if seeing it for the first time. Then, remembering the night before, they plunged again into the trees to gather wood.

They were scattered widely when the first flakes fell.

Darkness came in moments, a gloom born of giant crystals wet and sticky. Malcolm and Romig came back to the pit with loads of wood. They had been quite close. Arnold and Davis were already there, the Mormon rubbing snow on Davis's swollen ankle. Arnold raised his head so naturally toward Malcolm and Romig that it was difficult to remember he could not see.

"That's an awful heavy snow," Arnold said. "It's nearly dark anyway, isn't it?"

Romig nodded, and then remembered to speak.

Arnold raised his hand, palm up. "Everybody better get back here quick. A man could get lost in no time in that."

"They're not very far away." Malcolm peered into the gloom. He shouted.

Muchow and Art Rutledge came stumbling into the pit. "Whew!" Muchow said. "You can't see that fire twenty feet away." He threw a load of wood toward the pile. "Who's left out there?"

Leibee, Will Greene, Jake Rutledge, Ruthven and Roberts were still out.

Several men began to shout at once. Answers came from scattered points, the sounds muffled by trees and snow. Arnold cocked his head. "Somebody is 'way downhill."

The shouts of several went from the pit again, mixing, scattering. Some of the voices that answered from the gloom seemed farther away than the last time.

"Let one man yell," Romig said. "Or let's fire a gun."

"I got it!" Malcolm cried. He took his bagpipe from

its carrier. In a few moments shrill notes sliced into the murk.

Ruthven and Leibee came in together, carrying a long log. "We stood still and waited, and even then it was a long time before we were sure where the noise was coming from," Ruthven said.

Malcolm stopped piping. They listened. From somewhere on the slope came a voice with hoarse panic in it. "That's Jake!" Art Rutledge said. Someone else shouted, and it was impossible to say from what direction the voice had come.

"I'm a-going after Jake," Rutledge said.

"Stay here," Ruthven ordered. "You'll be one more man lost."

Romig watched the Kentuckian's face. Rutledge hesitated. He scowled. It seemed that he was considering the reason and not the source. He stayed.

"Come to the feast!" Malcolm piped.

Gaunt-faced men stood tensely when the pipes stopped again. Jake Rutledge shouted from so close they recognized his voice easily. "Here!" his cousin yelled, and a few minutes later Jake tumbled into the pit, breathing hard. He had no fuel.

The pipes shrilled once more. Greene and Roberts were still out.

Ten minutes later they came in. Greene was trembling, and his face was blank with terror even after he had stood beside the fire for several minutes. "We went the wrong way twice," Roberts said. "We couldn't remember whether we were above or below the camp." He was nervous, shaken, but when he saw Romig watching him, he sneered and said, "Now thank the Lord, Preacher, that your little flock is safe."

"I'll thank Malcolm Alexander for having sound sense," Romig said.

Ruthven nodded. "That was about as smart an act as I ever saw, Alexander. It was a quick, keen thing."

For an instant Malcolm's face was boyish. He started to reply, but Roberts said, "What a lovely bagpipe you have, Mr. Alexander."

Whatever Malcolm had started to say was lost in anger, at Roberts, at himself, with enough to spare for Romig and Ruthven.

"A lovely rifle, a lovely bagpipe, Mr. Alexander," Roberts said, and gave Romig an insolent look.

In an hour the snow stopped. Romig and Art Rutledge felled a large dead tree near one corner of the pit. Others enlarged the shelter, piling snow around the edges until the refuge was five feet deep. Fire watches were set at two-hour stretches. The party slept in comfort that night.

It was snowing again in the morning and had been since before dawn. When it stopped near noon, Leibee fought his way outside the pit but came wallowing back a few minutes later. "To dere!" he said, and rapped himself across the chest. "Dot is very bad."

The stout German's pessimism was reflected in the bearded faces of men standing silent in the pit.

"If we have to stay awhile, and if we run out of food, we can eat you, Dutchy," Roberts said. "You're nice and plump."

Leibee raised his arms and shook his fists chest high. "No vun eats me all up!" he shouted.

Laughter raised above the pit, but its run was brief, and reddened eyes in snow-burned faces grew thoughtful again.

Malcolm was for striking out at once. Arnold said it was better to take at least one more day of rest. Arguments started, with only Malcolm quite sure of what was best.

The matter was settled momentarily when more snow began to fall, not as thickly as before but smaller flakes that did not melt. It grew colder.

"Let's get wood and stay another night then," Malcolm said irritably, and cursed the weather.

He was in the pit stacking the supply to conserve space when he decided to move his pack and rifle farther from the growing pile of fuel. He had his rifle in his hand when Ruthven came to the edge above and threw down an armful of limbs. One turned end for end on the pivot of a small branch. The limb came down on the barrel of Malcolm's Ferguson and knocked it from his hands.

Coming to the pit behind Ruthven, Romig heard the words, "I'm sorry, Alex—"

Ruthven slid into the pit as Malcolm grabbed him by the ankles. When Romig looked down, the pair were fighting with the silent ferocity of two bitch setters.

Roberts scrambled down the other side.

"Stop it!" Romig yelled. He leaped, caught his foot in the straps of someone's pack and fell. He saw Ruthven knocked flat at Roberts's feet by one of Malcolm's blows.

Roberts cursed and kicked Ruthven in the side.

Romig and the black-browed Scot rose at the same time, Ruthven to knock Malcolm back against the wall. All Romig remembered afterward was the sneer on Roberts's face and then the feel of the Virginian struggling in his grip. Romig tried to hurl him out of the pit. He did throw him beyond the fire into a pile of gear. Roberts's head struck a rifle barrel. He was still.

Ruthven and Malcolm were down, wrestling, rolling toward the fire. Romig tried to separate them and caught somebody's elbow in the nose. His eyes went misty with tears, and he cursed savagely.

Above him Art Rutledge yelled, "Gouge the Yankee's eyes out, Malcolm!"

"Use your knee, Ruthven!" Muchow shouted.

Someone grunting like an angry bear came pumping in to aid Romig. It was Leibee. Together, he and Romig tore Ruthven off Malcolm and brought him to his feet. Leibee drove Ruthven back with a shoulder in the belly. He wrapped his arms around the big Scot's legs, lifted him off his feet and tried, it seemed, to drive him through the wall of snow.

When Malcolm came up, Romig spun him and pinned his arms from behind. Blood and profanity flowed together as Malcolm struck backward with his head against Romig's eyebrow.

Leibee was crying in a muffled voice, "By Gott, I haf no patience! I haf no patience!"

After a while Malcolm said, "All right, Romig! You don't have to bust all my ribs!"

Romig released him. Leibee let Ruthven go. Convinced that the two would not resume the fight immediately, Romig looked around. Men were looking down from the edges of the pit. Now that the fight below was over, they eyed each other, making offers with their eyes.

"Get your wood!" Romig roared. He went over to Roberts, who was coming back to life, and rubbed snow on the Virginian's face and neck until there was awareness in his eyes. Roberts lurched to his feet, throwing one arm against the wall to hold himself.

With the other hand on the butt grips of the pistol in his belt he said softly, "You miserable Yankee bastard, you!"

For a tick of time Romig was of a mind to knock him back into courteous insensibility, Navy Colt and all; but he turned away and strode to the other end of the pit, and stood there staring up at treetops until he had gained control of his anger.

One by one, the spectators around the pit returned to their wood gathering.

There were two fires in the close space that night, and once again, as in the cabin, there was little talk. The last man to bed down was Will Greene. He had been sitting at the Southerners' fire, seeing and hearing nobody. Into a silence broken only by crackling flames he said, "I got to get Samp out'n that hole soon's I can."

Silence ran again. Greene went to bed. The wilderness night pressed in and the fire watcher dozed.

CHAPTER 8

BEFORE DUSK THE NEXT DAY, the soft arms of winter were folding in on their victory. The Blue was only a short distance away, but it seemed that none of the men who had fought toward it was ever going to reach it. Four of them lay at the end of a scrawl of agony traced among trees and punctuated with abandoned gear. A tiny scratch against the body of winter, the trench down which they had come had lost its sharp edges during the heat of day when each sparkling snowflake had thrown splinters of sun into tortured eyes.

Terrible cold came when the sun died.

One man lying on his side had his arms wrapped around a shovel handle. His burned eyes were closed. His beard was damp and yellow on the snow. He had said he could break trail with any man, and this day he had proved he could. Now he lay on his side drifting into sleep. He held no shovel . . . it was a long pole, fuel he had to carry back into the prison. He had been out to bury dead, while sallow men and boys with rifles watched listlessly. Now he would take the pole to his comrades in the blanket tent.

Hans Leibee had never known Andersonville Prison to be so warm before.

Christian Muchow lay with his head almost touching Leibee's feet. Muchow's eyes were blinking. He was going to get up in a minute. It was his turn to carry the rope ahead and tie it to a tree so the others could haul

94

themselves along it. How that big Romig had been able to carry Job Davis on one shoulder and still drag along the line through chest-deep snow was more than Muchow could understand. The snow was so damned heavy; the rope alone had been like a hawser to drag ahead. In a minute, just another minute, he was going to get up and go on. . . .

The deck was smooth beneath him. He could feel the sun on scrubbed planks, hear the slap of water against the hull of the sloop, feel the rhythmic lift of the sea. The sky was blue. Blue was a beautiful color. Muchow sighed. So beautiful and warm. . . .

Joel Roberts, one-time Confederate cavalry captain, had slumped down for a short rest. Only a little rest, but now it didn't matter. . . . He was riding a black Kentucky horse toward a rail fence where men in blue spat puffs of smoke. The horse went effortlessly over a run edged with cool moss. Then Roberts was up the hill and among the blue men, scattering them, slashing at them. But there was no venom in the enemy. They moved away from him with smiles; they parted and let him pass and waved at him. A large, unshaven, hawk-nosed man stood with another on his shoulder and looked at Roberts sternly, but when Roberts tried to ride him down, the horse would not obey. It swerved and carried Roberts among wounded men who lay upon the ground and waved their knees from side to side. Again the horse would not obey. It leaped the threshing knees and would not trample the men.

The smoke vanished, and Roberts was riding down a lane toward a big stone house. The air was heavy with summer. Someone came running from the porch . . . and then everything changed. The house was sullen wreckage. The fields around it were filled with grass and weeds. He dismounted beside three brown mounds among slabs of stone defaced by rifle fire. Anger lifted in him until he was choking; his face turned toward the sky with a curse.

Roberts groaned in his sleep.

Will Greene was lying on red leaves. The tiny deer came toward him. "Lay still!" he whispered to his brother Sampson. "You'll fright him off!" Samp grinned and raised his rifle slowly, and the deer kept moving toward them. It was warm and dry here in the leaves. Will Greene forgot about the deer, or else it vanished. He put out his arm and laid it gently on his brother's shoulder and fell into the sweet darkness of sleep.

"How many are down?" Romig asked. He had been snowblind since early afternoon. His eyes were grinding in their sockets. He had one arm around Job Davis, who was leaning against the side of the trench.

"Six," Jake Rutledge said.

"Seven," Art said. They must be leaning on each other, Romig thought; their voices came from the same place.

"Let's get 'em up, and let's dig in," Romig said. They should have stopped an hour before. They had been exhausted then, but Malcolm had said the Blue was no more than a half mile away—and then cold had come all at once. Romig turned his face in the direction from which he had last heard Malcolm's voice. "Has Leibee still got a shovel?"

"I'll get it," Ruthven said.

"Where's Malcolm?" Romig asked.

"Right here. Anybody got dry matches?"

At noon somebody had tried to build a fire, but it had fallen into the snow. There had been few dry matches then. It was hard for Romig to remember whether it had been that day . . . or the day before. He heard someone pushing on ahead.

"We've got to have matches!" Malcolm said.

Arnold's voice came from close to Romig. "Someone used mine at noon. They were the only dry ones left."

It was Arnold who had tried to talk Malcolm out of trying to build a fire at noon, Romig remembered. A little later he thought of the waterproof tube Eph had given him so long ago. It was hard to find. His fingers did not obey readily. At last he had the tube in his hand. Someone took it. By then Davis had fallen and was lying against Romig's knees, doubled in the snow.

"C'mon, Art," Jake Rutledge said dully. "Let's get 'em on their feet."

Romig heard the cousins floundering away. One of them must have fallen, for he cursed in a muffled voice. Davis was a heavy weight that made Romig's eyes throb with the lifting, but he got the injured man on his feet and began to shake him. The effort seemed to drain all Romig's strength.

At last the Tennesseean said, "Lemme sleep . . . lemme alone, Zeke."

"Wake up!" Romig felt surprise at the hollowness of his voice.

"Keep on your feet. Stay awake." Arnold must be on the other side of Davis, for when Romig's strength was gone, someone was shaking the injured man. Davis began to sag; then he hunched his shoulders and cried out.

"Your ankle isn't frozen at least," Arnold said. "I'll kick it again if you don't stand up."

Romig leaned against the side of the trench. It did not seem so cold now. Somewhere ahead Ruthven was having trouble with Leibee, who was shouting in German. The sounds were all mixed up with the yelling of the Rutledges, groans and slaps and the muttering of men as if in a huge dim hall. Arnold must be able to see now, Romig thought, for he heard the Mormon say, "Get that little dry bunch right close to the trunk."

Another voice said, "For a minute I thought the Dutchman was frozen to this thing." The dry swish of a shovel working snow came to Romig, who kept blinking and shaking his head. . . . He knew he must have dozed a moment, because he had heard no one coming close, and yet Jake Rutledge was saying to him, "They're all up now, Chaplain. Hey, Chaplain! You awake?"

"Yes," Romig said, and did not open his eyes. He was not cold. He was not even stiff, except that his arms felt leaden when he tried to move them, and his fingers were sort of numb; but he was not cold. All he needed was rest. Rest. Then he would pick Job Davis up once more, and they would go on. No. That was not right. They were going to stop here. He shook his head violently.

"Don't everybody stand around!" Malcolm cried. "Help get some wood."

Romig listened to grunts and the sound of cracking twigs. Someone muttered, "My hands is almost froze. Can't even grab a little bitty limb."

It was cold, Romig realized suddenly, that was sending that drowsy feeling into his body. He opened his blind eyes wide and stared around him. The swish of the shovel went on, and a long time afterward Ruthven said, "This will do for a start. Who can hold a match?"

All activity stopped.

Moments later Art Rutledge said, " 'Less'n it's with my teeth—I can't."

After another silence Ruthven said, "Give me the matches, Malcolm."

The snow made little creaking sounds as men came close. Romig was awake now. He tried to flex his hands. They barely moved, and he thought his mittens must be stiff with ice. Then he realized he had lost his mittens. He put his hands under his arms. Little balls of ice were clinging to his coat sleeves. He pulled his arms inside his coat.

"There goes one," Muchow said. "How many's in that thing?"

"Eight or ten," Ruthven said.

"Light 'em all at once," Malcolm advised.

"Like hell I will."

In the middle of the next little silence Romig heard a tiny crack of breaking wood. Men muttered and stirred.

"You busted it against the guard of the knife!" Roberts complained.

Someone was rubbing his hands together vigorously. The noise of it stopped suddenly, and Arnold said, "Let me try, Ruthven."

There were more short silences, each followed by groans or oaths wrenched up from despair. They were watching life slip away from them in little flares, Romig knew. There should be a way to start a fire. From somewhere in the long ago some advice about that stirred in Romig's brain, but he could not remember what it was. Then he smelled smoke and heard crackling twigs, and no one seemed to be breathing.

Muchow cried, "God's sake, Rutledge, what were you trying to do!"

"I was fanning it!"

"You pud id oud!" Leibee shouted.

"There's two left," Arnold said quietly. "Everybody stand back."

At last Romig remembered the candles Ephraim had given him. "Wait!" The fumbling of his fingers made him tremble, but finally he got one candle from his pocket, surprised to feel the greasy warmth of it. High in his shirt pocket he had carried it, against his service Bible.

Someone took the candle. Romig heard a curse. The stub had dropped into the snow during transfer. Several moments later Arnold said, "I've got it. Now, look, men, stay clear and let Malcolm hold it while I light it under the twigs."

There were sounds of men shifting positions.

"Hold it sidewise, Malcolm," Arnold said, "and don't push it against the twigs until it's going good."

"Keep it clear of that blood on your thumbs," Greene said.

"The blood is frozen." Arnold's voice was calm.

More vividly than if he could see, Romig had a grasp of the picture. Malcolm's hands were bloody from breaking twigs with freezing fingers; his hands were so stiff he had to use both to hold the candle stub, and Arnold's could be scarcely any better.

"Sink or swim," Malcolm said. There was no fear in his voice. "Light both matches."

Arnold hesitated. "All right," he said.

Romig heard the searing of two matches and then no other sounds until Art Rutledge shouted, "It's caught! It's a-going!"

The crackling of twigs and the smell of smoke came pleasantly.

"Oh, God, let it burn," Jake Rutledge said.

Ephraim would be glad to know about his matches and the candle, Romig thought. He took his hands from under his coat and felt for Job Davis's shoulder. "How's the ankle, Job?"

"Pretty good—now," Davis said.

The crackling sounds were growing louder.

And then someone let out a curse that was almost a shriek. There was a hissing sound. Smoke came warmly against Romig's face, and then it was gone and the cold returned. The fire was out. Romig was the last of all to know what had happened. A section of the bank had sloughed and covered the flames.

There was no cursing then. Men looked for matches. Several had them, but all of them were wet. There were no guns left. Even Roberts had abandoned his pistol, and Malcolm's Ferguson was in a tree somewhere on the back trail. He spoke of going after it, but Arnold told him that the rifle was at least a mile up the mountain, and that by the time he went up and back—if he could make it—the cold would have the others. Moreover, they had no moss or anything else that the flash of powder would ignite.

The cold lay on them hard.

Job Davis sighed and sat down against Romig's legs.

"How far, Arnold, to some settlement on the Blue?" Muchow asked.

"Must be ten miles to Fort Marabee," the Mormon said. "Maybe one of us . . ." The pretense wedged down to silence. They all knew they had not made three miles that day.

Romig reached down and hauled Job Davis to his feet and began to shake him.

"I vill go for help!" Leibee said.

Romig heard him plunge away.

After a while Art Rutledge said, "He do have the spirit, but he ain't a-going very far."

Romig knew they all must have stood numbly, watching the German, for a few minutes later, someone grunted and somebody else expelled breath in a defeated sigh. Leibee probably was still trying, Romig thought; it was the way of the man. But he was not getting any place.

Heber Arnold spoke up strongly. "I've got a couple of matches against the bare hide under my arm. After a while they may get so they'll light. Everybody stay on their feet."

Cold was probing into Romig's stomach. He beat his hands against his chest, and the thumps seemed to come from objects that were detached from him.

"Can you make a sound on the bagpipe, Malcolm?" he asked.

He knew by the silence that Malcolm must be looking at him curiously. "Why?" the Scot asked at last.

"There could be some other idiots within hearing. Try it."

The wailing of the pipes made no tune, but Malcolm's wind was good. Notes scattered across the frozen wilderness. They broke against silent trees. They rode the freezing air. They died. Moisture from Malcolm's breath had frozen in the pipes.

The silence and the cold seemed to come together heavily then.

"Leibee's laying there beating the snow with his fists," Muchow said dully. "I'll go help him back."

"What's the use?" Will Greene asked thickly. "It's getting dark. What's the use?"

"I'll help you, sailor," Roberts said. "That Dutchman is a man!"

Romig heard them moving away. They didn't go fast, for they were a long time within his hearing.

"How do the matches look, Doc?" Malcolm asked a little later.

Everyone would be looking at Arnold now. In red-eyed desperation with frost on their beards, they would be looking at Arnold, reaching with their eyes. toward life, while rigidity was growing in their bodies. Romig tried to lock his knees. He was going to stay on his feet. This stubborn clinging to life had no quality in it save brutish fight, but he was going to stay alive as long as he could.

"A little while longer," Arnold said. "I want to keep them there as long as possible."

It came to Romig that the Mormon had no matches under his arm.

"It's almost dark," Greene said. "Look at those trees. Look at those dirty trees! They'd burn if we only had some way—"

"Shut up, Will." Romig tried to shout. His voice was a sleepy croak, but it sounded all right to him.

"It's getting dark!" Greene cried.

There never would be darkness that men couldn't conquer, Romig thought. Men made their own darkness, and they could defeat it. He wanted to say that. For the first time since the war he wanted to thunder a sermon. Bright thoughts ran through his mind and disappeared, and other glowing thoughts came to replace them. He was going to speak. He was going to keep these men awake. He felt his knees unhinging slowly, his legs trembling as he fought to stay erect; and when he was sitting in the snow, he was surprised to find that Job Davis was already there.

"There goes the preacher!" Jake Rutledge said, and there was terror in his voice.

Romig made a last effort to keep awake. "I'm just resting a minute, Jake."

"Pray for us, Chaplain?" Jake asked.

"God, let us help Thee," Romig said.

"Amen," Jake Rutledge muttered, and then a moment later he cried, "He didn't say no prayer—not the right way! He's all mixed up!"

"No," Heber Arnold said. "He isn't mixed up."

Romig heard the voices, but they meant little to him. He heard more voices later, coming from a great distance. They swelled, they receded. Someone pounded his back and shoulders. Someone fell against him. Men shouted at him, intrusions that did not quite get through his numbness, but still they kept him fighting against something that no longer seemed to have significance.

Sometime later he heard Malcolm shout, "There's a man on snowshoes!"

Romig heard, but the words had little meaning; they were just part of the muttering that kept him from rest. And then the noises found some cell of consciousness, and grew and spread until he had the thought. He struggled to his feet, not knowing which way to turn his sightless eyes. He stood there so long with silence around him that he began to think his senses had tricked him, and that he had heard no shout from Malcolm.

He heard a clacking noise, and his mind went to the night in the tiny cabin below the pass when the freezing mules were shaking their ears. But this clacking sound was regular. It came close and stopped.

"I'll have you a fire," a strange voice said, a voice filled with the quick rise and fall of Swedish speech. "Some of you go help the three who tried to go ahead."

There was a large, red-faced, raw-boned Swede out there on snowshoes, Romig thought, a man who knew the snow, someone like little Eph. Romig's mind shifted quickly to Ephraim's weathered, sturdy face. There was a man for you!

He clung to that thought when he found himself sitting down again with his legs across somebody's body. In a moment he would rise and lift Job Davis to his shoulder. . . .

At times he was dimly aware of sound and movement. Once it seemed that he rose and walked and smelled smoke hot in his face. And then he was warm, and the fight was over. . . . He stood and looked at snow-covered waves of granite and felt a gentle breeze against his face and neck. It blew past him and bent and rippled banks of flowers that grew along the edges of the snow.

CHAPTER 9

WHEN ROMIG'S CRAMPED ARM ran its signal through his stupor, he came from sleeping in little drowsy steps. He was under a bough roof. Outside the shelter he saw snow walls with the orange play of firelight on them, and only then did he fully comprehend that his blindness had passed, although his eyes were still hot and aching.

Sleepers jammed against him neither stirred nor

protested when he got awkwardly to hands and knees and began to crawl outside. He was crouched like a red-eyed animal emerging from its den when he saw the man squatting near the flames.

Firelight glistened on a wide forehead and two wedges of skull flesh where tight black hair receded. The man's lips were wide and full, his nose uncommonly long and thin. He was dressed in a buckskin shirt and leather pants.

He was a black Negro.

Romig got to his feet. He was stiff. His muscles were sore, and one arm was still hanging like a weight divorced from blood and nerves.

"Where—where's the Swede?" he asked.

"I am Teteluki Olsen. I speak English as one of Norway, but I am what you see." The voice was slow, as solemn as the Negro's eyes.

Romig went toward the fire, rubbing his arm. "Wolof?"

The quiet eyes seemed to sharpen. "My mother was half Wolof, half Eboe. My father was a Zulu." Olsen rose and leaned against the wall, a poleax he had been using as a staff between his knees. He stood as tall as Romig, who was four inches above six feet. He was as wide as Romig too, but not as heavy.

Romig stared at Olsen until the solemn scrutiny he got in return disturbed him, and then he looked around. They were in a snow pit. One end and side held an L-shaped shelter made of poles and boughs, with frozen blankets on top. Behind the fire was a log reflector that was throwing heat toward the sleeping place.

"You must have worked all night," Romig said.

Olsen nodded.

"Was everybody all right?"

"There will be frozen toes and fingers." Olsen glanced at the sleeping men. "Are you hungry?"

"I could eat the south end of a half-cooked skunk."

Olsen reached to one side and set a small iron kettle on coals at the edge of the fire. "I have some elk meat."

Life began to flow into Romig's arm with tingling ecstasy. He saw the Ferguson, packs, guns, and other gear that had been abandoned the day before. This elk meat—Olsen surely hadn't brought it with him the first time; he must have gone back to his camp. "Where is your camp?" Romig asked.

"On the river, about a mile from here."

"By yourself?"

Olsen nodded.

"You heard the pipes?"

"I did."

"We would have died if you hadn't come."

"That is so."

It would be a long time before Romig grew used to hearing a Norwegian accent coming so casually from a black man. He had talked to thousands of Negroes in the South, and he had watched and listened to scores of others huddled in his father's stone barn when they were on their way to Canada before the war, but he had never heard one speak so tersely and so calmly as Teteluki Olsen; and he had never seen one so solemn and yet so unafraid. The very name of Zulu was symbolic of barbarity and ruthlessness to make an American Indian pale by comparison. Perhaps this man . . . but Romig didn't know what he thought. He rubbed his arm and stared at Olsen; and then he dug his pack from one corner of the pit and got out sodden tea leaves and dried apricots that were already swelling.

Across a fire in a snowy pit where flames beat back a frozen wilderness Jonathan Romig, Vermont born, an ordained and licensed minister, and Teteluki Olsen, one-time bloody Zulu warrior, shared their food and reached their minds toward each other in friendship. Dawn was near when Olsen began to talk freely. Before that he listened, studying Romig's words as well as his face, and seemed to find at last something that satisfied him.

"I was born in a hut of mud and grass in Matabeleland," Teteluki said, "one of forty children of the chief." His deep voice wiped away continents and oceans. "My mother had been sold in slavery to the Dutch at Natal. When they took her north, she was captured by the Zulus in a dawn raid against laagered wagons of the Boers. My uncle told me how she died by the assegai after I was born—when she protested turning me over to the military system of the impis."

Romig brushed sparks from his knees and stared thoughtfully. He knew something of the bloody history of the Zulus, of their despotic military discipline, which for singleness of purpose probably outstripped any warrior creed that ever existed.

"Our camps were not homes," Olsen said. "They were barracks. Except to practice with the assegai I never remember playing with another child. No woman's hand ever touched my childhood. And later, until I killed in battle, I could not sit or eat with warriors. I crouched apart and waited, and in time some warrior would take a scrap of meat, wipe it in the dust, and hurl it toward me with a jeer. I killed. I was many times a warrior until Dingaan's Day, as the Boers call it."

Romig watched the play of light on the long black face. "Dingaan's Day?"

"It was then Pretorius led his Boers against us and crushed our regiments—the impis—with fire we could not stand against. Killing was Boerish nature, too. It seems to be the nature of all men I have seen." Teteluki squatted by the fire, his hands clasped before him. There were no dusty age wrinkles on his hands, but strong veins and the sheen of firm flesh. Deformity or injury had given Olsen unusually long thumbs with enlarged main joints.

"Since then you've come to God?" Romig asked.

Teteluki's black eyes swung quickly. They glinted. He shook his head slowly. "To the Carpenter God, you mean?" He shook his head again. "Have you? Do you know Him?"

"I look for Him among men," Romig said.

"You were born a white man with your God already prepared for you—and white. I was born a Zulu with other gods to fear." Teteluki shook his head. "No man comes to the Carpenter God quickly, as you find death by the sharp thrust of the uncleaned assegai, or from the knife of the chief's assassin—or as one becomes a Zulu warrior by washing his spear in human blood.

"No. I try to love the Carpenter God. I have not yet. I try. Even in these mountains I have seen the jerking that follows the shouting of your God-speakers, which they say is a sign of Godness. I have seen men thresh in the dirt like dagga smokers, while the God-speaker raised his hands and was pleased. If I thought the Carpenter God touched the minds of people like dagga smoke, I would long ago have gone back to Africa."

Romig stared in amazement. A thought that one holds himself is doubly enhanced when another states it. "When the Lord is upon them, Son," an older minister once had told him, "they'll jerk like beheaded chickens—and then you'll know how to measure the job you've done!"

"No," Teteluki said. "I have not seen your gentle God. Even now, when the thunder roars, I sometimes wake in fear of Unkulunkulu and Inkosi. Old wild fears run in my heart, and I want to seize an assegai and defy the heavens to hide that fear."

Olsen placed a limb upon the fire and watched flames curl around it. He brushed wet bark fragments from his palms, and they glistened brownly in the light. "Only once before in this land I told my story, to a Mormon bishop, who was kind but did not believe me. Afterward he said there was white blood in me. I no longer care because many people have said that after listening to my speech. But I am a Zulu, and I am proud to be one, for if your Carpenter God is what I've tried to learn of Him, He made us all."

The centuries that stood before and after Christ—the centuries when the minds of men had frozen on little things, like the minds of excited hogs—lay heavy on Jonathan Romig. This black man, with the understanding of Christ himself, had said that he was proud to be a Zulu. Romig wondered if he could say that he was proud to be a white man.

"There is something in your face that lets me know you will believe," Teteluki said. "And I have wanted to speak to someone who would listen and not tighten one side of his mouth and turn his head. Your face was good, even in the blindness of your sleep when we led you to your bed. Your mates say you serve God. I do not see God in your eyes—this Carpenter God who is yours, not mine—but I see goodness. I will tell my story, and then I must go up the mountain for packs and other things I had no time to get last night."

Smoke curled past the black face. "After Dingaan's Day we fled north. There was much trouble among the impis. My uncle killed my father and sent a knife for me where I lay wounded in a hut, but I strangled the chief's knife and fled that night with some of my people north to the lake called Victoria to live with our cousins, the Angoni. There was more murder among us; brothers killed brothers. I went then to live with Bushmen, learning to stalk the open places, learning something of their painting. But I was not one of them, so I went again where the long grasses bend and took refuge in a mission station."

Teteluki was silent for a long time.

"There was a Norway man called Schreuder, who taught me of the Carpenter God, and in time taught me to read and write. There was blood in my mind, and I was still a Zulu with an unwashed spear, but my mouth was ready, and I stayed because there were no Boers to shoot me. I stayed for years, and sometimes I saw glimpses of the Carpenter God in Schreuder's eyes. He was a man the Zulus never bothered. At last I went back among my own people to teach them of the Carpenter God. But they cared nothing for a man who never sought revenge and never killed. They taunted me. They angered me. I killed three of them and had to flee again, this time going to the sea itself. I sailed on ships. The first one was a Norwegian ship, whose sailors named me. I went to many places in this world, until one day we landed in the green land of California with half the crew rotting from disease. There I ran away."

Olsen rose and looked at the sky. Dawn was not far away. "I learned of gold in California, and later in the Mormons' land I helped to dig a ditch, and listened to new talk of the Carpenter God. There were good people there, but an army came and made bad tempers. I went with trappers in the mountains—rough, quarrelsome men, like Spanish sailors. I left them for the Black Indians of these mountains, and among them I have wandered for several years, walking in the forests. They have another god, somewhat like Inkosi—one called Manitou."

Teteluki's breath lifted past his face in vapor streams that mingled with the smoke. "Is the Carpenter God the chief of all—or do the other gods watch him closely, as officers in the impis watch to see if another becomes a favorite who must be killed by night?"

"There is one God," Romig said. "His name does not matter."

"You serve Him?"

"I try," Romig said. "But I am confused."

The dawn had come. Olsen reached above him to feel the crust. "We may be able to walk on that today," he said. He took a pair of web snowshoes from a corner among the packs. "I will go once more to see if I can find anything that was overlooked when my way was lighted only by pitch knots."

"How old are you?" Romig asked. The question had been bothering him for some time.

"I suppose somewhere between forty-five and fifty." Olsen began to lace on the webs.

"You're mining on the Blue?"

"I will be when spring comes. Late last fall I found a small, rich gravel bank." Olsen glanced toward the bough shelter. "There will be enough for all—unless greed grows among them."

He went up the back trail.

Romig put more wood upon the fire and sat staring at the flames until Heber Arnold woke and came from the shelter. The Mormon began to rub snow on his eyes. "Where's the giant?"

"Up the hill."

"He looked a hundred feet tall when he walked in on us last night. We were done, I suppose you guessed?"

Romig grinned. "I didn't have to guess."

Arnold came over to the fire to dry his hands. "Did he talk to you at all?"

"A little."

Arnold nodded. "There's a man with a deep intelligence, Romig, a man who doesn't even impress you as being black after you listen to his voice. I'll swear there isn't a drop of white blood in him, either."

"There isn't," Romig said.

"Warm that tea up, will you, please?" the Mormon said. "Whew! It's cold out here. I'll bet a bull could walk on this crust!"

Under a dark sky with light snow falling, they came at last into the valley of the Blue. Teteluki was carrying Davis. The Negro had said scarcely a dozen words since his talk with Romig before dawn.

They crossed flats where scrubby willows showed above the snow, skirted an enormous beaver pond that showed black water in the middle, and went downstream. Romig looked curiously at the river they had worked so hard to reach. It didn't seem important now, this swiftly moving snow-edged stream that ran as if cold had thickened it.

Where the river split to surround a little island that looked like a white iron-clad with bow upstream, they saw Teteluki's camp, a domed hut of mud and willows. Log footbridge connected the island with both banks. They crossed the south bridge, slick with ice, and crowded around the hut. Part of an elkskin lay hard as flint on the domed roof; another piece of hide covered a low opening which faced a large boulder on the downstream end of the island.

"My camp is small," Teteluki said, "but you are welcome."

Roberts started to speak. A tight cough jarred him. His eyes were showing fever, Romig thought. He saw Arnold watching the Virginian sharply.

They cleared the island of snow and built a large bough shelter behind the hut. Wood was plentiful on the north bank, which was several feet higher than the south side of the river. For two days and nights the cold was intense. They kept fires before the shelter at all times.

Boots were cracked and leaking. With the exception of bacon and salt pork most of their supplies had been ruined by the snow; but there were still some lumps of salt in cans, and they scraped the bottom of their packs, among sodden messes of corn meal and beans and swelling rice, to salvage what they could. Olsen had twenty pounds of salt, which he offered freely. Hanging in the trees on the north bank was almost half of a small elk.

Reaction from their murderous struggle was strong after they had reached safety. Romig was barely able to keep awake whenever he warmed himself at the fire. On the second day, when men were dull-eyed from too much rest, they put Roberts in the hut with Teteluki; the Virginian was too sick to know that he was lying on Romig's sleeping bag. Ephraim's bottle of brownish medicine had been consumed without effect on Roberts's fever or his cough.

Others had toes and fingers that would have to be removed, Arnold said. Jake Rutledge's left ear was drooping badly.

"Well," Arnold told them after dinner, when they

were loafing at the fire, "we'd best get at it."

Jake Rutledge felt his ear. "God! I'll look like that little Eph feller."

"Not nearly as smart, though," his cousin told him. Art looked at Arnold. "I know you figure all the toes on my left foot got to go, but I need the big one and that long, crooked one next to it. I knowed a feller back home got caught in a painter trap. They taken all his toes—and he wasn't no good for dancing, hunting—or nothing!" He shook his head. "I got to have that big toe and the other."

"*Ja!*" Leibee nodded violently. "Ven you die you must haf the two big toes to tie together!"

Andersonville again, Romig thought. Leibee had told him how the prisoners tied together the big toes of dead who had to be carried from the stockade each morning. For a time Romig had thought the snow had washed some of the vile mists of Andersonville from Leibee's mind, but they were still there. The German was haggard. Each day he retired to the lower end of the island, behind the boulder, and secretively examined a small, silk-wrapped packet.

Arnold, too, had been watching Leibee, but now he turned back to the business at hand. "All right, Art," he said, "we'll take a chance on leaving two toes; but if they start to go bad, they're coming off—even if I have to have Jake tie you up with Muchow's rope."

Art grinned. "He ain't man enough, even with that officer's hat he swiped. The toes will be all right. I'll wiggle hell out of 'em. I'll spit tobacco juice on 'em all the time."

"Take off your sock and put your foot on this log," Arnold ordered. He took out his knife.

Art Rutledge pawed at the hair on his forehead and gulped. "Can't you do it quick-like—with Luki's poleax?"

"I could, but the splintered bits of bone might start trouble when they begin to work out."

Art removed his sock and put his foot on the log. He stared at it in terrible fascination. Men crowded in to watch. Romig caught himself wiggling his own toes in sympathy.

Arnold's work was quick. He severed three toes at the joints closest to the foot. One that he tossed toward the river fell short. Muchow kicked it into the water—and then began to vomit.

"Hell! That warn't bad," Art Rutledge said, and fell fainting against his cousin's legs.

Job Davis, his tongue working in and out of the gap in his broken mouth, lost two toes. His ankle was drum-tight, but Arnold said it would heal in time. Will Greene lost both little toes. Then Arnold cropped Jake Rutledge's right ear. He smeared all his surgery with pine gum, scoured his knife with sand, and looked sadly at the broken boots the Southerners had worn across the mountains.

"A little cutting," the Mormon said. "Any fool could do that. But Roberts—that's the sort of problem that makes you curse your ignorance."

"The man is dying," Teteluki said. "By morning he will be choked to death. If you wish, I will show you what I saw done once in Sweden."

"Show me," Arnold said. "Come on, Romig."

They raised Roberts on a thick bed of spruce boughs and made a blanket tent over him. They heated stones and carried them in frying pans, placing them beside the sick man and pouring water over them until the hut was fogged with vapor and bits of mud began to fall from the roof.

"I have seen Indians do this too," Teteluki said gravely.

Romig wiped sweat off his face. "Did it help?"

"Sometimes. Sometimes they died."

Men got on hands and knees to peer in through the low door, and then returned to the big fires shaking their heads. At dusk Roberts seemed to be breathing with less effort.

"Now we roll him in the creek," Teteluki said.

Romig grunted like a startled bear.

Arnold cocked his head in doubt.

"The man is dying," Teteluki said.

They plunged him naked in the icy water and rubbed him with it. Romig slipped to his knees during the operation, and the shock of water was like a blow in the groin.

"Now," Luki said, "we take him inside and beat him lightly with switches."

"Good Lord!" Romig muttered.

They were squatted by the sick man, flicking him with small spruce boughs when Malcolm peered inside. "What in hell's name—"

"The Swedish method," Romig explained weakly.

"You tried to drown him, and now you're trying to

beat him to death!" Malcolm shouted. "By Jesus Christ—"

"Do *you* know what to do?" Arnold asked softly.

"No, but . . ." Malcolm went away.

Romig observed that Roberts was barely breathing.

They put him into warmed blankets and steamed him all night long. Just before dawn, when it seemed to Romig that the Virginian was dying, he began to cough loosely; and an hour later his eyes were focusing on movement.

"He has a chance, I think," Arnold said, "but I don't know why."

CHAPTER 10

EXCEPT FOR ROBERTS, who was mending slowly, none of the twelve had a dainty appetite, and in less than a week Teteluki's meat was almost gone. Before the last stripped bones—cracked, the marrow sucked from them or dug out with knives—had been thrown into the Blue, Muchow came stumbling from downriver on Olsen's snowshoes. The sailor had been practicing with the webs each day. He shouted that he had just seen a herd of animals twice as large as buffaloes.

"The elk yard," Teteluki told Romig. "I was going down in a day or two to kill another small one."

Men were shouting, running for rifles. They had been idle, without tools to mine the frozen ground. Their bellies were full. There was excitement at hand.

Arnold came to where Romig and the Negro stood.

"One would be plenty now—with the weather threatening to turn off warm any day," the Mormon said.

Teteluki nodded and watched men inspecting rifles. And then he went to the hut for his heavy Samuel Hawken.

Six men followed the Negro downriver through rotten-crusted snow, along the edge of spruce trees. Muchow, who had left his Jenks too far back on the trail for recovery, had borrowed Roberts's rifle. Romig's rifle had been stolen from him in Pueblo. Arnold didn't choose to take his weapon.

They went into the timber and started up a small hill that overlooked willow flats. Their breath came faster. They hurried, crowding close to Teteluki. Romig looked at tense mouths and eyes alert and eager. Killing, he thought, must be born in the blood. For hunters they made an unearthly crashing and crunching, but when they crossed the little hill, fanned out so that no one had the lead, the elk were still there in a yard a hundred and fifty feet away.

"One is plenty," Romig said loudly.

An old cow was watching him. She jerked her fleshy head, twisted in the trench among rust-colored willows, and ran stiff-legged toward the central pit. Muchow shot her through the neck and whooped.

That touched off every rifle in the party, excepting Olsen's. Death whistled down the hill. Romig and Arnold began to shake shoulders and shout. A man would stop firing, look up with unseeing eyes. Another would shoot. Then, having missed a chance to fire, the first would turn away and shoot again. They quit when nothing was moving in the bloody yard. Surviving elk were fleeing downriver. Marked by his tremendous height and velveted horns well started on new growth, the bull fled screened by cows, coughing explosive warnings as he ran. Buff color had begun to show in the triangular markings of his rump. He stumbled, and the cows lunged past him. He kicked snow wildly and gained his feet. Almost six feet high at the shoulder, his orange-brown mane strong against the whiteness, he paused one foolish moment broadside.

Malcolm steadied his Ferguson across a limb.

Teteluki took one long step and slapped the rifle down with the flat of his hand. It fell into the snow. Yellow flames ran wild in Malcolm's eyes as he turned and struck. It was a streaking blow, straight from the natural twist of powerful shoulders. It was enough to fracture bone.

Luki took the fist on an open palm, leaning backward. Then he moved ahead, striking Malcolm's chest with his shoulder. In the instant when the Scot was motionless and off balance Teteluki stooped. He came up with Malcolm's ankles, and sent young Alexander flipping backward so hard his feet doubled over his head.

Jake Rutledge clubbed his rifle. "I'll kill that nigger!"

Romig tore the gun away so savagely that Rutledge went spinning into the snow. His gray hat flew off. The strip of shirt hanging over his maimed ear fell across his shoulder.

"Sit there, damn you!" Romig roared.

Rutledge reached for his knife. He grasped the handle, then he looked at Romig's face again and sat still.

Malcolm was calm when he rose. He smiled. He went toward Teteluki slowly, shoving his feet for careful footing under the snow.

Teteluki's anger was gone now. The Negro turned away. He retrieved his rifle from where it leaned against a tree, glanced at Malcolm and nodded down the hill. "We have work to do," Olsen said.

He walked away.

Malcolm looked amazed, then foolish. He took a few quick steps toward Teteluki. He watched the broad back moving off, the straight set of neck and head crowned by a dun Scotch cap. Malcolm whirled to see what lay on the faces of the others, flinging a challenge with his eyes. He was dangerously angry, Romig knew, more dangerous because he was bewildered. But no one spoke, and no one showed much expression. Malcolm Alexander looked back in perplexity at Teteluki.

Jake Rutledge rose from the snow. "I don't like no man's hands on me," he said.

"If you had swung that rifle I think I would have killed you," Romig said. He looked at his hands. They were clenched hard. He opened them slowly and looked at Rutledge.

Rutledge picked up his hat. He put it on and felt his injured ear absently, and all the while his eyes were hard on Romig's face. The latter stooped and recovered the piece of shirt that had fallen from Rutledge's shoulder. He held it toward the Kentuckian. "Don't forget this. You don't want to catch cold in that frozen ear, Jake."

Rutledge took the cloth. He stuffed it under his hat so that it hung over his ear. "We both got mighty tempers, Romig."

There were seven dead elk in the yard after Luki finished two crippled cows. Tons of meat that would spoil lay in the red-splashed snow. Romig took Muchow's rifle and went down river on a bloody trail. He found one more dead elk and killed two wounded ones. For a moment he stood looking down at the last dead cow, watching the dullness of lost life turning the fluid brightness of her eyes to ugly jelly.

Most of the tension was gone when he returned to the yard. Men were staring as Arnold ate liver raw and smoking.

Muchow, always the experimenter, sliced a chunk and. tried it gingerly, and then he began to chew more surely. "Laugh at me for puking over a cut-off toe!" He sliced himself another piece of liver. "Let's see some of you try this!"

They butchered without plan or direction for a while until Arnold suggested taking some of the skins and only the choicest meat, loins and haunches.

They were carrying their burden of meat back to camp in skins when they heard the cries and saw Leibee, knee-deep in the river, throwing water wildly from Olsen's gold pan.

"Golt! I haf found golt!"

Teteluki had said there was gold here, but now the German's frenzied cries ran like the contagion of killing that had been in their blood a short time before. Malcolm fell off the north footbridge in his haste. Davis, Art Rutledge and Will Greene were hobbling along the edge of the island, shouting at the German. Coherence was still having a struggle when Romig and Arnold reached the island with their load of meat. By then Leibee had been pulled at, shouted at and questioned until he had retired behind the boulder at the lower end of the island. He was sitting on the gold pan, refusing to answer questions or talk at all.

"He found a little gold and then a nugget, I guess," Will Greene explained. "He throwed everything over his head and begun to yell like a pig caught in a gate."

The creek was full of splashing and shouting. Men slid and slipped, bumped against each other and fell down, all trying to find the nugget Leibee had thrown away. They used frying pans, tin plates and messkits, scooping up gravel, scooping up mud.

Arnold shook his head, smiling. "How does it lie here, Luki?"

"There's good gravel and sand on the north bank—and then nothing, as far as I know."

"Have you staked ground?" the Mormon asked.

Teteluki shook his head. "There is no district along this stretch. There was no hurry."

"There is now," Romig said.

Arnold nodded. "Tonight we'd best organize a district."

"Right now we'd better get the rest of the meat," Teteluki said. "You and I and Romig."

No one came to help them get the meat and hang it

in the trees beyond the north bank, where a little depression showed that the river had changed its course years before. Romig explained a plan to Arnold and the Negro. "If men work together they get along better. Now, I know nothing of placer mining, but I'm learning about men . . ."

The plan, Teteluki and Arnold said, was good.

That night they bound themselves with law. Twelve men stood around a huge fire, with cold nibbling at their necks, and took unto themselves land that had come to the United States forty-seven years before by the Florida Treaty. Public ownership was not even vaguely felt on this island in the Blue, and Romig observed that private ownership came to some as a matter to wonder about.

Before they started and even after they started, they were suspicious and resentful of the laws they were about to make. Men moved worn boots uneasily, scratched tangled beards, and stood ready to complain and shout. Their covenant would have to be simple.

Art Rutledge rocked back and forth on his healing foot. "We don't want nothing that don't give everybody the same chance."

"No stinking nabob stuff," Will Greene said.

Romig laughed. "You fellows sound as if you thought the regulations were going to be thrown at us by somebody who isn't here. *We* are going to make the rules."

Leibee greeted that remark with interest.

"I suggest," Romig said, "that we make Arnold chairman of the meeting, since he has had experience with mining and miners' law."

"That's all right," Art Rutledge said, and nodded at his cousin.

"I second the motion," Malcolm said.

"So do I," Greene said firmly.

"And if nobody has any objections, I will write down the rules we make in the back of my Bible," Romig said.

"Just so you read 'em afterward so we all can hear," Art Rutledge said. "I don't want no law I can't hear right out loud."

"All right," Heber Arnold said. "To start, this is Olsen's claim we're standing on. As the original locator of a district, he's entitled to two claims. The rest of us get one apiece."

Some stared with displeasure at the Negro.

On Arnold's recommendation they set their district as extending one mile each way along the Blue from where they stood, and one half mile on each side.

Romig started to write. "We've got to have a name for it," he said.

Silence ran. Men pulled their hot garments away from their legs and turned their backsides to the fire, or did their shifting in the opposite direction. They gave the problem serious consideration. Smoke drifted into their beards and filtered upward past their hat brims. A wolf howled down by the elk yard. Will Greene proposed Jubal Early City. Muchow said why not Sheridan or Lincoln.

"Let's be sensible," Heber Arnold said.

Jake Rutledge stroked his wiry beard and stared a

long time at a weak moon. "How about Calla Ella Della?"

Art snorted. "That fly-up-the-crick! Every man and boy along the Little Mossy—"

Jake put his boot on his cousin's foot. "Take it back! Eat it without salt!"

"My toe!" Art yelled. "My froze big toe! I take it back! My froze big toe!"

"I say Calla Ella Della," Jake repeated, and looked around for disagreement. It was solidly there in downcast eyes and hidden smiles, but Jake was too flushed to see it.

Ships of state had broken keels on lesser points, Romig thought. He said that while he thought the name one of the most interesting he had ever heard, he hesitated to name a rough camp in the mountains after a delicate girl so young and beautiful as Miss Della must be.

Jake blinked and got tangled up in the words. "It ain't Miss Della," he said. "That's just part of her first name. Her whole name is—"

"She ain't exactly a delicate girl neither," Art said, and covered his toes with both hands.

The cousins grinned at each other.

"How about Moonbeam Placer on the Blue?" Jake asked. "Now that's a right pretty mouthful."

They settled on Moonbeam. It wasn't bad at that, Romig thought. He wrote it, and then he stared at the page, thinking of moonlight on the broad Ohio; and suddenly Charity Megill's face was clear before him. She had an uncommonly disturbing habit of rising in his thoughts. He scowled and went on with his writing in a tiny, cramped style.

Arnold deftly directed the way to agreement, suggesting, waiting, controlling. They set a six-day citizenship requirement for owning ground, that being the length of time they had been here. No man could pre-empt more than one claim from now on, but anyone could buy as many as he cared to from others. Unless ill, each man staking ground had to do some work on it within ten days. "A reasonable amount" was enough. Fifty cents was the fee for recording ground.

With Teteluki casting the deciding vote they elected Ruthven recorder. That whetted appetites for the personal issues of voting. Too late Romig realized he should have introduced his plan for co-operative working of the claims before the matter of permanent officers was raised. That was the idea that he had told Arnold and Teteluki about, but now a sudden tensing around the fire told Romig that he had missed his chance and had better wait.

"What other officers are there?" Job Davis asked.

"President of the district," Arnold said.

"You'll do for that," Muchow said.

The Rutledges nodded at each other. "Anybody got any arguments?" Art asked belligerently.

He found no opposition.

"Arnold's president," Art said. "What else we got to elect?"

Malcolm looked disappointed, Romig thought.

"We'll have to have a judge for a miners' court—and a sheriff," Arnold said.

"A court?" Jake Rutledge felt his mutilated ear and scowled. "What's that for?"

"To settle claim disputes and other troubles," the Mormon explained. "There'll be lots of miners in here as soon as the word gets around. Stealing from sluices—that's generally punishable by twenty, thirty lashes. Hanging if the court decides. Killing is a hanging offense, unless it's done on the square. For petty stealing or general orneriness you can run a man out of the district or even banish him from the territory."

"How do you figure that?" Malcolm asked.

"Miners' courts stand pretty well together," Arnold explained. "The territorial legislature has already upheld their laws and rulings."

Will Greene looked incredulous. "You mean things like we're doing here tonight?"

Arnold nodded. "You're the law, Will—and you're helping make the law."

"Why, hell!" Greene shook his head. "I always figured folks that made the law was all crooks and cheats and carpetbaggers and such."

"Now this judge business," Jake Rutledge said. "I'm no hand for judges and courts. I figure—"

"I don't blame you, Jake." Art Rutledge laughed.

"I been in a couple of messes, all right," Jake said, "but no real big meanness." His face went somber at some thought. "Leastwise that no man can say about. But I don't see no need—"

"We could let it go for now," Arnold said.

"And get outvoted by a bunch of Johnny-come-behinds?" Malcolm asked. "Let's do it now, I say."

Jake Rutledge was looking at Teteluki. "Maybe we better do that. I say Malcolm for judge."

"Vromig vill be the judge!" Leibee said explosively.

"*He* don't vote." Jake looked steadily at Teteluki.

"Why not?" Arnold asked. "He already has."

"Them other things don't matter so much," Art said. "But I don't want no judge that some nigger voted for to have a say over me."

His cousin nodded. The Southerners showed agreement in stubborn looks.

"Teteluki saved our lives," Muchow said angrily.

"He did," Jake Rutledge said. "I'll fight any outsider that says a word against him—but I ain't having no judge over me that a nigger votes for."

Romig found nothing inconsistent in the Kentuckian's thinking. Jake Rutledge, like thousands of others in the South, was trapped by a prejudice that had been growing since the day the first black slave was landed in America. Jake was no more responsible for his attitude than Teteluki was for his color.

Without a word Teteluki turned and walked away.

Hans Leibee waved his arms. "I haf lost patience mit these people!" He too left the group.

The issue was not changed. It was merely shifted to a new ledge in men's minds. Now the matter was one of North against the South. Malcolm thrust quickly for advantage. "As president, you can't vote, Arnold," he said.

Arnold smiled, "The hell I can't. I'll resign and vote if you make a technical point of my office."

In spite of a deep anger that he held against no individual because of Teteluki's retirement, Romig said evenly, "This matter hasn't enough value to squabble over. I suggest that—"

"I say let's vote," Malcolm said.

By hand they voted. Four for Malcolm and four for Romig, including Arnold. Muchow went to Leibee and tried to get his vote, but the German only shook his head. He had lost patience, he said. To hell with their voting and fighting.

Malcolm smiled. "Arnold, do you want to get Roberts's vote to make it official?"

That war should have colored petty bickering in these distant mountains was something to wonder at, Romig thought. He had fouled his own plans to further understanding by standing smack in the middle of the squabble. Again he'd fumbled.

They listened to Arnold explaining to Roberts in the hut.

"I vote for the Yankee preacher," Roberts said.

The Southerners stared at each other. They rushed to the hut door and began to talk all at once.

"You heard me!" Roberts cried weakly. "Get to hell away from here!"

Jake Rutledge's face was grim when he returned to the fire. He looked darkly at Romig and Arnold. "Sickness tetched his mind," he said. "What was in that bottle of stuff you given him?"

"Liquid from the boiled roots of Oregon grape plants," Arnold said. "Harmless. I have drunk gallons of it."

"Yeah?" Jake Rutledge was dubious. "Well," he said

with more vigor, "there ain't a-going to be no election for sheriff tonight. We'll just wait awhile."

At daylight the Southerners moved to the south bank and began to build a camp of bough huts. The Unions took the other bank and started to build lean-to shelters. That afternoon everyone staked ground, men from both parties doing the work for those unable to wade snow. There was no arguing or fighting, but the comradeship was gone.

That evening Arnold, Teteluki and Romig were left on the island with Roberts.

The Virginian was weak and coughing the next day when he gathered his gear and crawled from the hut. Arnold tried to make him stay, ordered him to, but Roberts only shook his head. He smiled at Olsen and said, "Thank you, Luki." He looked at Romig and said, "You helped save my life, and for whatever that's worth, I owe you thanks. I voted for you because you happen to be one of those rare fools who is honest. I voted for you, Yankee, because if there ever was a test you could stand above personal things—and Malcolm couldn't. But I don't have to like you, Romig—and I don't." Roberts's eyes were cold and clear. He refused to take Romig's sleeping bag. He walked unsteadily across the south footbridge, waving off Arnold's efforts to help him.

Teteluki asked, "Why do men hold hatreds as tenderly as a mother holds a child?"

Romig had no answer.

"This word 'Yankee' I do not understand. They speak it as a Spanish sailor flings a curse. At sea the Yankees were red-faced, frozen-looking men who always stole lines from ships—or whatever else was loose when they came alongside in port."

Arnold turned away with a smile. Romig tried to explain. "A Yankee is to them what a Zulu, I suppose, is to a Boer."

"That is bad then," Teteluki said.

CHAPTER 11

THERE WAS COARSE GOLD where Teteluki had said, but recovering it with the tools at hand was another problem. After the first few days of individual flurries with sharpened poles to loosen the bank and with makeshift equipment for panning, even the most sanguine began to appreciate the problems of mining.

"It ain't a matter of just picking nuggets up by the pocketful—like I used to think," Job Davis said.

Teteluki's gold pan had gone from hand to hand, and there had been fights and quarrels over the use of it. His pick and shovel and the one shovel that had been carried across the mountains had given similar trouble. Leibee had carried the shovel, but original ownership was impossible to determine, for the German had picked up discarded tools thrown down by anybody.

Jake Rutledge and his cousin came to the island one day at noon, complaining that Union men were hogging the gold pan. Teteluki recovered the pan from Muchow and gave it to Art Rutledge, saying, "If you will, please, I wish you'd see that each party gets the same use of it."

Art said he would. He shifted clumsily on his bad foot, turning the pan in lean, dark hands. "I ain't got nothing against you, Luki—like it seemed the other night—and I ain't forgot what you did for all of us; but it was just that—well . . ."

"I understand," Teteluki said gravely, but Romig knew that he did not—except to sense that Rutledge was confused by something beyond his grasp.

"Perhaps it would be well if Art apportioned use of all the tools," Arnold said. "I will talk to everyone about that."

He did. They agreed with him, and thereafter Art Rutledge hobbled about and made a nuisance of his authority, but no man could complain about his fairness.

Having observed this sensible procedure, Romig tried to think of some similar stroke to use on Roberts, but he had to give up because he knew the Virginian's bitter-sharp intelligence required the most subtle kind of handling.

"You can do nothing with that one," Teteluki said. "He has demon memories. I know. I have them, too. No man can kill them for somebody else. That vote you had from Roberts may be the greatest victory you have ever had—and you don't realize it yet."

Arnold nodded. "Luki is right. Someday there will be a branch of medicine that will deal exclusively with sickness of the mind, but now"—he looked at the western mountains—"I don't know why I concern myself with any thoughts of medicine at all."

Romig's mind was on an immediate problem, a plan to bring the two groups together.

"What we need here is a cabin," he said suddenly. "Right smack on this island, big enough for everybody to meet here evenings if they want to."

Teteluki looked from one bank to the other. "Idleness is never allowed at sea," he said. "It breeds trouble. This is much like being at sea."

An hour later they had wrecked the hut. They went to the north bank and began to cut cabin logs. Romig had seen axmen before, but never one with the power and precision of Teteluki. They built a second bridge above masses of anchor ice floating in the Blue, and used it with the other as a ramp to roll logs to the island. They had laid the base logs of a cabin twenty by twenty when Art Rutledge wandered over. He stood around and watched for a half hour before Teteluki began to ask him questions about notching.

Art said, "I'll show you." He went for the other ax.

Others drifted in to watch. On the third day everybody was working, even Roberts, who was chinking with moss. Work relaxed old tensions. The two groups refought Pittsburg Landing, Pea Ridge and Seven Pines. They scoffed and argued, campaigning once more from Richmond to New Orleans; they galloped up and down the Shenandoah from Rockfish Gap to Shepherdstown, capturing prisoners by the thousands. Malcolm explained all the fine points of Gettysburg, and how Lee and Ewell had thrown the whole thing away by not supporting Jubal Early the first afternoon. "Now, if I had been in charge . . ." Malcolm said.

Muchow personally took Farragut and the *Hartford* past the bluffs at Vicksburg so many times that Jake Rutledge wanted to know if the admiral had been hauling cotton from New Orleans to Cincinnati like all the other Union grafters.

After every extravagant exploit—and most were— both sides shouted, "My froze big toe!" They manhandled green timber, wading snow in broken boots. Many had elkskin lashed over their footgear. They strained and shouted and laughed together. Teteluki said nothing, but it was plain he did not understand the change.

The Rutledge cousins took charge of notching, quarreling happily with each other. Ruthven and Muchow got the moss for Roberts, carrying it in an elkskin from the old river bed beyond the north bank. Leibee took charge of fireplace construction, grumbling a great deal because of lack of chipping hammer and real mortar, but happier than he had been for a long time. Malcolm helped him, giving a great many suggestions which Leibee did not hear at all. Six feet wide they made the fireplace, laying stones in clay that Romig and Arnold dug from under the snow. Greene and Davis made the door of hide lashed to a framework of small poles. It did not fit well, but it was a door. They made similar barriers for long windows on both sides.

The roof was of close-laid trimmed poles, the cracks stuffed first with humus and then the whole covered with six inches of dirt. When Jake Rutledge scraped in place the last shovelful of leveling dirt on the floor and tamped it with a big foot, he asked, "Now we got a cabin. What for?"

Romig looked around. They were all here.

"We've got a place for all of us to use anyway we see fit," he said. "It belongs to all of us, and let's keep it that way. We've been children at times and we will be again. One thing to remember is that everything we've won we've won together, and everything we've lost we've lost the same way. It's too much to think that we can forget some of the things that have been stamped in our minds from the war, but we can go on from here together—like men."

His face still pale from his illness, Roberts smiled faintly.

"We're not going to get very far working individually on our claims," Romig said. "There's too much stuff to move."

"That's right," Davis said. "We found that out."

"We can work all these claims together," Romig said. "Just as we built this cabin. Luki says he'll go up the mountain and get the whipsaw for us any day. We can make lumber for one big sluice and move it upstream as we tackle each man's ground. What comes out of a man's claim is his—and then we move on to the next claim—or any way you want to work it."

"That sounds right sensible," Jake Rutledge said.

The rest agreed slowly, with looks or nods.

"Let's do it then!" Romig said, and watched a tiny smile curve Roberts's lips. "Now—about Arnold and Luki and me living in the cabin. With your permission, we'll do that—along with anybody else who wants to move in."

Nobody did.

"All right," Romig said. "It's still a gathering place for all, a storeroom, a place for the sick, the headquarters of the Moonbeam Mining Corporation."

Jake Rutledge savored the name, grinning.

"There's just one rule," Romig said quietly. "This island is neutral ground. No war was ever fought here."

"Nein!" Leibee said. "No war was fought here!"

When Teteluki, Romig and Arnold were alone in the cabin, Arnold said, "Your plan worked out very well. I hope it holds."

"I'll make it hold," Romig said.

"Don't get too many 'I's' in God's work. That's what I warned you about in Oro City—the path your terrible drive may lead you to. You've won a pleasant victory, but God was moving with you. Remember."

It was another pleasant victory for Romig when he knew that he had taken the rebuke without offense.

Teteluki was staring at the boulder outside the doorway. "Why do they grow so deadly over little things—like the voting the other night?"

Romig cleared his throat and looked at Arnold. Together they tried to explain the war. They knew they could not make it clear, and in the end they looked at each other and knew they had not.

Teteluki said, "We had slavery among the Zulus too, far worse than what you describe. But our gods are cruel. Your Carpenter God is kind. Do not all your people follow him?"

"In different ways," Romig said.

"In different ways?" The Negro's voice was deep

and puzzled. "If there is one God, as you said, there must be one path to Him for all. Is that not so?"

"People grow bitter over the rightness of their paths—just as they grow bitter over their rightness in any matter," Romig said.

"You are a God-speaker," Teteluki said. "What is *your* path?"

Romig looked helplessly at Arnold.

"I am beginning to see now that there were many things which Bishop Schreuder wisely did not tell me." The Negro walked outside and leaped to the boulder, and stood there looking out upon the wilderness.

Irritated by his own ignorance, Romig turned some of his vexation on Arnold. "You can explain medical facts as they are known, Heber. You deal in facts, but who can explain the spirit of Luki's question with facts?"

"A fact in medicine is good and true only for a day. As we learn, the truth changes. And if you're wise, before you break your head and spirit trying to discover some great universal truths about religion, you will allow that God is flexible, and that some of his rules must seem to change as he presents them to meet the needs of man's enlarged understanding of himself and God."

"Mormonism, eh?"

"Yes. You might find some of your answers there, but you have the look of a man who never will be satisfied with any answer."

"I am uncertain and confused, but—"

"When Joseph Smith had been pulled and tugged at until he was confused he went to a wooded hill—"

"And received a vision," Romig said. "I will look for my visions in the faces and acts of men, where God has always been—or never. I will find my answers there."

"First, you'd best find yourself—or burn yourself up with your seeking."

"How about you?" Romig asked. "I always have sensed that you're unhappy about going back to the Mormons."

"My mind is at rest." Arnold walked from the cabin.

Later, Romig looked out and thought: A man whose mind is at peace does not run from questions and pace the bank of a river in evening cold.

Dusk came softly. Campfires gleamed on both sides of the Blue. Voices from them carried clearly. On the rock before the cabin the tall statue in buckskin skirt and leather pants looked out on purpling mountains.

CHAPTER 12

SPRING CAME ON DAINTY FEET, sprinkling tiny flowers along the edges of the snow. Little rivulets chuckled with their flow. The inhabitants of the big beaver pond above the island came forth and threw a splashing study on their dam, inspecting winter damage. Long grasses in a meadow below the high dam bent in the direction of the passing of the snow.

Rust-brown wood ticks crept from winter refuge and battened where they could. Men tore them fat and bursting from each other's backs, then rubbed against rough trees to scratch the bites.

Teteluki and Muchow had gone up the mountains and brought back the whipsaw, the latter wearing snowshoes of his own making—elk tendons lashed across willow frames that had been steamed to shape. And now the saw was busy. On an open framework of poles the miners cut lumber for sluices. One man standing on the framework and one underneath in the pit wiped the five-foot saw through logs. The man above took the backache from constant bending; the one below took sawdust in his eyes. Gradually the pile of sap-sweet fragments grew, as logs became planks and planks became twelve-foot sluice sections, held together by whittled dowel pins driven into holes made with Teteluki's auger.

Arnold showed them how to set the sluice, gently pitched, with the riffles tight and properly spaced. "Even in the best sluice half the gold goes right on through," he said. He looked at Malcolm's corduroy shirt. "A few yards of that would make the best natural riffles you ever saw."

"This," said Malcolm, "is the only shirt I've got."

When the boxes had been set and the flow of water had been regulated, there was heavy work for all. Two men still sawed because Arnold said the longer the sluice the better. Two men shoveled. Two picked. The rest hoisted boulders or rolled them clear of the gold-bearing sand. They started on Muchow's claim, downstream from the island.

After the initial cleanup three days later, Muchow's

face held a surprised look.

"Hot cannon balls!" he said. "We're going to be rich!"

The salt can that held his gold grew heavier. He left it under the bunk that Arnold and Romig occupied in the cabin. There were two double bunks there now, a large table and benches of whipsawed planks. Teteluki had taken from his pack a hammock no one knew he had, and slung it above the unoccupied bunk. It was a relief, he said, to be able to sleep once again in a hammock.

When the frost was gone from the ground, Roberts and Leibee went one evening to the old river bed and were secretive afterward about their actions there. Ruthven came to the cabin before breakfast the next morning, something on his mind. "I don't know what Roberts and Hans were up to last night, but there's trouble likely to come of that old river course. I should have told before, but I thought I'd let it ride along, since things were going so well."

Arnold was at the fireplace, cooking the last of the elk meat that he thought safe to use. He rose and faced the big Scot. "What is it?"

"When Much and I were digging moss from under the snow over there, we ran into some pretty good-looking sand and gravel. I went back and panned some of the stuff from the old bed. It's rich."

They had looked for gold, almost died because of it, and now they had found too much gold.

Whatever Teteluki thought, he merely looked at faces and said nothing. Romig was thinking of the strain this new find would put on human relationships. By their own laws, each man already had as much ground as he could hold. They could amend regulations to suit their purposes, which would be bowing to greed and opening the door to all sorts of other weakening compromises.

Ruthven sat down on the end of a bench. "We don't want to be hoggish, but still we went through a lot to get here. Why should somebody who comes tripping along later—on dry ground—fall into gold that we discovered?"

"We discovered nothing," Romig said. "Luki did."

"Yes, we've all taken the gold for granted," Arnold said slowly. "In fairness to those who are sure to follow, we limited our ownership. I wouldn't want to see that changed. At Tarryall I saw the result of greed, and it wasn't pretty." He squatted by the fire and put the frying pan over the flames again. "How do we know Roberts and Leibee know about the gold in the old river course?"

"They took a shovel with them, and they carried two loads of water in those skin buckets Luki made," Ruthven said. "I shouldn't have kept quiet about that gold, because when I have to admit I did, this whole bunch will be split wide open again, worse than ever."

"Legally no one here can stake the ground," Romig said.

"Legality will go to hell fast and so will peace if what Ruthven says about the river bed is true to any large extent," Arnold said. "If Roberts and Leibee discovered nothing, no harm is done. I say let's keep quiet until we know for sure. If anything breaks, we'll have to call a general meeting and try to work things out."

Arnold and Romig had a look at the old river bed that afternoon. There had been recent trenching, now carefully smoothed over with rich mold. They said nothing about it except to Teteluki, who had nothing at all to say in return. Several times during the week Roberts and Leibee wandered off together toward the spot.

Two miners from a gulch camp down the Blue came by on their way up Hoosier Pass. They were amazed to find so many men at work, and watched cleanup at the sluice with narrowed eyes.

"You fellows must have come over Hoosier pretty early," one of the visitors said.

"We came over there." Malcolm pointed at the mountains.

The miners looked at each other, either too polite or too greatly outnumbered to speak what they thought. It had been a very bad winter in Breckenridge, they said; snow fifteen feet deep in the street.

"Breckenridge?" Arnold said. "Where's that from Fort Marabee?"

"Marabee *is* Breckenridge now. It was named after that Tennessee vice-president under Buchanan, the one that went with the South and became a bigwig in Davis's cabinet. Folks changed one letter of the name so the town wouldn't be named after a lousy Reb."

"I'm a lousy Reb," Arnold said. "Half of us are."

Romig stifled a smile. He cleared his throat and set his brows and mouth to match the fierceness of his nose. Personally he considered the expression quite harmless, but he knew it always seemed to have an effect. The visitors looked at him quickly and looked away. They glanced at Malcolm, who was scowling. They looked at Leibee, who was squinting.

"That was a damn dirty trick—changing old Breckinridge's name," Job Davis said.

"We wasn't there then," one of the miners said hastily. "I reckon the war's over anyway."

The two men went on up the river.

Arnold grinned. "We forgot to ask them about the chances of getting supplies in Marabee—Breckenridge."

For several days they had been living on snowshoe rabbits that Teteluki and Muchow hunted in the evening, and crimson-streaked trout that Romig and Arnold took from the huge beaver pond upstream. The rabbits were tough and lean. There was no strength in fish, no matter how many they ate.

"One pork chop off'n the leanest hog in Kentucky would beat all the fish there is in that dam," Art Rutledge said. "By God, I'm starving!"

A party of six men went to Breckenridge, returning with a sack of beans, more salt, a side of lean beef, and two jugs of whiskey. They could have got some frozen potatoes too, Malcolm said, but the man wanted a dollar a pound for them. They divided the food equally. Muchow had paid for it in gold dust, airily waving away any discussion of later sharing of the cost.

Muchow reported that he had seen a woman who owned a corduroy skirt that was just what they needed in their sluice. "She wouldn't sell it, and she took a swipe at me with a pewter mirror when I tried to steal it out of the clothes-press."

"I'll get it," Malcolm said. "Next time down."

That night in the cabin they had a feast of beaver-tail soup, pan bread and steak, and afterward drank the whiskey. Greene and Davis talked to each other about their brothers. Leibee passed out after a few drinks. The Rutledges quarreled about which of them could play the violin better, and then Jake wept because they had no musical instrument of any kind. Roberts drank steadily, his cold eyes getting colder. Teteluki did not drink at all. Ruthven and Malcolm pounded the table and argued about ancient Highlands battles that no one else had heard of.

In the middle of an argument about the Macdonalds and the Forty-five, Malcolm said, "There's a Scot down in Breckenridge who's got the bugle he used to sound the Charge of the Light Brigade. You ought to hear him blast out 'Peas Upon the Trencher.'"

"I heard a hell of a racket down there today," Ruthven said, "but what's that got to do with the Macdonalds?"

"All the Light Brigade was Scots."

"No," Ruthven said. "No, Malcolm, there never were six hundred Scots who could stay on their horses at one time."

The pair had another drink and blinked at each other with drunken gravity. Watching, Romig saw two healthy, powerful young animals who would have to test each other's strength to satisfy themselves about their unfinished fight in the snow pit. At the moment drinking had made them cautious. They had examined several subjects together, and finding insufficient cause for violence at the moment, they had postponed their meeting until later.

The Rutledges decided that the only way to prove who was the superior violinist was to go to the south bank and fight. Davis solemnly assured them that they were right, but before anything more developed Muchow accidentally kicked over what was left of the beaver-tail soup. It spilled into the fire and filled the room with smoke and ashes, and diverted the cousins from their intended course.

The whiskey jugs were empty not long afterward. Those who lived on the banks started off to bed. Ruthven and Malcolm lurched up, blinked at each other, and vowed to see each other home. Since they lived on opposite banks they had somewhat of a problem.

It was settled when they both fell off the south bridge into icy water that rolled them over several times before they came up bellowing like rutting buffaloes.

Already in bed, Arnold began to laugh. "A barrel of whiskey every night might solve all your problems, Romig."

The whiskey had not hurt a bit, Romig thought, having long before observed that men who drink together often feel more kinship afterward than those who fight together.

After men began to sweat the next morning at their work, they were in a mellow mood, each accusing everybody else of being drunk the night before. This day at least, Romig thought, no one could have told who was Union and who was Confederate. Only Roberts was still unreconstructed.

Six men came up the Blue that day and staked claims above the last ground owned by the Moonbeam men. In the afternoon four men came off Hoosier Pass on their way to Breckenridge. They, too, looked around and stayed. Ruthven was diligent in collecting recording fees. "I'll have to have a couple of deputies," he said. "This book work is killing me." All his writing was on a tag taken from the sack of beans.

It was good to hear sober Ruthven make a joke, Romig thought.

Five more miners came up the river the next morning. The word was spreading fast.

Each night the island cabin was full of Moonbeam men. On the boulder outside Arnold set up a barbershop, his tools consisting of his razor-sharp knife and scissors from Romig's sewing kit. Inside the miners shared a comradeship of talk and laughter. They listened wide-eyed to Luki's tales of strange things he had seen around the world, and no one ever doubted him because his eyes and manner crushed all thoughts of doubting. He told of a quartz reef he had seen in Africa, miles of banket along a low ridge the Boers called Witwatersrand. "It is filled with gold," Luki said. "I know that now."

"Why don't they mine it?" Ruthven asked.

"I doubt that white men have ever seen the place."

Malcolm was excited immediately. "Let's all go there and get rich!" His eyes were glowing. "This place will be overcrowded before we know it, but in Africa—"

"Let me tell you more," Teteluki said. He did, and Malcolm calmed a little. But when he left the island that night he was still talking of gold in Africa.

Before he swung into his hammock Teteluki said, "I, too, have thought of mining some of that gold." Something savage came to the surface of his eyes. He seemed about to say more, but he looked at Romig doubtfully and turned away.

Little Ephraim Bull, Old Malcolm Alexander, and fifteen men arrived in Moonbeam the next afternoon, coming off Hoosier Pass with six pack mules. Excepting Leo Gorham, the Kansan whose arm Roberts had broken, the Moonbeam men knew no one in the group of fifteen. Ephraim said the rest of the two parties that had paused in Oro had scattered, most of them retreating to Denver. Eph and Old Malcolm, now partners in trade, had gone to Denver to pick up goods, and the fifteen men had followed them here on the chance that the merchants were going someplace where fresh gold waited to buy the pile of goods on the mules.

Eph still wore his beaten furs, but he was clean-shaven and had new life in his eyes. He spat and grinned and looked the scene over with quick eyes. He shook Luki's hand when Romig introduced the Negro. He looked at the men milling excitedly around the laden mules. "The other twin in the fur cap?" Eph asked.

Romig told him about Sampson Greene.

"We'll get the body out of there," Eph said.

Job Davis came up with a question in his eyes.

"I hauled your brother in to Oro on a canvas toboggan," Eph said. "We buried him there, and Old Malcolm wrote a letter to your mother."

Davis nodded and turned away, his scarred lips twisting a little.

Romig watched Old Malcolm greet his son gruffly. "Ye lost the Ferguson, no doot?"

"Hah!" Malcolm grinned. "A little thing like that? I scarcely knew I had it with me. I'm sorry now I didn't bring an anvil—"

"Two or three of them," Old Malcolm snorted. He stepped away to shake hands with Ruthven, and then he came up to Romig and grinned. "Aweel, ye made it, but I hear ye had to bellow a time or two befoor ye were fair started to keep them from each other's throats."

"They're all right." Romig looked to where Muchow and Roberts were laughing as they unlashed a copper wash boiler from a mule pack.

"We can boil our clothes!" Muchow shouted.

Eph rubbed his nose and gave Romig a sharp look. "We saw that big Irisher—Matt Sullivan—and the Megill gal in Denver with a curly-headed blond fellow. I talked some to Sull. He said they'd been scouting around for a likely camp to start a business. That's why they'd been in Oro."

"What kind of business?" Romig asked.

Eph shook his head. "Sull didn't say."

Arnold asked. "How was the boy—Timmy?"

151

Eph shook his head. "Just like always."

The newcomers were already rushing to stake claims. Only darkness stopped them. Art Rutledge managed to get three quarts of whiskey for his services in showing the latecomers where the best ground was. He did not know and neither did the men he advised, so the transactions worked out well. Art shared his whiskey all around.

The cabin walls threw back the roar of voices until very late that night. The merchants moved the X-legged table athwart the fireplace end of the room and did a sellout business in California-made red flannels, blue woolen shirts, tough cowhide boots and other gear. Muchow financed those who had no money, selling his gold to Old Malcolm and Ephraim, and then lending greenbacks to anybody who wanted to buy anything.

"What's gold?" he said. "The crick's full of it!"

"Maybe," Old Malcolm said, and kept a record of Muchow's loans.

There were other trades, exchanges and loans to such an extent that the tangle of finance would never be unsnarled, but no one cared, and least of all Jonathan Romig. Not caring about the use of gold seemed to be a disease engendered by the country.

Gorham had a banjo, which immediately endeared him to the Rutledges. Trading done, the cabin rocked to song. Art hobbled out among the newcomers camped up the creek and somehow managed to obtain five more quarts of whiskey. The evening went along.

During the celebration Teteluki drew Romig outside

by the rock. "Have that little man and the big red-faced one stake the old river bed. Two claims will cover it," the Negro said. "And then someone in this group—or all of us—can buy the claims back for a dollar."

Romig laughed. "You should have been a lawyer!"

"You can trust the two who came today."

"How do you know?"

"It is in their eyes," Teteluki said.

They were silent for a while beside the rushing water. Cold starlight lay above the rounded outlines of the forests. Late campfires tossed flames against the night. "I'll get Arnold and the others," Romig said.

They held the conference near the latrine on the north bank.

"Simple enough," Eph said.

"Aye," Old Malcolm agreed.

Ruthven shook his head. "Not if Roberts and Leibee get sore when they find out. If they hadn't covered up their trench—"

"Hell!" Ephraim spat. "You mean the place in the old river bed where someone planted radishes that just started to sprout?"

"Radishes!" Romig began to laugh. Now he knew what had been in the silk-wrapped packet that Leibee had treasured.

At daylight the merchants staked the old river bed. Ten minutes later they sold their ground to the Moon-beam Placer Company for two dollars. Ruthven made his records. "We meet by night at a latrine," he said, "to circumvent our own laws."

CHAPTER 13

I T TOOK THREE DAYS to find the body of Sampson
Greene—three days after the party reached the
long ice-sheathed trough where he had fallen.
Everybody had come except Art Rutledge, who
couldn't walk well enough yet, and Leibee, whose
strength was failing rapidly.

On the peaks above them the sun was bright and
warm. The almost-perpendicular wall of the gorge,
along the base of which they probed with long poles,
went up in dark ledges untouched by the sun. It was
gloomy down here, and their mission made it
gloomier. Looking upward Romig wondered how, half
blinded by snow, staggering with exhaustion, they had
ever followed the ridge along the sky.

Mostly they worked in silence.

On the second day, a bit of fur came up in an ax nick
near the end of Malcolm's probing pole. They dug with
snowshoes and hands and shovels and found Sampson
Greene's cap. Twenty feet or more to the side, on the
third day, they found the body. Ledges had done brutal
work. One glance was enough to prove that Greene
had not struck alive in the snow.

Kneeling beside him, his brother said jerkily, "It was
like a Minié ball in the heart, wasn't it? Just like a
Minié ball . . ."

"We'll take him down to where the trees are green,"
Romig said.

"Away from these dirty rocks! The dirty screeching

wind!" Greene stood up and cursed the black gorge, windless now and wet with melting snow.

Malcolm lifted the two ragged blankets the dead man had carried. The shoddy tore in his fingers, and he stood scowling at it. "We fought the war with junk like that," he said, and looked at Ruthven accusingly.

"My men's shoes were made of paper that fell apart in the mud," Ruthven said. "Don't ask for sympathy, Rebel."

Their anger was springing from natural rebellion at the sight of death, from old memories revived by it, Romig thought. "Let's not quarrel here," he said.

"Rebel, eh?" Malcolm's eyes were bright. "When we get on solid ground, Ruthven, I'll ask you to repeat that."

"I should have said childish adventurer, Alexander. A turncoat, something more appropriate." Ruthven's lips were flat and tight. "I'll repeat anything you want to hear."

"Not now," Eph said crisply. "We got hard work."

The Scots did not wait for dry ground. They fought on a ridge where snow was a foot deep. Like bulls they pawed their feet for solid purchase, measuring each other as if they had never been close before.

Eph kicked snow from a log and sat down.

Greene's body lay on a pole litter, unnoticed.

Malcolm feinted and crouched. Ruthven knocked him flat with a long left hand that cracked against one cheekbone and laid it open. Malcolm came up smiling. Again he feinted and crouched, and again Ruthven's left went out. Malcolm knocked it up and went under it, inside. The blows that went into Ruthven's stomach made Romig wince, for the sounds were dull, solid, painful to the ear.

Ruthven went back, his guard opening as he started to bend. Malcolm caught him on the jaw then, two sliding blows that made dull red smears through the black roots of Ruthven's beard stubble. The black-browed Scot staggered and clutched a small spruce that could not hold his weight. He fell sidewise.

Malcolm laughed. And that brought Ruthven up from the snow with more eagerness than caution. He rushed in with his hands held close to his body. That earned him another trip into the snow. He sat there glassy-eyed, with blood running from his mouth. He came up slowly, pulling himself with the aid of a tree. He swayed. One knee unhinged and made him stagger. He spat blood and stared at Malcolm.

"Rebel. Turncoat, huh?" His lips set in a cold grin, Malcolm went in to finish it. He went too soon. Ruthven trapped Malcolm's arms and pulled him close. He hit Malcolm twice under the chin with a heavy shoulder, and then he pushed him clear and knocked him to the snow with an uppercut. Malcolm lay there with his face stupid, his mouth opening and closing. He rolled over on his hands and knees, then he pushed himself up and ducked sidewise as Ruthven came rushing in.

Ruthven tripped over the foot that Malcolm thrust out and could not check his lunge. With arms reaching for nothing he crashed headlong into a clump of small spruces. They bent but held enough to send Ruthven rolling sidewise.

Malcolm laughed again.

Jammed against a rotting log Ruthven grunted as he pushed away to regain his feet. When he rose he held a piece of limb torn from the log. Malcolm cast around in the disturbed snow and snatched another short length of wood. They rushed together with their clubs held high. Malcolm took the brunt of Ruthven's blow upon his forearm. His own stroke, delivered with a grunt, caught Ruthven squarely on top of the head.

Romig started forward, expecting to see Ruthven go down with a cracked skull. Eph reached out and caught Romig's coat.

"Rotten wood," Eph said. "Both pieces."

Both clubs had broken. Ruthven's knees buckled, but he did not go down. He shook his head, rotten fragments of wet wood in his hair. Malcolm's left arm was momentarily useless. He was rubbing it and staring at Ruthven.

"They won't do much now," Arnold said.

He was not quite right. Ruthven dropped his broken limb stub and moved in. The two Scots stood close against each other, pounding with short blows. They slipped. They grunted. Their breath came in gasps. They leaned against each other and kept going, spitting blood over each other's shoulders, their faces sagging with exhaustion.

They had no control now of anything. They had forgotten the cause of their fighting, the direction of their efforts. They were two columns of bruised and aching flesh, going on because some locked signal in their brains said they could not quit.

Then Malcolm seemed to weaken. His blows stopped entirely, and he went on the defensive, putting all the weight he could on Ruthven, who, dimly sensing victory, tried to finish it with a flurry. But Malcolm had been resting, trying to weave the frayed ends of energy into strength for one last try.

It came. He struck hard against Ruthven's chest with his shoulder. Ruthven went back. Malcolm reached down to try Teteluki's ankle-catching trick. He was too tired, too slow. His grasp was too high. Ruthven kicked one leg free and stiffened the other. He clubbed his fists against the back of Malcolm's neck.

Malcolm fell face down in the snow.

Romig let out a long sigh.

"Wait," Eph said.

Malcolm was getting up. Slowly he reached a kneeling position. He used one hand to brush reddened snow from his face. Staring up at Ruthven he blew, rather than spat, bloody dribble from his mouth. He grinned crookedly and got on his feet.

"Let's fight," he muttered.

The two men fell against each other and tried to go on. Then they fell together in the snow and tried to wrestle, striking weakly with their free hands. And after a while they were still, lying side by side with their legs intertangled. They lay there trying to draw life into their lungs through battered mouths.

Once more Eph stopped Romig from going toward the prostrate pair. The little merchant looked at the others, some still open-mouthed, and pointed down the mountain.

Jake and Romig picked up the litter and started. The others followed.

The fighters caught up two hours later, coming in together. They had washed their cuts and bruises with snow but they were a sorry sight. No one spoke to them, and the Scots had no words of their own. They relieved Muchow and Roberts of the litter and carried it until they were stumbling, neither willing to be the first to say, "Enough." Will Greene and Teteluki finally relieved them.

"I will show you both that ankle-catching trick someday," Teteluki said.

Romig saw Muchow and Roberts grin slyly at each other.

CHAPTER 14

A FEW DAYS AFTER THE FIGHT on the mountain—an event which became a handy reference point for time—Charity Megill came riding up the river with Sull. Romig was shoveling at the sluice head with Malcolm and Ruthven. Malcolm whistled under his breath. Ruthven grinned. His deep-set eyes swung to Romig, who dropped his shovel without a word and waded across the stream.

Sull gave him a nod, civility and nothing more.

"Tell her she can stay!" Malcolm yelled from the creek.

Sull threw a hard, watchful look toward the sluice.

"Welcome to Moonbeam." Romig bowed.

Charity's eyes were full of smiling. "Thank you, Mr. Romig." She looked around at the trees, at the budding valley and at sun-bright patches of snow high above. "You picked a beautiful place, I must say."

"I find it greatly enhanced now," Romig said. He watched sun and shadow cross her face as she moved.

Sull was studying him impassively.

"I trust Dr. Arnold and your other friends are well, Mr. Romig?" Charity asked.

"Fine. You plan to locate here?"

"We do," Sull said. "We have three wagons coming up the river." He looked at Charity. "We'd best ride back and report the trail."

The woman wheeled her black horse easily. It reared, but she controlled it without taking her eyes from Romig. "I hope you're finding as much gold as we heard you were."

"There's never that much," Romig said. "But we're finding some."

He watched the pair ride down the valley. He felt beard stubble on his chin and looked at gravel in the cuffs of his muddy trousers. Tonight he would shave and have Heber cut his hair.

Later at the sluice Malcolm asked, "Cat got your tongue, Romig? Tell us all about things."

"She's—they're bringing wagons," Romig said.

"What's in 'em?" Muchow asked.

"How do I know! I wasn't *that* curious." Romig grinned at the sudden laughter all around him.

There were twenty-five or thirty men with the three

oxen-drawn wagons that reached Moonbeam that afternoon. Those at the sluice watched Sull and Charity lead the drivers upriver to a flat near the beaver pond where most new residents had already settled.

Men who had been following the wagons descended on the sluice. Among them were five lanky, dark-faced fellows who stayed close to a tall, stoop-shouldered man who seemed to be their leader. Sharp-faced Muchow had a way of prying information from almost any person, but all he got from the five was that they were Missourians—Ozark men. They seemed more interested in details of the sluice construction than they did in gold itself.

Irish rogue ran liberally among the other visitors. They were interested in everything; at least they were everywhere and talking loudly, peering into huts and bough houses, poking fingers along the upstream side of riffles in the sluice until Young Malcolm shouted angrily and banged a couple of wrists with the handle of a shovel.

A quick-moving slender man introduced himself to Romig and Arnold. "Barney Garrison," he said. "We've heard a lot about this camp." He looked across the river at Ephraim's and Old Malcolm's mules picketed in the willows. "I see that Malcolm Alexander and his partner are around."

Romig nodded. "They went down the river somewhere to look over a gulch camp this morning." He studied the man more closely. Garrison was in his late twenties, perhaps a little older. His hair was short-cropped, blond, as crisp as frosty grass, with curious steely glints in it. It matched the crispness of his move-ments, the quick flash of his green eyes, which seemed to settle briefly on a point, absorb the salient features, and then move on to something new. Garrison must be the fellow Eph had seen with Sull and Charity in Denver.

Like Young Malcolm, this man was thoroughly charged with energy, Romig thought; but unlike the Scot, Garrison's drive was carefully controlled and directed. He was a man to sort and classify whatever came to his attention, discarding much, keeping the tools of knowledge that would serve him. That was the way Romig read his eyes and movements.

"You plan a business here, I understand," Romig said.

"A saloon—to start," Garrison said.

"Come on over to the cabin," Arnold said, glancing at the island where some of the newcomers were poking around.

Teteluki was already on his way across the north footbridge.

Not until he was in the cabin did it occur to Romig that there was gold under the bunks in buckskin pouches Teteluki had made. The Negro was standing just inside the doorway, looking at six or seven men who seemed to have been arrested in the act of brazen exploring. Possessions had never troubled Romig, having them or not having them; but discourtesy always made his temper rise.

He saw that Arnold, too, was nettled.

"Here is the man responsible for founding the

camp," Arnold said, and introduced Teteluki to Garrison.

"A Swede naygur!" someone said when Teteluki spoke. A laugh ran around the room, and Romig scowled.

Garrison's eyes rested on Teteluki longer than Romig had seen them steady on any object. The curly-headed man spoke civilly, but he did not offer to shake hands. "I hear the bunch upstream have been doing pretty well too."

"I guess so." Romig knew that Leo Gorham, who came almost every night to the cabin with his banjo, had been doing fairly well with straight panning, and that others had found gold in side gulches. "Anyway, there are a good many new claims recorded—all fees paid, too."

"Oh?" Garrison's roving look had been on Luki's hammock and Hawken rifle on pegs beside it. "Then you've organized a district?"

"Yes," Arnold said. "The laws, such as we have, are written in Romig's Bible. We elected—"

"Jesus Christ, boys!" a man standing by the fireplace said. "We walk all the way from Kansas to find a camp where the rules are wrote in a goddamned Bible!"

Romig held his temper. He looked at the speaker, a keg-chested man with a thick reddish beard and bloodshot eyes. "Object to the Bible if you wish," Romig said. "But the rules we all agreed on when we started this camp will be enforced."

The man laughed, a sound that started deep in his chest and grew in explosive, unhumorous grunts.

"Don't start giving orders, mister. There's quite a few of us that may not like your lousy rules. Just because you stumble onto something first don't mean you're going to hog it all."

"We didn't try to," Arnold said. "That's the reason for the laws."

"Gentlemen," Garrison said, including Teteluki in his glance, "I would apologize for the behavior of Haring"—he indicated the man near the fireplace—"and these other bounty-jumping apes, but they don't belong to our party. They merely joined us."

Haring laughed again. He hawked and spat against the fireplace stones, and then he reached for the Ferguson rifle that Young Malcolm had left above the mantel rather than expose it to the doubtful protection of a bough hut.

"Put that down!" Romig said.

Haring ignored the order. He tried with thick fingers to force the trigger guard down, obviously ignorant of the screw mechanism of the block.

Romig stepped toward him.

"No use to get sore and have that big nose bumped," Haring said. He started to return the rifle to its resting place on pegs driven between the stones. Either through intent or carelessness he missed one peg and the breech came down upon the mantel. Haring laughed. "Well, what do you know!"

Romig did not try to hit him. He merely jammed the heel of his right hand into the red beard. Haring's head rapped the fireplace, and his eyes went foggy. By belt and shirt Romig carried him outside and threw him sidewise into the river.

The cabin was empty then.

Disinterestedly, Garrison said, "He's had that coming. All the way from Denver he tried to run his bluff on everyone but the Missourians."

They watched Haring scramble from the water. He turned on the north bank and looked back. He nodded his dripping head slowly, leaving the threat unspoken, and then he went off upstream.

"You've made a dirty enemy," Garrison said. His eyes flashed over Romig's face. "But I doubt that you've ever worried over things like that."

Romig was wondering now why he had not thought of a better way to handle the affair. "Making an enemy has never pleased me."

Garrison started across the footbridge. "You boys come up and see us when we get organized."

Standing at the boulder near the door, Leibee looked across the river and muttered, "Raiders!"

Leibee had told Romig about the Raiders of Andersonville, bounty-jumping scum who had robbed and murdered other Union prisoners, until gaunt dying men had risen with clubs to smash the Raiders' headquarters and hang six of the worst offenders. A large part of the gang had been Irish, mainly from New York.

Arnold went over to Leibee and touched his shoulder. "You can't blame all the Irish for what happened in prison, Hans. Do you hear me, Hans?"

Leibee said, "New Yorkers! Raiders!"

Young Malcolm came leaping across the bridge, grinning. "Hey! You sure gave the red-whiskered guy a heave for his money. What happened?"

"His hands and mouth were careless," Romig said, and wished now that he had thought to replace the Ferguson on its pegs.

"Yeah! They were like that at the sluice. I had—" Malcolm glanced inside and saw his rifle. He strode through the doorway. "Now who the hell was fooling with this?"

"No harm is done," Arnold said.

Malcolm's voice was an outraged shout. "The nipple's blunted!" He jumped to an accurate conclusion. "That's why you threw the bastard in the water!"

"Slow your horse," Romig said. "Eph can fix that soon enough. He used to be a gunsmith."

"Fix it!" Malcolm said. "The man had no right to touch it. I'll bust his face for him!"

Davis and Greene came in together. "What's wrong?" Greene asked. "Did they steal something?"

"No." Romig looked from the north window. The visitors had left the sluice. Muchow and Ruthven were coming to the island.

"Where's your soap and razors?" Davis asked. "I seen 'em right here on this shelf this morning."

Romig frowned. The soap and razors were gone, and so was a ragged piece of shirttail used as a towel.

Muchow and Ruthven walked into a silence. "What's up?" Muchow asked.

"That bunch is all damned thieves!" Malcolm yelled. "They busted my rifle! They stole everything in sight! They—"

"Now wait a minute," Arnold said. "Maybe we misplaced the stuff. Maybe—"

Teteluki said softly, "No. They took it. I saw them from outside."

"You *seen* 'em?" Davis cried. "Why didn't you—"

"What they stole is worth little," Teteluki said. "What we learned of them is worth much. One of the razors was mine. I had small need for it. Let them have it."

Romig's razor had been a gift from his father. It galled to think that it had gone into the pocket of a sneak thief, but he said, "Maybe Luki is right."

"What about my rifle?" Malcolm's voice was down. His anger was up.

"The man was punished," Arnold said, "and Eph can fix the rifle."

Roberts and Jake Rutledge came in.

"There's more manners in one cabin in Kentucky than in that whole tribe of prowling bastards!" Rutledge said. "Me and Roberts had to run three of 'em out'n our camp by hand."

Muchow's sharp face jerked. He went out and ran toward the north bank.

Ruthven said slowly, "Thievery is something I wouldn't want to see started around here. I had enough of that in the army to last me all my life. I think we'd better find some way to get back what was stolen, or else admit our laws are not worth a pebble."

"You're damned right!" Malcolm said. "Let's go up—"

"Before you set the heather afire let's consider the thing," Arnold said. "I agree. We can't let stealing get started. The next thing somebody will try robbing a sluice, and then we'll have to hang him." He shook his head. "That isn't a pretty thing to see, boys. On the other hand, we don't want to start a fight if we can help it. I suggest that a few of us go up and talk to the men that Luki saw steal the stuff. You'll know them, Luki?"

"No." Teteluki walked out.

Art Rutledge limped in. "Jake, you and me and Roberts thought they didn't take nothing, but them three messkits that were hanging on that tree are gone."

Jake threw his hat on the floor and began to curse. "That settles it! I'm a-getting my rifle now!"

"Wait a minute," Arnold said, but the Rutledges did not pause.

Muchow returned. He nodded grimly. "They hit our side, that corduroy shirt Malcolm gave me to put in the sluice, one of my blankets, two of Job's—"

"We've talked enough." Malcolm looked carefully at his rifle. He nodded, yellow lights glinting in his eyes. "It'll work, well enough."

Romig and Arnold tried to stop them, but it could not be done. Without rush or waste of movement the miners armed themselves. They gathered in the trees on the north bank, and Malcolm looked them over.

"Where's Dutchy?"

No one knew.

Romig and Arnold went along, unarmed. Teteluki hesitated, and then he came too, his only weapon a broad-bladed knife. Muchow was carrying the Negro's rifle.

Like skirmishers they drifted through the trees

toward the flat near the beaver pond. The wagons were there. The oxen had been freed and were standing in mud and sand near the shining water. One new tent had been pitched. Charity Megill was at the flap, her eyes on a group of silent men standing near Sull. The Irishman was the center of attention.

The sleeve of Sull's checkered shirt was slit. Blood showed on his hand and wrist. He was looking unemotionally at a man lying on the ground. It was Hans Leibee, his fair beard clotted with dust and pine needles. He was motionless, the fingers of a broken hand extending toward a knife.

Charity was the first to see the island men. She ran forward with a cry, and then a man near Sull looked up and shouted, "Hey!" There was silence for a moment, with one group closing in on the other in a tight semicircle. Those close to Sull fell back quickly.

Romig saw Haring standing on a wheel hub, his wet clothes tight against his body.

Sull did not move back when Arnold and Roberts went forward and knelt by Leibee. Close behind them, Romig looked down and saw that the German had been kicked and trampled.

Sull spoke to Romig, looking straight at him. "He came at me with a knife. He was yelling, 'Raiders.' I tried to take the knife away." Sull held out his bleeding hand. His eyes were hard and alert.

"You didn't have to use your feet," Arnold said. He grasped Roberts's wrist when the Virginian started to draw his Navy Colt. Roberts's narrow face gleamed like a hatchet as he crouched and looked up at Sull.

"Get some water in your hat, Roberts," Arnold said.

After a moment or two the Virginian rose and walked toward the beaver pond, first handing his rifle to Romig.

Charity came running around the flank of the crowd. She glanced at Leibee and looked away quickly. She faced Romig. "There was nothing unfair here. This man"—she didn't look at Leibee again—"attacked Sull without the least warning—"

"This ain't no woman's business!" Haring yelled from where he stood on the wheel hub. "Get her out of there!"

Barney Garrison came out of the crowd. He took Charity's arm. "For once that loud-mouth is right, Charity," he said. "There may be trouble here." He nodded toward the tent.

"If there's trouble," she said, looking at Romig, "it's because you all stand around inviting it—instead of speaking up!"

"Get her out of there!" Haring yelled.

The man was right, Romig thought, but if he had been close enough he would have broken Haring's mouth. He looked at Charity. "You'd better—" He pointed away from the crowd. Men had loosened guns in their belts. Some of those near the wagons had picked up rifles.

Charity gave Romig a scornful look and walked away.

The island men had lost all the advantage of their surprise, Romig knew. He looked at them and saw that they knew that as well as he—and that they were more determined than ever. They had right on their side, but Leibee had been wrong—and from the combination a dangerous situation already had developed.

"We take the responsibility for what our friend did," Romig said. He could not have spoken so if he had been looking at Leibee. "But someone in this group stole from our camp. We want him—or them." He looked at Teteluki in appeal.

The Negro gauged the situation and did not hesitate. "There." He pointed at a thick-lipped, burly man standing forward in the crowd. "He was one who stole from the cabin."

Garrison whirled and went toward the man, who began to back into the crowd. The Missourians caught him and flung him forward. Garrison stopped before him.

"Did you steal from the cabin?" he asked.

"Hell no!" the fellow said.

Garrison kicked him in the side of the knee. The man cried out and bent forward, staggering. Garrison kneed him in the face, and knocked him backward, and when the fellow hit the ground Garrison landed on his stomach with both knees. Romig did not see where the knife came from, but it was there in Garrison's right hand, the steel twinkling as Garrison put the point against the bridge of the man's nose. "Wiggle the least bit—and it slips into one eye or the other. Did you steal?"

"Mother of Christ!" the man whispered. "Yes!"

The knife twinkled, disappeared. Garrison dragged the thief to his feet and began to search him. There was a razor with Romig's name on the handle. Garrison tossed it, and Romig caught it from the air. He dropped it into his pocket, thinking that no material possession or its recovery could be worth the terror in the thief's eyes.

Garrison's tapering hands moved on. He held up a gold watch in a hunting case. "Who was it that had a watch stolen in camp two nights ago?"

"Stoker! Charley Stoker!"

A big freckled youngster came forward. He wore a wrinkled blue shirt that was torn across the back. Bright anger moved across his face. "I can see the engraving from here!" Holding his watch in his left hand, Stoker swung his other arm and elbow back. His under lip pushed out.

"No, no!" Romig pushed the youth away with a palm against his chest. "You've got your property. Stand back."

Romig's act caught Garrison's attention long enough to bring an odd expression to the blond man's face before he turned again to the thief. "Who are the others?"

The thief gave two names. The Missourians, their faces showing satisfaction, grabbed two men from the crowd and brought them forward. Only one struggled. A Missourian thumped him casually on the crown with a pistol barrel, then looked at the weapon as if inspecting for damage.

Garrison gave Romig a quick grin. "Leave it to a Puke to jump when he sees a chance to work over a Jayhawker."

Recovery of the stolen articles was swift. They were

piled on the ground beside Leibee, who was still unconscious. And now the miners had three thieves to deal with. Garrison looked at Arnold. "What's the procedure now?"

"Let them leave this district," Arnold said.

"Give 'em fifty lashes!" Haring yelled. He was still standing on the wagon hub. "Whip hell out of 'em!"

Young Malcolm was licking his lips and watching Haring steadily.

"Let them be gone in ten minutes," Romig said. "As judge of this district, I say that; but if you want a trial we can have a trial."

"Naw!" someone shouted. "Let 'em git!"

The thieves left quickly. That should settle things, Romig thought. And then he looked at Leibee, with Roberts and Arnold kneeling by him. He looked at the island men. They had a victory—this miserable pile of small possessions lying on the ground, but that was forgotten now. It had been too quick and easy, for one thing. There lay Leibee, his broken fingers twisted in the trampled earth, his face misshapen from heavy kicks. Sull had not moved away.

The faces of the island men were plain to read: they were confused a little now, more dangerous in their confusion than they had been before. This Sull was large and arrogant. He had trampled a man who had walked stoutly through death with them. Right or wrong, no matter. This Sull had beaten a friend, a man whose mind was dying. Goddamn Sull and all the rest with him.

It was time to move away before that thought grew too strong and dangerous.

"Let's go back to camp," Arnold said.

"The hell we will!" Jake Rutledge said.

Muchow moved his rifle casually until it bore on Sull. Behind one of the wagons Romig heard the dry clatter of a breech, and moments later he saw the glint of steel as two men rested rifle barrels on the spokes of a wheel.

"What about that Dutchy?" Haring yelled. "How about that Dutchy? He tried to kill a man for no cause."

"He was not responsible. He has had his punishment," Romig said, not talking to Haring at all.

"You vapored about your highfalutin' laws wrote in a Bible!" Haring shouted. "Do something about that Dutchman!"

There came a little growl of approval among those who faced the island men. Heads nodded. Hands moved swiftly toward weapons.

"You'd better go," Garrison said to Romig.

"Who says we have to go?" Muchow came a step forward.

"We just might stay awhile," Jake Rutledge said. "We might stay and see who's got the guts to start something."

Art took off his hat. He stood there with his lank hair hanging on his forehead, a wolfish, happy look upon his face. "The two behind that wagon wheel first off, Jakie."

"I seen 'em," his cousin said.

Teteluki went several paces toward the beaver pond. Motion was a dangerous thing. It caught all eyes. The Zulu took the knife from his belt and sank it into the ground with a careless flick. He looked at Sull.

"You like to use your feet. Try them on me. I have no knife."

Sull hesitated a moment, then he went out to face the Zulu. A feral sigh stirred in the crowd.

Big, utterly unafraid, Sull was no closed-eye slugger. He moved lightly. He used his fists straight out from his body. But he struck Teteluki only once, and even then the Negro was moving backward away from the blow. Sull's face went white when he hit the ground after Teteluki's ankle-grabbing trick.

Luki feinted the same pass after Sull got up. The Irishman dropped his shoulders and his guard. Teteluki leaped and kicked. The impact made a sickening sound. Sull went to his knees, then forward on his hands. He got up slowly, eyes unseeing. The blue-black of his jaw was oozing blood like a sponge. He stood there swaying, his hands moving weakly in defensive gestures.

Teteluki picked up his knife and strode away, back through the trees, going downriver.

Timmy, the boy who had been with Sull in Oro City, ran from the crowd and began to beat against the Zulu's leatherclad legs. "You dirty nigger, you! You dirty nigger!" he screamed.

During the instant when Luki glanced around at the puny attack Romig saw sheer horror in the Negro's eyes, and then Luki almost broke into a run to get away from Timmy.

The tension was broken. Someone laughed and said, "Y'God, that kid's the best man we got!"

Charity came running up to Sull, now being supported by Garrison. "He's all right," Garrison said.

She turned on Romig. "Get out of here with your gang of murderous brutes!"

Malcolm started for Haring, but Ruthven dragged him back. "There's a time to go," Ruthven said. "This is it." He picked up Leibee and started, and the island men went with him, walking backward until they were in the trees. Leibee was still unconscious.

"How is he, Arnold?" Roberts asked.

"He'll never be all right," Arnold said. "It might have been a blessing if . . ." He walked on, his face set in gloomy cast.

Across the river where scrubby willows ran to the edge of timber, Teteluki was walking toward the mountains. Muchow shouted at him. The Negro did not look back.

"I've been thinking," Ruthven said, looking at Malcolm. "Why don't we all move together on the north bank? Timber is handy. It isn't damp of a morning, like out on the flat on your side."

Davis said, "We'd only have one camp to watch then."

"It might be a good idea," Malcolm said.

CHAPTER 15

IN A SMALL VALLEY jeweled with beaver ponds, Teteluki leaned against a yellow-pine tree, turning thoughts that no friend in Moonbeam would ever hear, not even Jonathan Romig, the second man

Teteluki had known who tried to help another merely because the other needed help.

Bishop Schreuder, the Norway man, had been the first.

The two of them, Romig and the missionary Teteluki would never see again, had ruined a dream that had begun the day Teteluki learned the power of gold. That reef of banket the Boers might find someday could do for the Zulus what Teteluki's uncle, Chaka, had only started to do. Chaka had taken the long spear from the warriors, giving them the short assegai so that they had to close with the enemy.

Teteluki knew now how to give the Zulus guns, and that had been his plan until one evening not long ago when he had been looking at a dead sky, telling himself that Inkosi was more powerful than the Carpenter God, who never made a sign or caused a sound.

Then from the frozen mountain had come strange music. Teteluki had been startled. He had been afraid, but at last he had gone to investigate.

One look at those freezing men, and he had thought to turn without a word and go back to his hut. Then his mouth opened and said words he did not intend to speak. Bishop Schreuder would not let him turn and leave.

Yes, it would have been a terrible thing to have let those men die, especially Romig and Heber Arnold. The latter was another who gave help only because it was needed. They both must be true followers of the Carpenter God.

But they had helped destroy Teteluki's plan of being

a chief, not of a miserable *kraal* or two, but of villages and citadels days apart; leader of a Zulu nation armed with rifles, owner of every warrior's life.

Teteluki could not say with words how it was that Romig and Arnold had killed his last thoughts of returning to Matabeleland, any more than he could tell how he knew Schreuder had kept him from leaving men to die; but both things were true.

Now the Zulu did not know whether he regretted the loss of his dream or not. He knew he was unhappy, more so than he had ever been since first becoming confused by talk of the Carpenter God.

Once he had thought every white man followed the Carpenter God.

On his second ship, a Dutchman, the captain had not paid him at the end of the voyage. The captain had ordered him thrown overboard to swim five miles to land, if he could. On his third ship, a Spaniard, he had hung six hours by his thumbs for spilling a drink of water. His back had been lashed to bloody froth on another ship . . . Teteluki had learned how difficult it was, even for those born to parents who knew the gentle God, to follow His teachings.

Now he feared he had abandoned one course for a second he could not travel to the end, for he had never heard of the Carpenter God until long after he was a Zulu warrior.

The scene of a few hours ago tormented him. He had been pleased when his plan to stop men from killing each other worked as it did. And then the boy had run after him. . . . All fair-haired boys looked like the little one who had made Teteluki a warrior long ago south of the Tugela River; but the one today had been especially ghostly.

Black, solemn, the agony of ages running in him, Teteluki put his face against the tree and wept.

Pastel colors were streaking the western sky when he started back to Moonbeam, the same hues he had seen in boyhood above the Drakensberg. He would never see the Drakensberg again. Perhaps he would always be confused and unhappy, but he had come to final decision.

He would go toward the Carpenter God.

CHAPTER 16

ON A SUNDAY AFTERNOON Romig paused a few moments on the north footbridge to look at miners swarming among the willows as far as he could see both ways along the Blue. High above them the sun was bright on blue timber and gray slopes. Cottony blobs of clouds were scattered in the sky like bursts of baby breath in a blue bouquet. But the miners had no time to look. They were busy with the yellow witch that ran their fevers high.

The island men could rest a little now. They had worked eight claims. They were veterans, founders of the camp of Moonbeam, although they lived almost a quarter of a mile from the town proper. Section by section their long sluice had crept upstream. It lay now like a square-jointed snake under a caving bank on Leibee's claim, with undermined willows hanging crazily over it. The last twelve-foot section was lined along the bottom with corduroy, Malcolm's shirt, stolen and recovered; two skirts that Eph had brought from Denver; and the skirt Muchow had seen in a Breckenridge brothel. Ruthven had brought it back, and would not say how he had got it.

Romig smiled and resumed his way above muddy water.

There was little timber on the north bank now. Saul McAllister and his dark-faced sons and nephews—the Ozark men who had learned much while asking little their first day on the creek—had used the trees to build cabins where Northerners and Southerners now lived as one group.

Before the first cabin Muchow, Roberts and Teteluki were sluicing clothes with soft soap in a copper wash boiler over a fire. Muchow gave Romig a glance of devilment.

"All shined up, I see. Headed for the saloon to preach?" Muchow grinned.

"If I were looking for sinners, I wouldn't have to go that far." Romig went on to where Leibee was boiling mercury from gold amalgam.

The German still lived alone in the bough hut he had built when there were no cabins near. He would not move. He had accepted Romig's sleeping bag, and he had not protested when Davis and Greene covered his shelter with canvas, but he would not move into any of the cabins with the others.

"Be careful of those fumes, Hans," Romig said. There was not much anyone could say to Leibee. He was living in another world. He worked every day, although his strength was gone. Taking care of the little wooden cups of mercury that were fastened below auger holes in the last sluice section was his special task.

"I haf boiled this before," he said. "Don't tell me about the fumes."

"Sure, Hans. You know." Romig hesitated. "Are you still going to buy that land in Iowa?"

"Land?" Leibee looked up with a cold stare. "Golt is the stuff, Vromig." He pointed at the frying pan he was using. "Very rich golt."

There are so many ways in which the dreams of man are broken, Romig thought.

He walked among stumps toward the store Old Malcolm and Eph had built after their second trip from Denver. They had misjudged where the town would rise, but they were close enough. In addition to the store, they carried gold to Denver to bank, for a fixed percentage of each pouch.

Leo Gorham and Old Malcolm had their heads close together at gold scales on the counter when Romig entered. Gorham's banjo was slung under his shoulder.

"Six ounces, close enough," Gorham said. "I'll never get rich on that lousy claim, but I won't starve either." He saw Romig and grinned. "The boys at home?"

"Art and Jake fell back into bed after breakfast, but plunk that banjo a few times and you'll have them out." The Rutledges had a violin now, the first major item they had ordered Old Malcolm to get for them after their claims began to pay. Sometimes Young Malcolm insisted on joining them with his bagpipe, saying that it blended well with any kind of music. Opposition never troubled him; he merely played louder.

Thinking of that, Romig smiled. He watched Gorham take a receipt for his gold and leave the store.

"Fine lad," Old Malcolm said. "Saves his money."

"What if he didn't? What would he be then?"

"Busted." The Scot put the scales under the counter.

It was a keen enough answer. Romig had learned that there was little to win from Old Malcolm. He sat down on the wide counter that almost closed the front end of the store. "Since those two men were robbed the other night, there's been talk of filling the office of district sheriff."

"Aye?"

"We can't elect anyone from down here, but we could elect Gorham. He would make a good man."

Old Malcolm nodded absently. "He's honest. He's tough. No doot, the lad would do." He looked at Romig's freshly shaved face, and clothes that had been smoothed by careful drawing over a peeled aspen log before they were spread on willows to dry. "Ye'll be walking with Charity again today?"

Romig nodded. "Eph leave this morning?"

Old Malcolm began to fill his pipe. "Last night. Eighteen thousand he had."

The Scot really had something on his mind, or he would not have let information like that slip out easily, even to a trusted friend. His pipe going in fierce bursts, Old Malcolm scowled at Romig, so that a man looking through the doorway might have thought the Scot was getting ready for an angry outburst.

"Little Eph went too late to marry a lass he'd left in the States. Ye ken that, Romig?"

"He told me about it when we were deer hunting."

"Ye're twenty-five. I was married at seventeen." Giving advice was not Old Malcolm's forte, and now he was half angry at himself for doing so, and angry at Romig for making the doing necessary. "Ye can't be wandering always after something ye canna find, Romig, looking for the true religion—or whatever it is ye want."

"You think I should marry and settle down?"

"Aye." Old Malcolm put both hands on the counter. "Ye're a strange mon, Romig, restless and dissatisfied. Marriage—" He shook his head. "I have done with my talk. A mon is a fool to give advice."

Romig went up the road slowly. He had told himself weeks before that he was staying in Moonbeam because the human complications of a quickly thrown together society would spark with friction and quarrels wherein he could help others, and while doing so, help find himself and take a step toward the God he sought to know. Sometimes, he felt, he had helped a little, and often he had been trapped by his own weaknesses. But the reason he was still here after he had felt the urge to be gone toward another Shining Mountain was Charity Megill.

She knew, and so did he.

He walked more slowly, reluctant now to hurry to a meeting that had been a happy thought a few minutes before. He remembered his father standing by the white gate long ago, with the sun breaking in fresh glory after a rain. His mother knew when the times came: after a rain and at sunset. She would stay in the house as long as she could, and when she could stay quiet no longer, she would come to the front porch and call, "Jedediah!"

Romig's father would not hear.

"Jedediah, what are you staring at out there?"

When his father did hear, he would turn guiltily and walk toward the house, smiling at his wife. Romig's mother and father had been in love all their lives; but still at times Jedediah Romig had stood bemused with gazing far beyond the Ohio lands that held him fixed.

Romig knew that his mother must have lived always with the fear that someday her husband would walk toward the blue horizon, pulled by a power he could not resist, not hearing when she called. That marriage had not been fair to either, though neither was at fault.

Romig came into Moonbeam nursing bitter thoughts about his heritage. What had those other Romigs searched for, or had they searched for anything? Was it God that Jonathan Romig sought, or was he driven by a curse that would forever send him wandering without cause?

No man could walk in Moonbeam without the thrust of the town sweeping private thoughts away. Men bumped against Romig. They hailed him. Newcomers with packs and tools still on their backs wandered here and there, asking questions, listening, veering toward any group where claim-owning residents were panning cans of rich sands, which might or might not be from ground that was for sale.

Mules, horses and oxen crowded the bumpy street, with their owners leaning against them while they talked. A sweating teamster trying to get his wagon out of town stood up and cursed and cried for passage. Raucous bluejays swooped above him, sawing with their voices. He finally got clear by swinging his team between two tents. He pulled one down in the process, and a man in red flannels, his long black hair awry, came scrambling from the folds waving a revolver. He cursed the teamster. The teamster spat through stained whiskers and cursed him back and told him to crawl into his hole before he caught a cold.

Those panning and those watching the panning scarcely looked up at the incident.

Romig stopped where Saul McAllister and his kin were throwing up a new building. Fourteen hours a day they worked. They owned claims, but Saul said carpentry was sure, while gold in a river was another thing. Sometimes his lanky sons and nephews stared thoughtfully at nuggets displayed in Barney Garrison's Shenandoah Saloon, but the next morning at daylight they were back at their building.

Saul said, "Howdy, Romig." He looked at his hammer. "Likely day." He went back to work.

Near a patched brown tent two men in faded blue cavalry jackets were spreading blankets near a seething cone of pine needles. "You reckon them ants know enough to bite a bedbug when they see it?" one asked doubtfully. The other laughed. "You watch and see!"

Romig went on past tents, half tents and huts, coming into the part of town where more substantial board shacks stood close together. He bumped against a rumbling ox that ploughed a straight course across the street toward the cool mud of the beaver pond.

Three married women came from the Elkhorn butcher shop, where one could buy wild game and cuts of oxen that had spent themselves upon the plains and nearly died upon the passes. Some claimed they *had* died on the passes.

Two of the women would have gone up the street, but the third, Mrs. Wallace Frisbee, saw Romig and held her companions with a low word. Mrs. Frisbee was a woman with shrewish eyes set in a plump pale mass of flesh buried in a gingham bonnet. She was going to ask again that Romig organize religious services and preach, he knew.

She asked. It was more an order. Romig smiled and thanked her and said, "I know too little of God to tell others all about Him."

Mrs. Seth Marmett, a little woman, pregnant, whose face still showed the fine strain lines of the trip over the mountains, smiled nervously, and said, "I'm sure Mrs. Frisbee understands, Mr. Romig."

Mrs. Frisbee waited until Romig was crossing the street and said loudly, "Too little of God, indeed! No wonder, the way he chases that Megill thing!"

The Shenandoah had no sign, but neither did the house of Madam Olga Munson. Customers had no difficulty finding either place. The Munson home of carnal joy, two stories high, had been built by the McAllisters right after they finished the Shenandoah. It sat discreetly off the street a few dozen paces, creating an illusion of privacy, but giving unobstructed view of the intentions of any man who left the propriety of the street on any of the trails that led to the house as spokes run to a hub.

Madam Olga, according to Young Malcolm, was the only person in the Rockies with speed and heft enough to stand up to Teteluki in a fair fight. After the rather stormy opening of her establishment, Young Malcolm had exhibited, in proof of his contention, a large lump above one ear, where she had struck him with her fist when she found him searching closets in quest of corduroy garments suitable for lining the bottom of a sluice.

Thereafter the Madam and Young Malcolm had become friends, and he had the choice of the house, which was hardly outstanding on the Blue in 1866; but at least he never was assigned to the charms of the War of 1812, a working member of the firm who had no back teeth and who wore a red wig under a bandana. Miss War of 1812 had been so named by Art Rutledge, who swore his grandfather had seen her at New Orleans in charge of a British cannon, red wig and all.

Timmy came along the shady side of the Shenandoah, leading a mouse-colored burro Sull had bought him. Sunlight had not changed the boy's pale look, and his queerness was still with him. Arnold had examined him several times and always watched him thoughtfully, but the Mormon never had voiced his opinion about the injury to the lad's head. Timmy lived with Sull in a little cabin at the edge of the trees, next to Charity's cabin.

He saw Romig and waved excitedly. Alone, Romig was his friend. With Teteluki, he was a "dirty nigger lover."

Timmy wanted to go fishing, he said, but dirty kids would follow him and try to steal his burro and throw rocks where he wanted to fish. Old Sull was busy in the saloon. Couldn't Romig go along to knock hell out of the dirty kids?

Not today, Romig said. Why didn't Timmy go down to the island? No one would bother him there. Muchow and Roberts would see to that. There were lots of fish just above the island. Sometimes they got into the sluice and flipped and flopped all over before someone threw them back into the stream.

Timmy was delighted. He scrambled on the burro and started to get his gear. The burro plodded, head down, but the boy was galloping.

Romig watched Timmy go. God's will, Mrs. Frisbee once had said, and he had told her that a horse was not the instrument of God, nor had it kicked because He had directed it to injure a careless boy. Then he had asked her if it was God's will that her three boys were Timmy's worst tormentors.

Voices rolled out strongly from the Shenandoah. The bar was crowded. Men were two deep at the faro tables. The aromatic smell of fresh sawdust mingled with the sharp reek of whiskey. Romig saw big Sull watching a table where men were tense and craning.

Romig knew a little about the Irishman now. He had been master of a sloop owned by Charity's father, a Richmond merchant. Supporting to the last a hopeless fight, Romney Megill had been killed by looters during the evacuation of Richmond. He had tried to defend a warehouse filled with supplies to be hauled over railroads that were not running to an army that no longer existed.

Matthew Sullivan had been more practical. For two years before the end he had sailed every other load of goods from Bermuda to New York. When Richmond fell of age and inertia, Romney Megill's daughter had a bank account in New York—and then Sull told her. Together they left the vulture-ridden ruins of the South.

As far as Sull was concerned, Charity was his daughter now. He had known her from the day of her birth—the day his own twin daughters died of yellow fever in Bermuda and Charity's mother died in Richmond.

Romig went past the corner of the corral behind the Shenandoah. Troy Haring, the man he had thrown into the Blue, was unloading kegs of whiskey from a wagon. He worked for Garrison now. Young Malcolm had not caught up with him and probably never would unless the man angered him again, for Malcolm was too busy gulping at life to worry about Troy Haring, or even a Ferguson rifle that had been repaired by Eph in minutes.

Red-whiskered Haring stared at Romig with a surly expression. His head was wedged up from sweat-darkened blue flannel with little aid from a burly neck. He grunted when Romig spoke, then spat, and went on with his work.

Scalloped barge boards trimmed the front of Charity's cabin. Saul McAllister had sawed them out by hand and finished them with a drawknife. The frippery had startled Romig at first, but now he was used to it, just as he was used to the interior of the cabin.

"Come in, Jonathan."

Charity was only a few feet away, smiling at him from behind a cherry-wood table set with silver coffee urn and china cups.

Romig blinked when he saw Arnold sitting by the wall with cup and saucer balanced on the gray broadcloth of his trousers. Arnold's brown beard was neatly trimmed these days, and his hands and nails were always clean, although he worked at the sluice as often as any island man, leaving only when the sick or injured needed help. He did not look like a man who had come without curse or complaint over mountains choked with snow.

"Sit down, Jonathan," Charity said. "You make my home look small, standing there glowering."

"I was not glowering." Romig sat down by Arnold, and then he had to rise again to take the coffee Charity poured. He stood a moment looking at the soft curl of her hair where it brushed the cups of her temples.

"Heber and I have been talking about Timmy," she said. "Heber says he knows a doctor in Philadelphia who might be able to help him. I'm going to talk to Sull this evening."

"Anything I can do to help," Romig murmured, but

he was not thinking of Timmy at the moment.

This cabin . . .

It bothered him today as it never had before. Dark green carpet covered all the floor. The log walls had been sheeted, then papered with a pattern of dark wine with gold medallions; and on the ceiling more pale gold against a light green of the same tone as the rug. Hand-wrought bronze hardware . . . green plush chairs . . . The place did not fit a gulch camp. It represented solidity and permanence, the things that a woman wanted.

The things that Romig did not want.

She was watching him. "I see, as usual, you are disapproving of my sinful luxury, Jonathan. Would you have me live in a tent, with the rocks and dirt and stumps still underfoot?"

As usual. It struck him that he had never concealed his thoughts from Charity, even when he had tried. Then, thinking of Old Malcolm's advice, he was uneasy.

Arnold laughed. "He can't get over remembering that we were living in bough huts a few months ago—and neither can I."

"Is that so, Jonathan?"

She was pressing a small point, and yet it was a great point too, Romig realized.

"I have no quarrel with cabins of any kind," he said.

The answer did not please her. It did not please Romig either, because it was a lie. He rose and put his cup on the table. "Are we going walking, or do we talk all afternoon about a cabin that will be falling in ruins in a few months, when Moonbeam starts to fade?"

Charity gave him an odd look. "Now, you're speaking the truth." She rose. "We'll go walking as soon as I change."

Arnold was on his feet. "I've heard Richmond girls say that before, during the few months I was at Chimborazo Hospital, and I could have done ten operations while waiting."

"Oh?" Charity said. "You never mentioned being at Chimborazo."

"Perhaps I didn't." A shadow crossed Arnold's face. He seemed vexed. "I'll buy a drink, Romig," he said.

They went toward the Shenandoah. Troy Haring stared at Arnold's clothes as if they were an insult to an honest man who had to sweat at his work.

"You're still going on to Salt Lake, Heber?"

"I am."

"Why?"

"I have to."

"You're a doctor, Heber, not a farmer."

"I'm a Mormon, Romig. There were thirteen in our family. I'm the only one who strayed. My father is a bishop now, and it will be a glorious thing to him when I return."

"Would you serve your father or your God?"

Arnold walked on. "I'm going back, Romig. I never have forgiven myself for near-apostasy."

"What about abandoning medicine?"

"It will have to stagger along without my dubious skill."

They went into the Shenandoah. Sounds of happy

disorder rolled over them like a blast. The faro bank tables were rolling high. At the Wheel of Fortune, South Carolinians were whooping over the luck of Joe Ashfield, who was making a killing. His long tallow-colored hair was hanging in his face. He was dancing a jig, his mud-splattered hat in both hands. It was half filled with chips.

Sull was standing behind the group. He looked at Romig and Arnold and nodded. He might, Romig thought, have been standing once again in the doorway of the miserable hut in Oro where Romig had first seen him, watching everything with his tight-lipped reserve. Whatever Matthew Sullivan thought was evident in his deeds, not in his expression.

Romig and Arnold beat their way through the long room to the bar, where Barney Garrison was watching bartenders. It was said that all the money paid for drinks in the Shenandoah actually went into the tills. There was no guessing about the value of a pinch of dust. Near the middle of the room a cadaverous cashier sat in a doghouse, ready to exchange seventeen dollars in paper or minted money for every ounce of gold presented. Money or chips for the tables. A man had his choice.

All his bartenders were busy at the moment, so Garrison took care of Romig and Arnold. His green eyes met their faces in comprehensive flicks. He was not one to accept a man day by day, but had to give him new scrutiny at each meeting.

They ordered whiskey. Garrison set it out. "How's mining?" he asked.

"Good—while it lasts," Arnold said. "In here?"

"Good—while it lasts," Garrison answered.

He moved away to where three drunken men were getting abusive to a bartender. The argument did not last long, and Garrison went once more to the end of the bar and stood there, attentive to the whole room.

Without turning, Arnold said, "It's hard to think that Charity owns this place, isn't it?"

Romig had become used to the fact. She had some money. She wanted more, as everyone who came west did, and so she had invested in the Shenandoah. She also owned a freighting service over Argentine Pass, where her crews hauled bulky articles at five dollars a ton-mile. Garrison and Sull were the fronts for everything.

"This is not the place to discuss a woman," Arnold murmured, staring sidewise along the bar, "but yonder stands the man who will marry her one day—if you don't stir your stumps."

Romig grunted. The thought had occurred to him, but now it was a powerful thing, having come from Arnold. He looked along the bar at Garrison. Maryland man. He had not finished at West Point, but had gone south to become a Confederate army engineer. Charity had met him in Independence and had hired him against Sull's will.

"You think so?" Romig asked.

"They're alike," Arnold said. "She doesn't know it, but he does. They both want to wring things out of the country, out of life, things that you and I don't seem to want. We are standing on some of the last free land there will ever be in America. There's metal in these hills that will make our placering look like nothing someday. We are here, Romig, but just moving through. Men like Garrison and women like Charity will hold these things I speak of. That's how they are alike."

"That doesn't mean they'll marry—"

"The only time I've ever seen Garrison's eyes stop tearing things apart was when he was looking at her. Sull doesn't like him, but Sull can't stop him." Arnold drank his whiskey. "A few minutes ago we were telling Charity pleasant lies about her cabin. She didn't like our lies. Garrison would have told her the truth, whether it was a disagreement in principle or detail." Arnold nodded. "It would have been detail, Romig. You see what I mean?"

"Go on."

"I've finished."

"No more advice?"

"Advice be damned," Arnold said. He wiped his beard carefully with a handkerchief. "You don't want it any more than I do when you try to tell me what to do."

"But still you started to—"

"I did not," Arnold said. "I stated some facts as they appeared to me. You are quite fond of saying that all decisions, including the right to God, are purely individual. Practice that, and let me do so also."

"You started out to give me personal advice I don't need from you or any other man. Why don't you go on?" Unreasoning anger was lumping up in Romig. He wanted to quarrel. In the recesses of his mind he knew he was angry because Arnold had spoken what might be truth about Charity and Garrison.

Temper made fine lines on Arnold's brow and put glints in his brown eyes. "I should not have spoken at all," he said.

"That's right." Romig's anger had been fermenting ever since Old Malcolm gave his advice.

Arnold tossed a coin upon the bar. "To hell with you, Romig. Go on and blunder about and start yourself a new religion if you want. Sit under a juniper tree and look at your navel, for all of me."

Heber Arnold walked away, pushing a path through the crowd with discourtesy that was uncommon to him.

Romig started to take another drink and then pushed it aside. He saw Garrison's eyes flick over him and knew the saloonman had missed nothing, even if he had been too far away in the bumbling uproar to hear the words. Damn Barney Garrison. Let him say something now, and get his fine curly head knocked against the wall.

After a while Romig started out. Joe Ashfield stopped him at the Wheel of Fortune, thrusting the hatful of chips toward him. "Grab some, Romig! Play 'em on something. We're pushing luck today!"

"You'd better push 'em in your pocket so you can eat tomorrow, Ashfield."

"To hell with tomorrow! We're busting the house today!"

The Carolinians whooped.

Blinking in the hard burst of sunlight before the Shenandoah's unshaded front, Romig saw Arnold across the street talking to Seth Marmett. That's it, Heber, give husbands advice about their pregnant wives. It's more in your line than what you tried to tell me.

Before he passed the corrals on the way to Charity's cabin, Romig was ashamed of himself for trying to quarrel with Arnold. He would have gone back then to say so, but he saw Charity waiting for him in her doorway.

Far above the valley with its glints of busy shovels, Charity and Romig sat in a little clearing where the breeze was cool. Her arms were clasped around her knees, and she was smiling down upon the valley.

"You said today that Moonbeam would fade, Jonathan. It will. And then—where will you go?"

"Somewhere else." He did not add that he might not wait for the camp to decline before leaving.

"West?"

"I suppose."

"Why wander at all?"

"I have to."

"You mean you want to."

"I want to and I have to."

"What are you looking for, Jonathan?"

It seemed futile to say God, when God was everywhere. But it was not entirely restlessness that was pushing Romig. "I suppose," he said, "I am trying to find myself."

"Will aimless wandering help you do that?"

Romig stared at the valley. What had those other Romigs found? Had they discovered anything? His father had returned to settle down, dissatisfied and lonely for something he had glimpsed or had failed to glimpse. Had Jedediah Romig merely been bemused by memories of the campfires of his youth, of bright running water, and mountains ripping at the sky far from the steaming fields along the Ohio? His son did not know. His son had to find out for himself.

"What holds you here now?" Charity asked.

Romig looked at her steadily. He loved her, and he did not want to say so; he forgot for the moment that she might know that better than he. It was not all body hunger, though that was powerful in him too; but there were tenderness, a yearning for companionship and the thought that she could bring peace to him that would take the magnetism from far horizons.

"*You* have kept me here," he said.

She knew. She did not hold the thought with happy greed or selfish content, Romig saw, now that she had forced the truth from him.

She said, "From the day I saw you in Oro City I knew I would go where you were, and I knew you would live to get over the mountains."

Romig's face was close to hers. Everything inside him reached toward her. Then, like the whip of winter wind, there came to him the old scene that had lain in his mind till manhood before he understood it.

Jedediah, what are you staring at out there? Jedediah . . .

Fear and uncertainty and anger gripped him. He stood up quickly. What lies east or west or anywhere but now? What is there to seek when love is here? He was a fool. Old Malcolm had been right. Soft-spoken Arnold had been right, and Romig had not let him finish.

Romig told himself those things, but he did not turn back to Charity, for overriding all his logic was the memory of fear in his mother's voice when she had stood calling to a man who could not hear her.

Charity was standing beside him. He had not heard her rise. "It's late afternoon," she said. "Let's go down." Her voice was steady and controlled, but something was gone from it.

They did not speak going down the mountain.

CHAPTER 17

NOT LONG AFTER DAWN the next morning, Saul McAllister hailed the island cabin. Only Teteluki was awake. He swung out of his hammock like a huge cat. That, and something in McAllister's voice brought Romig and Arnold out of their bunks quickly.

"Found a man clubbed to death," McAllister said.

"Who?"

"Seen him around, that's all. Southerner." The flat cheeks and hatchet lines of the Missourian's face gave him a somber look in the poor light.

Arnold, Teteluki and Romig went with him. Moonbeam was stirring, but no one had gone to see why five McAllisters were standing in the willows. Saul motioned with his head, and his sons and nephews left without a word to start their day's building.

The dead man was Joe Ashfield. He lay face down in mud among willows at the upper end of the beaver pond.

"Seen his blue shirt from the ridge of the building," McAllister said. "Red Legs done it, most likely."

Teteluki barely had time to establish the fact that three men had carried Ashfield before the place was overrun with excited miners. The camp began to roar angrily. Romig and Arnold moved with purpose through the confusion. They got Sull out of bed, his face looking bleak and old.

"The lad played all day," he said. "Once he was about seven thousand ahead. He quit with three thousand and went out with his friends."

"When?" Romig asked.

"About midnight, I'd guess. Ask Olga Munson. That's where they were going."

Madam Olga rumbled irritably at the early pounding on her door. She let Romig and Arnold in and went back to her room to dress. "I ain't talking to no man at this hour in a kimono." They waited. She returned wearing a blue velvet gown with straps that made snug channels in her fleshy shoulders. She was big and blonde and grim, and her eyes grew harder as she heard the news.

"He was here with all them Carolinians sometime after midnight. He went out with 'em about two o'clock."

"Drunk?" Arnold asked.

Miss Olga bristled. "Do I have drunks in here?"

"No," Arnold said quickly. "Pardon me."

Ashfield had had no trouble with his friends, Madam Olga said, and she had seen no indication that any of them intended to rob him. "Better find the bastard who done it and hang him. Ashfield was a decent sort."

Romig and Arnold talked to Ashfield's friends. They were deadly quiet and determined on vengeance. They had left Ashfield at his tent door, they said. They figured he still had about twenty-nine hundred dollars.

Two miners who lived next to Ashfield confirmed the story. They had been roused, and one of them had stepped outside to see what was going on. He had seen Ashfield enter his tent and light a candle, and he had seen the other Carolinians resume their noisy way up the street.

At eight o'clock Arnold called a miners' meeting in the street. He stood on a wagon and told all the facts that were known. There was eagerness to hang somebody, but no one to hang. All that came of the meeting was a decision to elect a district sheriff within three days. Justice thereby served, the miners scattered to their work.

Romig spoke briefly at the grave of Joseph Conroy Ashfield, aged twenty-one, the first man to die violently in Moonbeam.

"I don't like it," Arnold said on the way back to the island. "A thing like this puts any man who had similar ideas one step closer to trying them out. We've got to be careful now about flashing money or dust around for anyone to see."

He said the same thing at the sluice that afternoon, and Leibee listened tensely. It was no secret that his dust was hidden somewhere near his lean-to. The island men had tried to persuade him to send it out by Eph, but Leibee had played innocent. "Golt? Vat golt do you mean? I haf no golt." And he had given them a crafty look that made them heartsick.

And now, listening to talk about the murder, he watched all faces with a cunning look, and no man could tell what he had in mind.

"McAllister said something about Red Legs," Teteluki said. "Who are they?"

"Them Fire Zouaves the Yankees had," Art Rutledge said promptly. "The ones with the striped pants that made such fine targets."

Arnold laughed. "No, Art. I talked to McAllister about it. He was talking about a gang from Lawrence, Kansas, that jayhawked into Missouri. As far as McAllister is concerned every Kansan in camp was a Red Leg once."

Leibee slipped away and went downstream toward his lean-to. The island men watched him go, exchanging significant looks.

Arnold shook his head. "We can't take his dust from him. It's all he has left to think about. But some way we have to protect him."

"I will sleep near his shelter every night," Luki said. "No man will bother him or steal his gold."

They fell then to talking about the election of a sheriff, agreeing that Leo Gorham was a good choice. The Rutledges went after him and brought him back with them.

"I don't know anything about a job like that," Gorham said. "But if you fellows are willing to back me, I'll try anything. There's talk that Haring is going to run."

Roberts was a spectator only. He did not like the Kansan, and had never spoken to him since the day Gorham arrived on the Blue.

Romig went that night to the Shenandoah to test the wind. Haring was going to run, sure enough. He was already campaigning.

"Gorham!" he said. "He's a pet of that downriver bunch that grabbed all the best claims and all the offices. They want to run everything, and they didn't do nothing about that crazy Dutchman that tried to kill Sull. Christ A'mighty! We could all be clubbed to death in our bunks and that gang wouldn't care a whoop. They know they can't elect anyone from down there, so they honey-talked Gorham into running, and then they'll tell him what to do!"

Romig smiled. Haring, he thought, was making as fine a speech as any politician ever did. He went over to the bar to talk to Garrison.

"How do you stand?" Romig asked.

"I don't," Garrison said crisply. "Let every man take care of himself. A sheriff, whoever he is, can't be anything but the instrument of a howling mob."

"Your view is plain enough."

"I hope so." Garrison moved away to help a bartender. Sull came up behind Romig. "Charity wants to see you," he said.

Two bronze ship's lanterns in the cabin threw mellow light on furniture and walls. Another lamp was burning in the bedroom, where Romig saw a dressing table with crystal jars and silver sparkling against a gilt-edged mirror. On a shelf at one side a busy clock sat in the belly of a porcelain Venus.

"Did you and Heber find out anything more?" Charity asked.

Romig shook his head.

"There's talk that the Shenandoah doesn't like to see a winner get away. I don't like that, Jonathan."

Romig's face went bleak. "I don't suppose Ashfield would like what happened to him if—"

"Don't misunderstand me. I mean that there are men saying Sull was behind the thing. Sull has been like a father to me, Jonathan, and I resent—"

"Of course. But you're in a business where you'll have to take a lot of that."

His words hurt. They took some of the color from Charity's face, but they did not turn her gaze. "I don't want to quarrel with you, Jonathan. The last thing on earth I want is to quarrel with you."

"What *did* you want? I can't stop men from talking."

"I wanted to tell you that Olga Munson and I have been talking—"

"You and Olga Munson!"

"You and Sull! You both act shocked to death. If I thought I needed a companion, I certainly would prefer Olga to that bleating cow of a thing Sull made me take along when we went to Oro City."

"But she—well, it isn't proper—"

"Good heavens, Jonathan! For a man who threw away all conventions, you still cling to some silly little scruples. Now let me finish. I talked to Olga—outside her house, if that helps serve your precious propriety—and we decided she has a better chance of someday finding out what happened to Ashfield than all the loud-mouthed men in camp. That's what I wanted to tell you, that sooner or later she may hear something useful, and then we'll let you and Arnold know."

After a while Romig nodded. "That may help." He looked at the lamp bloom in Charity's hair, at the steadiness in her gray eyes. She was wearing a low-necked blouse. The soft light put a faint dusky tinge on her bare shoulders.

"Why did you ever go into the saloon business?" he asked.

"It was a quick and certain way to make money out here. I didn't have enough to stay in Richmond, what with the way the Yankees were doing there, and I did not care to live in the North. It was my plan to make enough money out here so Sull and I could return to Richmond and live as we pleased, Yankees, carpetbaggers and all."

"What about Garrison?"

She raised her brows. "What about him?"

"Is he going back to Richmond, too?"

She seemed surprised. "Why, I don't know what his plans are. I hired him because he can get along with men much better than Sull. Garrison can take care of himself, as you've probably noticed, so when it's time to move he can do whatever he has in mind."

She believed she was using Garrison. The thought troubled Romig. No one should ever underestimate Barney Garrison. He had been attracted to the man at first, and Garrison had been friendly—until Romig's visits to the cabin with the barge boards became more and more frequent. Then, without discernible sharpness in the change, Garrison had shifted in his attitude toward Romig. The change must be interpreted as reflecting Garrison's own intentions, of which Charity seemed to be completely unaware.

"A penny for your thoughts, Jonathan."

"I was wondering when you intend to return to Richmond."

She came a step closer. "I'm not sure yet that I will."

"Why not?"

She stood there waiting, with the answer in her eyes.

Twice now, driven by his love for her, Romig had pushed forward to the point of decision. And for a second time, tortured by the fear of what his love could do to her in years to come, he turned away, and the moment went to ashes. He wanted to explain, but he was afraid of her logic, afraid that it would blind him now to what must be inevitable later. Someday he would have to explain. Right now he could not.

He looked back from the door. Her expression had not changed. She was standing there, still waiting.

"Good night," he said.

"Good night, Jonathan."

He walked far toward Hoosier Pass that night, with the cold on his face and the quiet trees around him.

Whenever he stopped, inaction brought back the silence of Charity's cabin during the moments when only the ticking of a Venus clock marked the waiting of a woman hoping for an answer that did not come.

The whooshing sounds of nighthawks catching insects came to him. All around the mountains watched. What lay beyond them that could be worth his love for Charity? Why would not that love help sublimate the wild streak in him, the longing of the Romigs for things they could not find?

Out of the cold night it came to him again: *Jedediah! Jedediah! What are you staring at out there?*

Even the Shenandoah was closed when he walked back through Moonbeam. In a tent near the upper end of the street Irish voices were singing:

> "What he robbed from the rich
> He gave unto the poor.
> Brennan on the moor!
> Brennan on the moor!
> Proud and undaunted stood
> John Brennan on the moor!"

Barney Garrison's tenor voice was in the group.

The gripes of Teteluki's hammock creaked in their pole rigging as Romig started past Leibee's lean-to.

"It's me—Romig."

The Zulu's voice came softly from the darkness. "Yes, I knew by your walk. Two men were robbed tonight. Beaten with clubs."

"Killed?"

"No. They will be all right."

"Who—"

"Arnold will tell you. He is still up."

A rich bed of embers in the fireplace showed the strain on Arnold's face. He was bone-tired, Romig knew, for he had been up the two nights before with a miner who had driven a pick through his foot.

"Gavail and Pierce," Arnold said. "They live behind Marmetts in a little tent. Mrs. Marmett couldn't sleep. She heard a groan and sent Seth out to investigate. But for that the men would have killed Gavail and Pierce, I think. They got their gold. Three men in burlap hoods. That's all we know."

"What are we going to do, Heber?"

"I called a meeting here tonight. Not everybody. We appointed a secret committee of twenty men. We'll watch winners from the Shenandoah. We'll watch men with rich claims who have not sent their gold away. All district officers are members of the committee, and Sull, Gorham, Marmett, McAllister, Teteluki . . ." Arnold named them all.

"We talked it over carefully. We may bait a trap or two. We made several plans that may let us catch the three men." Arnold rose wearily, his shoulders riding heavy. "I'll tell you the rest in the morning. We tried to find you for the meeting, but no one knew where you were."

"I was under a juniper tree staring at my navel," Romig said bitterly.

Arnold put his hand on Romig's shoulder. "I'm sorry I ever said that, Jonathan."

CHAPTER 18

HANS LEIBEE disappeared on the day set for election of a sheriff. He said he had some mercury to boil and did not go to the sluice with the others. When the mess detail, Muchow and Roberts, went to the north-bank cabins about eleven o'clock, Leibee was gone.

For a while the island men tramped around the lean-to, looking questions at each other. Teteluki shook the sleeping bag. "He kept his gold in this. It's not there now."

Ruthven went to the store. Old Malcolm had not seen Leibee pass that way.

"These robberies have touched him off," Arnold said. "He's taken his gold, and God knows which way he lit out. Does anybody know how much he had?"

"About twenty pounds of dust," Teteluki said. "I made the pouch for him, and I have heard him talking in his sleep."

They decided to split into three groups. Arnold would lead one up the mountain on the route by which they had come to the Blue. A man in Leibee's condition might go that way, Arnold said. The Rutledges would take the second party downriver, and Teteluki would lead the third group toward Hoosier Pass.

Before they left Teteluki pointed at a footprint. "He walks hard on his heels. See how his boot soles are worn along the outside edges. One stud is gone from the circle of hobnails on the left heel."

Romig went upriver with Teteluki and Ruthven. No one they found in Moonbeam had seen Leibee. At the blacksmith's shop they found the mail carrier watching his horse getting a loose shoe fixed. He had come off Hoosier that morning and had met no one, he said.

"He would try to let no one see him," Teteluki said.

Beyond the last upriver claims, the Negro pointed to a footprint in the trail. It was Leibee's. Later they found where he had left the trail when he heard the mail carrier's horse coming. Teteluki went on until the footprints came back into the path again. He stopped.

"He has about a five hour start. He is nearly running, and I doubt that we can catch him until exhaustion slows him down. We had better go back now and get horses and let the others know."

Charity gave Romig permission to take any of her animals. At the corral, Haring said no one was taking mules anywhere until he had talked to the boss, meaning Garrison.

"You'd better talk fast then," Ruthven said, "or they'll be gone when you get back." He began to saddle a mule, and Romig followed suit.

Haring went away. He returned glowering after talking to Garrison. The Rutledges and Malcolm came from their downriver search. "No tracks at all," Art said, and then Romig told him what they had found upstream.

Malcolm went at once to see Charity about more mounts, but he did not reach her cabin. He stopped and yelled, "Look! Indians!"

Ephraim Bull and a huge black Indian were riding

210

into town at the head of a mule train. Behind were fifteen or twenty Indian riders, squaws, bucks and children.

Four mules back in the column Leibee's body was lashed behind a packsaddle. He had been clubbed to death and scalped.

Death and Indians made a prime attraction. Within minutes, the street in front of the Shenandoah was buzzing. Men from claims far upriver and from claims below the island arrived as if by magic as the word went around.

Eph stilled the uproar momentarily. "These Utes came all the way from Garo with me. We found Leibee just below the pass, and this ain't no Indian scalping job!"

Laden with surly insolence that proclaimed his leadership, the giant beside Eph showed unveiled contempt for all the shouting over a simple matter of death. A giant he was, Romig thought, weighing at least two hundred and seventy-five pounds.

For a few moments the chief and Teteluki grunted back and forth in Ute, and then the Zulu went upriver, his leather pants flapping as he trotted.

Followed by a crowd, Eph led the Indians and the pack-train down to the store, where Old Malcolm scowled from under bristly brows and asked no questions. Eph dismounted and tossed a little canvas sack to his partner.

"As near as me and Colorow's boys can figure, three men did the job. They had sacks over their boots. It may be that Teteluki can trail them." Eph looked keenly at the crowd.

"Why didn't the Indians try to trail 'em?" someone yelled.

Eph put the question in Ute to Colorow, who grunted a surly answer.

"He says how many of you will go with him to trail some Arapahoes who killed two Utes last week in South Park?"

A miner cursed. "This is different. If all the damned Indians killed each other we'd be better off."

They put Leibee on a blanket inside the store. Scalping had let his facial muscles drop. That, and the beating he had taken about the head made it difficult to think of him as Hans Leibee. But there was his broken hand, his clothes that fitted so loosely now on a frame that had fought the snow with the strongest of them. The flies were obscene vultures. Job Davis fought them off with his hat until he got sick and went outside to vomit.

The evil of it drove Romig outside, too. He paced among stumps until a mighty rage subsided. Once he had thought that snow was a common enemy, and then it had been hatreds between two groups, and now it was man himself who was the common enemy.

Two hours later they buried Leibee beside Sampson Greene in a coffin Saul McAllister had started building before anyone thought to ask him. Five or six hundred miners stood quietly while Romig spoke among the pines on a hill overlooking the Blue and the lodges of Colorow, now camped a short distance below the store.

Immediately afterward, but not before a rumbling for

revenge began, Arnold explained once more every-thing that Eph knew about the killing. And then he told what Teteluki had found.

"Luki says three men had burlap over their boots. Leibee skirted the town, but apparently someone saw him. It was known that he had hoarded his gold. They followed him, staying mostly on the needle mat among the trees, so that Luki couldn't tell just where they started from. They came back along the river. They burned the burlap, standing in the river while they did it, and then they stayed in the river."

Arnold waited, looking at the funeral crowd. He let the facts of cold premeditation run their course, and he had in mind, as he told Romig afterward, that someone might remember three men absent and returning that morning.

But no one spoke, except to curse and say that this murdering had to be stopped. Many men looked scowling at the lodges of the Utes. Arnold saw the black looks and called on Eph, who explained that Indians never scalped neatly, or from the forehead clear around. "It's as old as the mountains—this busi-ness of blaming murder on Indians," Eph said. "You all knew the Utes were camped over the hill. So did three men who tried to shift attention by scalping Leibee. Send a committee up to read the marks, if you don't think I'm right."

That evening the island men were gloomy and vengeful. Teteluki had gone off someplace. At ease on the bunk under the Zulu's hammock, Colorow sat eating dried apples. He had already consumed the rations of six men.

"Does that noble Roman understand English?" Romig asked Eph.

"Enough—when it suits him."

Romig looked at the chief. "Don't you think you'd better move your camp? The miners are in an ugly mood."

Colorow kept munching. Then he said, "Move camp?" He scowled and spoke in Ute.

"He says," Eph said, "that the miners can move *their* camp. *His* people camped here since time began."

Romig grunted. "Fine."

"Sugar!" Colorow said.

Romig took the can from a shelf. He meant to pour some into the chief's hand, but Colorow plunged big greasy fingers in and conveyed what stuck to them to his mouth. Romig gave him the can. "You should move your lodges."

Colorow shook his head. He belched, spraying sugar.

Muchow rose suddenly. He had been tense and quiet ever since that morning. He went out quickly. Romig glanced at Arnold, then followed. The onetime Union sailor and Romig walked toward Moonbeam. Romig had guessed that Muchow was headed there.

"He had a right to live, didn't he?" Muchow asked suddenly. "Crazy or not, he had a right to live, didn't he?"

"Yes."

They went on. There was little they could do about Leibee at the moment, Romig thought. After the election of a sheriff, which had been postponed until the next day because of the funeral and excitement, perhaps some plan . . .

"All day I've been hanging on a line and seeing Hans drive a pick into a crack when you and Roberts were about gone." Muchow's words broke bitterly into the night.

"I know. I've been thinking of it too." And of Leibee plunging through the snow toward Sampson Greene; and of Leibee trying to go on for help when there was no help and death was coming in with drowsy warmth. "What are you going to do right now, Much?"

"I'm going to watch heavy spenders in the saloon."

"Isn't it too soon to expect—"

"Probably. But I just can't sit."

The Shenandoah was more crowded than usual. Talk of the killing was loud around the room. Romig wondered how loudly men would talk later on in lonely tents and cabins. Haring was again boosting himself for sheriff.

"I wouldn't let no Indian stop in this district!" he said. "The bastards all oughta be Sand-Cricked right!"

Romig saw Leo Gorham watching with an expression of disgust. The slender blond man looked at Romig and shook his head.

"Maybe they *didn't* do this killing," Haring said, and he had listeners. "For all we know that crop-eared little bastard that runs the mule train did it. They say the Dutchman was carrying a pile of gold. That Bull is friendly with the Utes, and they wouldn't give him away, seeing it was a white man he was killing—"

Romig started toward Haring, but he was too late.

Muchow was ahead of him. His sharp face white, his green eyes glowing brightly, Muchow tapped Haring on the shoulder. The Kansan turned.

"You're a foulmouthed liar, Jack," Muchow said. And then he hit Haring in the throat.

There were three more blows that Romig could not follow. It was over. When Sull came ploughing, throwing men aside, Haring was on the floor. There were men in the place who did not yet know there had been a fight.

Gorham moved in and put his back to Muchow and looked around for trouble. Romig took the other side.

"Take him outside," Sull said, indicating the unconscious man, then looking toward some of his friends.

Garrison knifed through the crowd. The light made odd streaks of the steely glints in his hair. His eyes took in the scene, then settled unwaveringly on Muchow. "Keep your political fights outside," he said. "Don't ever start trouble in here again." His voice ran cold and sure. He looked at Romig an instant, and Romig knew then what he had guessed before: Garrison hated him.

Romig accepted the fact with joy, for anger was clawing up the ladder of his thoughts. "No political fight, Garrison. You know it. Do you care to put things on a personal basis?"

"Ease down!" Gorham said. He had his hand on Muchow's arm. "You're wrong, Garrison. Back up."

All at once, instead of Garrison's set face, Romig saw before him two somber eyes and black skin. "Jon," Teteluki said in his solemn voice.

"Let's go," Gorham said.

Teteluki's calmness brought control back to Romig. He turned, and the Zulu followed him. Still holding Muchow's arm, Gorham led the party toward the door. Men fell away and let them pass and there was silence until someone said loudly, "Those damned island men! They never come up here unless they got a chip on their shoulder!"

At the corner of the saloon, Haring's friends had him on his feet. They stopped talking when the four men came outside. Sull went as far as the door with the islanders.

"I'll know if anyone who shouldn't have money begins to throw it around," he said. He went back into the saloon.

Sometime later Muchow said, "I feel a little better now."

Romig did not. He felt that he had acted from the instincts of a great ape. He had gone to keep Muchow out of trouble and had tried to start trouble of his own. If it had not been for Teteluki . . .

"Luki," he said. "You—"

"He's gone," Gorham said. "He faded off into the dark a minute ago—and I didn't even know it for a while."

A great ape, Romig thought. That's all I am.

At times he had controlled his temper, but he knew he never had conquered it. It was not likely that he ever would. And that other damning force, the surging restlessness to move and search—that was inevitable too. It would make a hell for him and Charity if they were married. It was as sure as the cold against his sweating face. And then he thought of Garrison having Charity, and that sharpened once again the knives of temper.

Just short of the store they met Young Malcolm bringing up the rest of the island men. Someone had run down with news of trouble. Young Malcolm was disappointed to find it all over.

"Where's Luki?" he asked.

"He's all right," Gorham said. "Nobody's going to bother that one."

"We still ought to go up and make a show of force," Malcolm said. "They might gang Luki."

Ruthven laughed. "God help them! No, Malcolm, let's go home. Moonbeam has put on lots of weight since the last time we overmatched ourselves and got away with it, thanks to Luki."

Colorow was still sitting on the bunk, still eating. He had opened canned peaches with an ax. He greeted the occupants of the cabin with a belch and went on eating.

The world could split, Romig thought, and that black mountain with his sullen face and sharp eyes would sit and belch contentedly.

The chief showed interest when Romig took something from the cupboard, but when Colorow saw that it was only coffee he grunted in disgust. He finished his peaches, threw the can under a bunk, and then stalked into the night.

"I had an ancestor who went to live with Indians," Romig said. "He must have been the craziest one of all the Romigs."

"You get used to Indians," Arnold said. "All you

have to remember is that they are Indians—not white men."

Romig put the coffee on the fire. He sat at the table looking at a three-foot spear on pegs below Teteluki's Hawken. Luki had carved this assegai from a wagon spoke. It was a sinister weapon, the fluted head worked to deadly sharpness with edges of broken glass.

Teteluki had kept it in his hammock when he slept near Leibee's lean-to. Fluting made the blood flow faster, the Zulu had said. Arnold had nodded gravely, commenting, "A bit of clever engineering as old as man."

At the moment there was a blackness in Romig that made him tell himself man's greatest distinction was knowing more of killing than of living.

Arnold got up and went to bed. It was quiet. The Rutledges and Gorham were not making music across the creek tonight. From the gloom of his bunk Arnold said, "I am glad that Hans never lived to see the inside of an asylum, so-called."

Sometime later the coffee pot boiled over but Romig did not hear it. He was standing at the door, looking at black mountains thrust into the stars. He would stay in Moonbeam until this present conflict was settled, he told himself, and then he would go somewhere beyond those waiting summits.

So strong was the urge to move on that when the Indians left the next morning Romig was of a mind to go with them. Except for the first part of his resolve, he would have gone.

CHAPTER 19

MOONBEAM ROARED and the Blue ran muddy, but the camp was dying, even as the Confederacy had been withering at the base when its flame was highest. The base in either case had not been broad enough. Although the cream was gone from Moonbeam, the sluices were no less busy, for there were always green, fresh men to bow their backs when veterans got from under.

A few men, not necessarily wise, but shrewd observers, realized the facts. Work on the surface was becoming a thing of the past. From now on wealth would come from where it lay in place deep underground. Already there were smelters over the range, a stamp mill at Sts. John on this side, and heavy machinery was beginning to dribble across the thirteen thousand foot passes.

Moonbeam had been a freak, and there would never be another California Gulch.

Old Malcolm and Eph knew. The future now was in silver and smelters, they told Romig one night in the store.

"We got a few investments at Sts. John and Montezuma and around Argentine," Eph said. "Ruthven is thinking of coming in with us." He watched Romig casually.

"The crags have nae been scratched," Old Malcolm said. "But let others do the digging. Smelters, Romig. Smelters for silver mainly." He cleared his throat.

"Why don't ye coom in with us?"

Romig shook his head. "I'm not fitted for business."

Old Malcolm looked at Eph and urged him with his eyes to speak, but Eph looked at Romig quietly. Exasperated, Old Malcolm scowled and made loud sounds with his pipe.

"Where to from here, Romig?" Ephraim asked.

"I don't know. Maybe the Salt Lake Valley. I—"

"Ou aigh, God! Ye maun be gaeing daft!" Old Malcolm bristled like a grizzly. "Polygamy and such! An' ye sae hardheaded ye pass oop the one lass—" He ground his pipestem in his teeth and shook his head.

Eph went on rubbing his tender nose. "I hear they're making a wonderful valley out there, but all valleys are alike."

"He'll find that oot!" Old Malcolm said.

Above his gently moving hand Eph's eyes were vague, as if he too had caught a glimpse of something far away. The expression came and left, and Romig knew that Eph was solidly in Moonbeam. Eph had found himself. He might have other moments when his eyes went vague and he heard the call of far-flung campfires, but business would provide him with enough adventure and satisfaction to keep him happy.

The door opened quietly, and Teteluki looked in. "Romig, would you come to the cabin, please?"

Since Leibee's death three weeks before, the Negro had been much absent from the island cabin, coming in silently at all hours of the night. He had his regular duties on patrol as a member of the secret committee, but he had been gone more than the job required. He always took his assegai.

There had been no more killings in Moonbeam, but the fear of them still hung in the air. There had been five cases of sluice robbing, and Romig had sat in judgment on the accused men. In three cases where the facts were clear, he had been forced to order twenty lashes and banishment from camp.

Troy Haring, badly defeated by Gorham for sheriff, had volunteered to do the lashing. He enjoyed the task.

There had been other thievery and trouble, with the guilty still uncaught. A miner who had sold his claim to a greenhorn for three thousand dollars had been robbed at gun-point by two men in burlap hoods. Two miners had been held up, robbed of their dust and beaten with clubs ten minutes after an escorting party left them a half mile from camp.

Twice traps had been set for Ephraim Bull when he was leaving with dust, and both times he had smelled out trouble and escaped. Once when he and Old Malcolm, Romig and Ruthven had gone to lodge in Breckenridge, someone had broken into the store and taken a strongbox with sixty pounds of sand in pokes. The gold, held for Denver shipment, had been in the ashpan of the stove.

Romig and Teteluki crossed fretting water and went into the island cabin. Gorham, Sull, Arnold and Seth Marmett were there, not talking. Marmett was a big-jawed, silent man who had given up working his own claim to build sluices for other men.

"This is not all of the committee," Arnold said. "But perhaps it is enough for what we have to consider." As usual, Arnold looked drawn. He had fought for four days to save a man with blood poison in his leg—and the man had died.

"In every case where there has been a robbery Luki has studied all signs closely," Arnold said. "At the store window, downriver where they almost waylaid Eph the second time, and on Hoosier where the last two men were beaten and robbed, there were the tracks of a man who walks, as Luki says, like a crab." Arnold looked at the Zulu and waited for him to speak.

"I have measured the footprints with my eye," Teteluki said. "I know that I am right. The man walks on the outsides of his feet, and he spreads his feet much farther than an ordinary man when he is hurrying. And now I know who it is."

The Blue made its sounds on both sides of the cabin. There were no sounds in the room.

"Wakarusa John," Teteluki said.

Romig looked around at grim, staring faces. He did not know the man, but he had heard the name.

"He works at the corral for Garrison," Gorham said. "A Missourian. A stringy man." He nodded. "Now that I think of it, he walks exactly like Luki describes."

The sound of water was again loud in the room.

"It ain't much to go on," Marmett said dubiously.

Arnold nodded. "That's the problem."

"With the way the miners feel, we might have a hanging on our hands if we let this out," Romig said. "The man has not been found guilty—yet."

"He is guilty," Teteluki said somberly.

"Just the tracks? That's all we have?" Gorham asked.

"It is enough for me," Teteluki said.

Marmett looked at Sull. "Has the man gambled heavily, shown gold he might have—"

Sull shook his head.

They stared at each other.

"We've set traps," Arnold said. "We've tried several stunts. They didn't work. Now what have we got?"

"Tracks," Gorham said. He looked at the Zulu. "I don't doubt you in the least, but . . ."

Romig knew there was in all their minds fear of being wrong. He asked, "Does this Wakarusa John go to Olga's place?"

Gorham grinned. "Who don't?"

"Let's talk to her," Arnold suggested. "It's possible the man has dropped something. Madam Olga could tell plenty about us all, I'm sure. And then let's talk to Wakarusa himself."

They went in a group to Madam Olga's house. She had just thrown out a drunken miner and was in an angry mood, but she took them to the kitchen for a low-voiced talk.

"No." She shook her head. "I don't suspect nothing about that scraggly-toothed hound. If he's swiped any gold he must have lost it, because all he does in here is whine about paying."

Wakarusa John was asleep on a cot in a smelly tent near the end of the street. He reared from twisted blankets with his hair on end and a terrible fear in his eyes when Marmett lit a candle and revealed the faces of six grim visitors. Recognizing them, Wakarusa expended breath shrilly.

"Gawd!" he groaned. "I thought that gang was here."

"What gang?" Gorham asked.

"The murderers."

Romig lit another candle. What was the face of evil? What was the face of murder? Wakarusa needed a shave. His long neck needed a wire brush if ever it was to be clean. His eyes were shifty, rather filmy. From sleep? From thoughts that crawled frantically around his brain?

They confronted him with the evidence they had.

"Oh, no, boys! Gawd no!" The whine was in his voice. The fear was in his eyes. "What can you prove by tracks?"

"Enough," Teteluki said from the gloom near the door. "Yours are the tracks of a jackal."

"We want the truth," Marmett said.

Wakarusa swung his feet to the dirt. Knobby, crusted knees stuck out through rents in his underwear. "On the Book, boys," he said, and raised a trembling hand. "I never was in on any of that hell." He looked suddenly at Gorham and his eyes widened. "You're a Kansan! That's it! You're after me because I'm from Missouri!"

"That's got nothing to do with it. Who are the others?" Gorham asked.

"Goddamn it, boys! You're after the wrong man!"

Sull had been ransacking the tent. He pushed Wakarusa out of the way and searched the cot, and threw the dirty blankets back upon it. He looked at the other members of the committee and shook his head. "Nothing."

"Why would there be?" Wakarusa whined. "I work for what little—"

"He lies. Look at his eyes," Teteluki said.

For just an instant it seemed to Romig there was a hard brute strength behind the filmy blue of Wakarusa's eyes, something that belied the craven outward look and acts. And then the man was pleading again, his lips writhing over scraggly teeth. What was the face of falsehood?

"I don't know," Marmett said, his big jaw clamped hard. "I don't know about this at all."

"Let me walk up the trail with him," Teteluki said. "When we come back he will tell the truth."

"Don't let that nigger—"

"No, Luki, we can't do that," Arnold said.

"What can we do?" Gorham asked. "Run him out of camp?"

Romig jerked his head impatiently. "That's no good! Either the man has the right to stay here like any of the rest of us, or"—he studied the filmy eyes again, and saw only fear and weakness—"he's guilty and must stand trial."

"I'll go! I'll leave!"

Teteluki's voice came solemnly. "He is guilty."

"He don't look it. He don't act like it to me." Marmett was edging toward the door, plainly sick of the whole affair.

Scowling, Romig tried to look inside Wakarusa's mind. Decision was a hairline matter. Luki was so positive, but there was no other evidence. They could bring Wakarusa John to trial. Considering the temper of the miners at the moment, Romig knew the man would hang. Better that a guilty man escape . . . And yet Wakarusa did not seem guilty. He was not guilty, Romig decided.

Sull's voice came low and harsh. "We have made a mistake, I think." He glanced at Teteluki, black and somber near the door. "And yet, if the man stays, something may happen to him."

Gorham smiled thinly. "I'm damned sure something will."

Arnold's face was strained with seriousness. "We've taken a lot on ourselves tonight. Now, what is the decision?"

"Guilty," Teteluki said.

Romig looked at the black face, then back at the terror-whitened man sitting on the cot, and again for just a breath of time he thought he saw behind the cloudy eyes to a cold, hard arrogance. But a man's life should not be taken on the strength of a vagrant impression, and this committee had assumed a terrible power even to consider the matter.

"Let him go or stay, as he wishes," Romig said.

"Suits me," Marmett said.

Arnold and Sull nodded.

"He'd best go," Gorham said. "But let him do as he pleases."

Wakarusa was already throwing a pack together.

The committee had come to a poor compromise, Romig thought, and saw the same thought on the faces of his companions. Only Teteluki had been sure. Now he showed no disappointment over the decision. He merely waited, fingering his knife, until Wakarusa rushed away into the dark.

The word was spread by miners in adjoining tents who had overheard. It caused an ugly snarl in Moonbeam. Wakarusa had been guilty as hell. Weren't the tracks enough? The wooden-headed committee, acting on their own, had turned him loose when he should have been hanged outright. But at least things ought to be a little safer now.

One man who thought so decided three nights later to slip out to Denver with his gold. He was clubbed and robbed a few hundred yards from camp. Once more: three men.

Studying tracks at daylight the morning afterward, Eph nodded. "Luki's right about one thing. There's a spraddle-legged crab-walker in the bunch."

Teteluki said nothing at all.

CHAPTER 20

HEBER ARNOLD had never worked before a gallery, and now he wondered why he had one. Men were standing clear to the water's edge around the north-bank cabins. It was Sunday, true, but what was that to miners?

"You ready, Heber? That sun's hotter nor the hubs." Job Davis was sitting on a stump, his back against a cabin wall, his long arms going down to where his fingers were already trying to grip the bark scales of the stump. Ruthven and Muchow were there to hold him if they had to, and Young Malcolm, cutting quite a pose, held a tin plate with razored pocketknife, cotton swabs and forceps that Joe Rasmussen, the blacksmith, had made from the levers of two broken carbines.

Arnold had another keen look at the gallery. He had amputated in the field while men walked by without a glance, and now half of Moonbeam was here to see him remove the roots of a few broken teeth. He picked up the knife.

The crowd pushed in closer, craning.

Any fool might know the handicraft of surgery; surgical judgment was something else. In the case of teeth, Arnold was not sure he had it. Davis's gums were ridged and swollen. What was left of the canines . . . Follow the procedure indicated.

Davis rolled his eyes at the knife. He had seen it a hundred times, but now it was a hellish thing. Scars on his mangled lips bunched in orange ridges as he opened his mouth wide. His shirt was dark with sweat, and his fingers clawed into the stump, while his body trembled like that of an eager hound.

"Nothing to it, Davis," a miner said. "Soon's as Doc cuts your head off the pain's all gone."

A laugh rolled out toward the Blue as Arnold went to work. The sun burned his neck. At times Ruthven's big brown fist reached out with a piece of shirttail to wipe sweat from two foreheads, or to pour a whiskey rinse into Davis's mouth. Dark yellow pus welled up from three of the extractions. Davis was white. His elbows jerked as his fingers worked against the sides of the stump, but neither Ruthven nor Muchow had to touch his arms.

When it was done, Davis spat blood and whiskey and grinned weakly. "That it?"

Arnold flipped a bit of bone and pulp from the forceps, looking appreciatively at the instrument. Rasmussen was quite a blacksmith. "That's the worst, Job. A little trimming and digging for bits of bone later on." Arnold nodded at Ruthven and Muchow, and they led Davis inside. Arnold reached out for his knife. He would boil . . .

Young Malcolm pulled the tin plate out of reach. The miners began to crowd in hard. Someone pounded Arnold on the back. "Never seen a better job of excavatin'!"

"Them long ones really went plumb to his brain, didn't they?"

"Not quite." Arnold smiled absently. What was this, anyway?

Romig came out of the cabin carrying a mahogany case with a silver plate that caught the thrust of sunshine. He looked at the crowd, and suddenly they were as silent as they had been during the operation.

"Heber Arnold, you've never hesitated one second when someone needed help. You've never asked a fee of anyone. The boys decided to take up a little collection and get you this. . . . Here. From everyone in camp."

Arnold took the case and blinked. His hands were unsteady. The little silver plate winked up at him, and he had to tip the case to read it. *Dr. Heber Guthrie Arnold, From the Citizens of Moonbeam, Colo. Terr., 1866*

His hands fumbled with the silver catch. He raised the lid. Clean and sparkling in their nests of black velvet lay scalpels, ratchet clamps with tiny serrations, bone saws made in one clean piece, curving needles, button trephines, two flexible probes with porcelain tips, a Hey elevator, a hypodermic needle!

Arnold felt Romig's eyes on him, but he did not look up; he was afraid to meet the piercing inquiry of the dark face. Arnold looked at the miners instead. He forced a smile, not wanting them to know how much he hated them all at this moment.

"Speech, Doc! I'm late at the Shenandoah already!"

"Up at Olga's, too!"

"Speech!"

They were grinning, happy, taking pleasure in their act. Arnold could not hate them long. He glanced side-wise at Romig. Damn him! It had been *his* idea, Arnold was sure.

"I—thank you all," Arnold said. "With—with a fine set of tools like this, I'll have to start charging double."

"Two times nothing is nothing!" someone yelled.

Arnold walked around the corner of the cabin, carrying the open case in both hands. He found a path between stumps and started toward the road to Moonbeam, not aware of where he was going.

He heard Art Rutledge yell, "Celebration! We'll get a couple of kegs and all keep Davis company!"

Old Malcolm called twice from the porch of the store before Arnold heard him. The Scot hooked his arm in a beckoning motion and went inside. Arnold turned that way.

"Aweel . . ." Old Malcolm blew a cloud of pungent smoke above the gleaming instruments. "A turrible mess of devices of torture. Whush!" He caught something in Arnold's face that brought doubt to his own for a moment, and then he stooped behind the counter and came up with a wooden box.

It held dressings, ligatures, ether, chloroform, morphine tablets, chloride of lime, creosote—an array of dark, glass-stoppered bottles.

"The Young Malcolm's and Roberts's idea," Old Malcolm said gruffly. "They want everybody in camp poisoned." He reached under the counter again and pulled out a physician's bag, black leather, silver mountings. "Noo this—"

"Your idea."

"Eph and me." Old Malcolm sucked noisily on his pipe. "A mon canna lug aboot a mahogany box, can he!"

"This all didn't come about overnight."

"Aye, it took a bit of time. The States are nae just doon the river, ye ken."

"Everybody trying to push me into medicine," Arnold mused softly.

"Ye've always been in medicine. There's a thousand men in this camp that know it. Even that selfish bairn of mine has seen—"

Footsteps beat on the porch, and Seth Marmett plunged into the room. "Doc! It's time! Martha—"

"Sit down a minute, Seth," Arnold said.

Marmett stared, and then he started to get angry.

"Catch your breath," Arnold said. "Then go to the blacksmith's shop and see if Rasmussen has finished polishing a pair of forceps. Get him out of the saloon if you have to."

Marmett started away.

"Don't run up the street with those forceps. You'll scare every woman in town to death. I'll be along in just a minute."

Old Malcolm watched Marmett run up the road. He shook his grizzled head slowly. "That wee wife of his has nae been looking good. She put me in mind . . ." He stared at the counter and his face was bleak.

Old Malcolm's wife had died a few days after the birth of Young Malcolm, Arnold knew. This one, too, was going to be a bad one. Arnold began to transfer instruments from the case into the bag, and then he dug into the wooden box.

Timmy's burro was in front of the blacksmith's shop. The boy was inside, staring curiously at Marmett, who was holding the forceps wide open, a scared look on his face. "They're polished, Doc," he said, as Arnold came in. "But great God, look at those things. Big enough to pull a stump!"

Arnold took the instrument. "I'll want boiling water, Seth."

Marmett nodded. He plunged away after a last horrified look at the forceps.

With his tongue Arnold tested the forceps for scales or rough spots, while Timmy watched in holy wonder. As cold as the dark iron it came to Arnold that his diagnosis was correct: it was no head injury affecting Timmy. The skull fracture in the thickest part of the frontal bone showed no indication of cerebral compression. The injuries must lie at the second cervical, undoubtedly fractured, and at the disk between the fifth and sixth cervicals.

There was no surgical help for that. Dr. Moses Bernard in Philadelphia had improved three similar cases by other treatment. Sull had agreed to send Timmy to Bernard. Arnold had written the letter, and Mrs. Marmett had offered to take the boy as far as her mother's home in West Virginia after the birth of her child. Ruthven had made arrangements for his brother in Philadelphia to get Timmy to his destination and handle other details.

"What are you licking that thing for?" Timmy demanded impatiently.

"It must be smooth. Timmy, will you tell Mrs. Frisbee—"

"The old hag is already there. Do women have kids just like oxen?"

Arnold blinked. "Well—I'll talk to you later about that, Timmy."

Charity was in the Marmett kitchen. One glance and Arnold knew how the other three women there resented her presence; and one more glance at plump-faced Mrs. Frisbee showed how she resented Arnold's being there. The cabin was hotter than the hinges, and Seth was bringing in more wood. Arnold put the forceps and his instruments into a dishpan of boiling water.

"Scrub that little table," he said to Charity. "Here, I'll show you how to make a solution of this lime." He looked at the other women. "I want compresses dipped in boiling water and wrung out." He left them bumping into each other and went into the bedroom.

Mrs. Marmett was a little woman with flaming red hair that now lay in two long braids across her outing-flannel gown. Her eyes were bright with fear and suffering. Her finely chiseled features were white and pinched. Someone had tied ropes to the footboard of the bed. She was clutching knots in the free ends.

In a few minutes Arnold was sure that for once a husband had not run for help too soon. Soon after that Mrs. Frisbee, who had grumbled loudly about putting her hands in lime solution, stood in the doorway and sniffed. "Chloroform! Well, indeed, Dr. Arnold!" She came to the bed.

He put the bottle and a compress into her hands. "There's enough on it now. I'll tell you when to add more, and when to let her breathe—"

"I'll do no such thing, Dr. Arnold—if you are a doctor!" Mrs. Frisbee put the bottle and compress on the kitchen table now ranged against the bedroom wall. She folded her arms and looked coldly at Arnold.

Charity picked up the cloth and bottle. She looked frightened, but she nodded at Arnold and went to the head of the bed.

"In sorrow shalt thou bring forth children," Mrs. Frisbee said. "It wasn't meant to be any other way. I have borne six of my own."

The birth started as a breech presentation when Mrs. Marmett's strength was almost gone. Arnold turned the child. Already the pelvis seemed to be contracting. He picked up the forceps.

Mrs. Marmett smiled at him gently, her eyes blank from pain and anesthetic. "Is—is it all over?"

Too much chloroform? Oh, gentle Christ! The sharp nose, the tightness at the temple cups, the discolored face, the warm smell of death.

"Mrs. Marmett!" he said.

"A girl?" Her eyes were closed.

From her vulture post against the wall Mrs. Frisbee said, "Uh-huh! Uh-huh! I thought so!"

Charity's voice was colored with violence. "You get to hell out of here!"

"You'd better, Agatha," another assistant said.

"Martha! Martha!" Arnold saw Mrs. Marmett's eyes focus on him wearily. "Once more, just once more. You're going to fight, you understand! The ropes. Pull hard, Martha. Every bit of strength you've got! You're going to fight hard just once more, aren't you?"

She looked at him drowsily, her mouth slack. She closed her eyes, and then she opened them in surprise, as if Arnold's words had just come through. "Why— yes—yes—Dr. Arnold."

She drew a deep breath and set her teeth and waited for the next contraction. It did not come. She released her breath and stared at Arnold in terror. "I'm dying."

He smiled at her with the taste of sweat upon his lips. "Why, Martha Marmett! You're going to fight!"

He thought she took courage from him; and that was all he had to give at the moment. Then he saw the rolling knots of agony start again as muscles and nerves, driven by the heritage of life, tried to do their task. This was the last, he knew. She would not have strength to help again after this time.

"Everything! Harder!"

Her courage, nature, and the forceps. . . . It was done. A girl, protesting against life before Arnold had her upside down. He tied and cut the cord, and gave her to a woman at his side. Curse this business of feeding a fetus to twelve or thirteen pounds! It made a weight to brag about—and almost killed the mother.

If there was life in Mrs. Marmett, he could not see it from where he stood.

The placenta came two hours later.

At sunrise, Arnold scrubbed his hands for the last time, blinking stupidly at water still boiling on the stove. There was wood stacked almost to the ceiling, and the sound of Seth's ax was still coming from outside.

A strong wrist and long fingers held out a towel to Arnold. He smiled his thanks to Charity. It must be true that women had a stronger cable of life in them, for she did not look as if she had been up all night.

Barring infection or hemorrhage or other complications, the mother would live. The infant girl was strong and healthy enough, and in time the scars left by the forceps would be only dimples. Arnold took a splinter from a log and carefully wiped lime solution under his fingernails. Great Tophet! It was hot in here!

Mrs. Frisbee came in, her round face bright with cold. "I'll stay now."

Charity said, "I'm sorry about last night. I should not have spoken as I did."

"It's all right, dearie." Mrs. Frisbee took off her bonnet and hung it on a peg.

It was not all right, and Charity was not sorry, Arnold thought. Women like the pair of them would always hate each other. "Send Seth to the island if—"

"Send Seth to my cabin," Charity said. "Dr. Arnold is going to have breakfast there, and then he's going to have a little rest."

Mrs. Frisbee made a tight-lipped grimace.

The two lanterns by which Seth had chopped all night were still burning. Marmett leaned on his ax, his big jaw drooping a little. "She'll be all right?"

"Both of them, I think," Arnold said.

Sunrise. You could think clearly then, no matter how tired you were. Perhaps it was the tiredness that drove all little things from your mind. Decision was as clean and shining as the mountains. Arnold damned Romig a little, but only with a sense of wonder. Romig had known from the day in Oro City when he asked his questions from the bunk in a miserable hut. The gifts yesterday—was it only yesterday?—had not forced decision, nor had this birth. They had not done so because decision had been there all the time, needing only a final push at a critical moment, just as the crude forceps had supplied power when needed most.

Last night in the agony of Mrs. Marmett, Arnold had seen again his twin sister's face. There had been a Gentile doctor only a mile away. No doctor, the bishop said. Everything was in God's hands, and His will must be heeded. The bishop had led the elders in the laying on of hands, and Clorinda had died; it was His will, they said.

The bitterness had drained into the years instead of into Arnold, but still he knew, and had known all along, that he had no place in Zion. They had told him that when he raged and cursed them at his sister's bedside. "You have no place in Zion unless you learn to bow to the will of the Lord."

Too many things were the will of the Lord or against His will. Michael Servetus dying in the smoke and flames of green wood on Calvin's orders because the book containing the greatest physiological discoveries of the time was "hugely scandalous and against the honor and majesty of God."

"Did you hear me ask you a question?"

Arnold smiled. "Forgive me, Charity. I was just thinking that not so long ago a doctor in Hamburg was burned to death for witnessing childbirth while disguised as a woman."

"The midwives, no doubt, were all ancestors of Mrs. Frisbee."

Arnold smiled. "What was the question?"

They were passing the corral behind the Shenandoah. A chipmunk ran up a post and warned the world.

"What is driving Jonathan away from me?"

Arnold looked into her face and saw a hurt that filled him with formless sadness. He loved Romig, and he loved this woman as gently as he had his twin sister.

"In a way," he said, "I think it is the same sort of conflict that was sending me back to Zion when I didn't want to go, but with Jonathan it is much stronger. It is not a matter of what to do as much as it is what to think."

"I don't understand."

They stopped on her porch.

"You would if you were married to him."

"I want to be," she said simply.

"I know." Arnold sighed. He looked at sunshine clean on long blue slopes, at trees and sky, and all the never-ending beauty of the earth. He thought that forever and ever a man like Jonathan Romig would go lunging toward that beauty in an effort to capture and hold some of the peace and strength and calmness of it.

It was in Arnold's mind to say that no woman would stand for long between Romig and his driving unrest, but he could not say so to Charity. Romig would have to explain himself—if he could.

CHAPTER 21

THE ISLAND MEN were almost ready. They had cleared the stumps from the old river course where Roberts and Leibee had planted radishes. Where the old run met the new one, they had built a rock dam. It merely detained the Blue, making it wait a moment before rushing through; but when the upstream face of the barrier was covered with canvas, and the huge beaver dam above breached properly, there would be water enough to scour the old river bed free of overburden.

Muchow, the chief engineer, said the beaver pond could be controlled by means of a head gate now being completed at the blacksmith's shop. The dam was a quarter of a mile wide. In places the water was fifteen feet deep. It was his plan to release an initial burst by breaking the dam just a little. The rush of water, aided by the rock dam, would raise the level of the Blue until some of the stream would return to its ancient course, cutting away leaf mold and other impeding matter that lay above gold-bearing sand and gravel. Thereafter, by means of the head gate in the beaver dam, and by experimenting with canvas on the lower dam, the flow of water could be adjusted to whatever was required.

The Moonbeam Placer Company would share equally the gold taken from the ground. Their test holes indicated that they were going to do quite well.

Romig was not thinking of the plan this evening when he stopped near the rock dam. The restlessness was in him. He looked at furry outlines of the mountains and thought how simple it would be to walk away and meet the morning sun on some new hill or in a valley he had never seen.

He was standing there listening to the splash of water through the dam when he heard somewhere behind him the sound of tearing cloth. A man soundly cursed all the stumps in the world, and then cursed the world to boot.

Roberts came lurching toward the river on a trail that led to the cabins. He had ripped one pants leg nearly off.

"How are you, Roberts?"

"Drunk."

They had passed as friends, but they were bound by mutual sharing rather than understanding. It would never be any different, Romig knew.

"Know what I did tonight, Brother Romig?"

"I smell one act and suspect the other. Drinking and gambling."

"Objections?"

"None."

"That's the hell of it," Roberts said. "You're full of love and understanding all the time, except when you're bashing my head against a rifle."

"I was sorry about that."

"There you go again." Roberts tried to put his foot upon a stump and could not make it. So he kicked the stump and staggered from the effort. "Know what I did tonight, St. Augustine?"

"No."

"I looked a long time at that flash-eyed Garrison, a long time, Brother Romig, and I just about decided to call him out."

"What for?"

"For you. I won't kill him. I'll just cripple him so no woman would want him, especially Charity Megill. Blow his jaw away, maybe, or smash his hip so even old Heber couldn't patch him up."

"Good Lord, Roberts!"

"Don't think I'm merely talking." The deadly sincerity of the Virginian's thought came coldly through his drunkenness. He made two more attempts to put his foot on a dark stump. "The floor's uneven, damn it! Where do you want him maimed, Romig?"

"I don't."

Roberts clicked his tongue. "You say no to the one thing I would do for you. I don't much care for you,

Romig, but I like Garrison even less. Another thing, I've halfway fallen in love with Charity myself." Roberts waved one hand vaguely. "You know, same state, we know lots of the same people. She's beautiful too, of course. What's the use of Garrison having her? Where shall I shoot him, Romig?"

"Just forget it."

Roberts suddenly fell over the stump that had been annoying him. "Never mind!" he said as Romig started to help him up. He gained his feet, swaying. "You lack the saving grace of hatred, Romig. A shame, too. In most ways you're normal enough. I made you a practical offer, and you refused it, so to hell with you. You're not much good."

"What is corroding in you, Roberts? What—"

"I'll tell you." Roberts's voice ran as cold as the river. "Men in Yankee uniforms raped and murdered my mother and two sisters. One of my sisters was twelve."

Romig released his breath slowly. "Guerillas?"

"Bushwhackers, yes. But who brought on the war and made them possible? I hate anything in blue. I always will, and you're no exception. There were six men. I've got three of them. My cousin beat me to another. The last two came out here someplace. When I get them, I'll go right on hating anything that wore blue."

"Ruthven lost two brothers, but he—"

"Too bad. My name is Roberts."

"Do you hate Muchow?"

"Yankee sailors—that's a little different. Don't try to

change the subject. Don't pull any of your little gentl-
izing tricks on me, Romig. I—" Roberts waved his
hands as he staggered. "Where were we? Oh, yes! We
don't shoot Garrison. We don't marry the girl. You just
go on looking for your gold-plated Grail. Maybe you
think you'll change your mind and come back
someday. You're a fool, Romig. Do you really think
Penelope just sat around and knitted socks all those
years? No indeed, you stupid spotless knight! There
was a Garrison around. There always is."

Roberts laughed. He turned and lurched away. "No
jaw, no hip shot, Roberts. Be a good boy, Joel."

Where the trail led close to a caving gravel bank
Roberts slipped and rolled into the river. He was up
and moving before Romig reached him. "Keep your
hands off!" he said, and went floundering down the
stream, falling and cursing as he fell.

Romig stood alone in the gloom, listening to thunder
clearing its throat somewhere above the ranges.

Another figure came from the shadows toward the
road. It was Sull. He walked close to Romig and stood
face-level. "He made a winning tonight," Sull
explained. "He was alone when he went out." The
Irishman stood there silent for a while, formidable
against the night. The smell of bay rum and cigar
smoke drifted from him.

At last he said, "Roberts is right about Garrison."
And then he turned and walked away.

When Romig entered the island cabin, Teteluki was
sitting at the plank table with the brownish print of a
Bible spread to the light of two candles on tin cans. It

was the first time Romig had seen the Negro reading his Bible, although Luki had mentioned once that he had one in his pack. He rose when Romig entered, closed the Bible, and stretched like a huge, long-limbed cat.

Above the mountains the thunder gods began to rally their mighty drum corps.

"More rain tonight," Teteluki said.

"Where's Arnold?"

"Sawmill accident down the river." The Zulu started toward his hammock.

"May I see your Bible, Luki?" Romig had heard often that strength, solace and inspiration came from the first verse that met one's eye after opening the Bible at random. It had never worked for him, but he was willing to try again.

Solace, strength and inspiration were delayed by the fact that Teteluki's Bible was written in Norwegian. Romig blinked. He put his finger on a verse and looked at Teteluki.

". . . we brought nothing into this world, and it is certain we can carry nothing out."

"Thank you, Luki." There was a solid thought. Romig grunted and started to go to bed. While he was putting his wet boots near the fireplace, he felt a rush of damp air and heard the hide door close.

Teteluki was gone into the night—and so was his deadly assegai. The drums above the mountains began their rumbling march in earnest.

Romig was roused by a fine drift of water on his face. The door had blown back and rain was slanting into the room. Rain was splashing from the eaves, hissing furiously into the river. Slowly Romig gathered will to get up and close the door.

And then he was staring, wide awake.

Marked sharply by a flash of lightning, Teteluki was standing naked on the rock outside, holding aloft his assegai. Another flash burned the air. Thunder bellowed. Teteluki was leaping now, thrusting his short spear toward the sky. Blue-white flashes illuminated him. Darkness left the naked, leaping figure still moving in Romig's brain, if not before his eyes.

Lightning caught Teteluki brandishing the assegai, whirling silently to stab at new streaks of fire. Water streamed from him. Long lash scars on his back writhed with his movements. He made no sound.

Romig watched until the thunder rolled away, sending back the sullen growl of a retiring but undefeated army. The rain fell harder then. Teteluki came inside and began to rub himself dry.

"What did you think?" he asked.

It took Romig a moment to realize that he had been as visible as the Zulu. "I don't know," he said.

"With oxhide shields and assegais we used to defy the natural forces that are the Zulu gods. Until this summer I still, at times, took fierce pleasure in doing so, but it is done now. Tonight was the last. I will go now toward the things that Bishop Schreuder tried to teach me long ago."

The memory of the voice, solemn, peaceful, stayed with Romig long after Teteluki had finished speaking. The Zulu's weight settled against the hammock gripes and then the cabin was silent. The rain began to lessen.

Romig looked at the dead fireplace. It must be nearing morning. "You weren't on the rock all night, Luki."

"No. I was moving in the darkness of the town, as I have done many nights, listening behind the tents of men, listening for something that would let me take revenge for Leibee. But I found out nothing, and now I am glad that I did not."

Long before he went to sleep Romig heard the even, peaceful sounds of Teteluki's slumber.

Not with the shouting and the moaning and the talking in the unknown tongue . . . but with peace He comes . . .

CHAPTER 22

YOUNG MALCOLM, Jake Rutledge, Gorham and Muchow were playing poker in the island cabin the night Eph came in with a Henry rifle Young Malcolm had ordered. The Scot leaped up and snatched the weapon, grinning like a boy.

"Where's the ammunition?"

"At the store, grabby," Eph said. "I didn't figure you'd need any before daylight."

"Oh, I got to try it out right now."

Ruthven rose from the fireplace, where he had been sitting with Roberts. For a man who hated anything Union, Roberts had been having quite a friendly conversation with Ruthven, Romig thought. "I'd better go with him," Ruthven said. He winked at Roberts and glanced at the Ferguson above the mantel. "Any man who's never had anything but a flintlock will have to be watched to keep him from shooting himself."

Malcolm was already going out. "Ha!" he said. "Come on, cocky, I'll show you how a Henry operates."

Muchow slapped his cards on the table. "I can't get rich off Jake and Gorham, and here I was figuring to make enough tonight so I wouldn't have to work when we start the sluice again tomorrow." He looked at Arnold and Romig. They shook their heads.

Eph raised one hand. "Don't give *me* the eye, Muchow. If I'd wanted to lose my shirt I could have done it in Denver."

Muchow glanced at Roberts, but only for a flash. Gorham was in the game, and the Virginian would not play with him.

"I got enough," Rutledge said. "It ain't no bargain to play against you and Gorham."

"Just get in?" Arnold asked Eph.

Eph put his back to the fire and crossed his hands behind him. "A little while ago."

"No trouble?" Arnold asked.

Eph shook his head. "Here?"

"Peaceful," Arnold said.

Eph's eyes were thoughtful. "Where's Luki?"

"Still out hunting. He left at dawn," Romig said.

"Uh-huh." Eph nodded. "Did he say what he was hunting?"

The room was quiet suddenly. Muchow's sharp face jerked up from counting chips. "What's up, Eph?"

"I know this. Wakarusa John didn't go over Hoosier

Pass. You say he started that way, but I talked to freighters camped on top, and they didn't see him."

"It was night," Romig said.

Eph shook his head. "They had two watchdogs with them. The dogs never made a yap that night. Wakarusa would have had to pass close to the camp, unless he took off into the trees on the low side—and why would he do that? He'd been turned loose."

"Hmm." Gorham looked at Romig. "So maybe he didn't clear out after all."

Eph nodded. "Luki thinks—"

Teteluki came in, his Hawker in his hands. His face said that he had overheard or guessed the conversation. They waited for him to speak.

"I found a camp today where he had been a few days before," Teteluki said. "In heavy timber. There were cans there. He is either slipping back for supplies, or someone in Moonbeam is taking food to him. His tracks are the same tracks that Ephraim studied where the last man was robbed."

Gorham folded his arms and looked around the room. "We made a bad mistake, I'm afraid."

"Uh-huh," Eph said. "I'm afraid you did." He looked at Teteluki. "He'd moved his camp, of course?"

Teteluki nodded. "But I will find it in time."

"We still don't know he's guilty," Arnold said.

"I will bring him in soon. Then the miners' court can judge his guilt." Teteluki poured water and began to wash his hands.

A sudden burst of rifle fire across the creek made Rutledge jerk with alarm.

Arnold frowned. "Luki, you don't intend to—"

"I will only bring him in," Teteluki said.

"I'll go with you the next time," Muchow said, his eyes hard and bitter.

The Zulu shook his head. "No, Much, I will go alone."

Muchow nodded. "I thought you'd say that. All right, go alone, but no one is going to keep me from hauling on the rope after Wakarusa is delivered."

Arnold was worried. "Your view is just what I'm afraid of, Muchow. We don't know that Wakarusa is guilty. When the time comes we must give him a fair chance. In the meantime, let's keep quiet about this."

"That's what you tried to do the first time when you had him cold," Roberts said. "It didn't work very well." The Virginian gave the room an insolent look. "Fair chance! What kind of chance did Wakarusa and his gang give Leibee—and the rest? I'll trust Luki's judgment from here to hell. I'm only wondering why he wants to bring the bastard in as anything but a chunk of cold meat."

Roberts stood up and stalked from the room, bumping against Gorham as he went.

"Someday," Gorham said quietly, "I'm going to lose interest in trying to get along with him."

When only the regular occupants of the cabin were left Arnold yawned and stretched. "We've had quite a group here. Pretty soon we'll be breaking up." He shook his head regretfully. "Where to from here, Luki?"

Teteluki was cutting bacon. He did not look up.

"When the Arapahoes gather for their fall hunting, I will go to get my wife."

"Your wife?" Arnold stared at Romig.

"A Ute. She was captured by the Arapahoes last summer near the hills of singing sands in Spanish Valley. I had thought to let it be so, but now I am going after her."

"And then?" Romig asked.

"I will have land and cattle in a little valley that I know of. My wife will always be a Ute, and I find no fault in that; but my children will know of God."

Arnold and Romig looked at each other, and then they looked away as if they shared some mutual shame.

Teteluki's shouting roused Romig and Arnold when the grayness of dawn was creeping under the door.

"Heave out! Get to the bank!"

There had been a loud thump somewhere, Romig thought, but it had not fully wakened him. And then he heard an ugly roaring sound that was coming closer.

"The beaver dam!" Arnold yelled.

Excited shouts were coming from the north bank. "On the island!" Muchow yelled. "Get clear!"

Romig was last when they ran outside and started across the footbridge. He had taken time to snatch Young Malcolm's Ferguson from the mantel. The shock of cold power striking an obstacle came to him. In the gray light he saw dark water spraying up from the rock dam. Willows and slashing foam leaped high. The shuddering sounds of rocks moving underwater came to him.

And then the dam was gone. Coming through the dawn was a roll of charging water half as high as the cabin. Romig's bare feet slipped on the dew-slick bridge. He fell into the river on his back, still clutching the rifle. As he struggled up, he saw Arnold and Teteluki, already on the bank, turn and rush back toward him. He thrust the barrel of the Ferguson toward them. He slipped on smooth river rocks and went down again.

He heard the water smash the cabin. The world blew up inside his head, and that was all. . . . He was sleeping in the haymow of the stone barn back home on a rainy day. Lowing cows were coming in from pasture. Louder and louder they made their sounds until his head was full of pounding pain that sickened him. He groaned and tried to burrow into the hay, and felt mud beneath him.

"Just let him lie there." That was Arnold's voice, and after a while Romig could see the Mormon and others standing over him, wet and shivering.

The right side of Romig's face was numb. His fingers touched a lump he thought was mud on his face, and then he realized it was a flap of flesh hanging below his cheekbone.

"Just lie there awhile," Arnold said. "An aspen log, I think, smashed you in the head."

Old Malcolm and Eph, in half boots and red flannels, came splashing through pools of water. Men were arriving from Moonbeam by the time Romig was on his feet. He felt sick at his stomach, and his head was full of great fuzziness.

Only the rock and a few large stones from Leibee's fireplace were left on the island. The north-bank cabins had been flooded three feet deep. Brown silt and logs and willows from the beaver dam clogged the old river bed. The sluice had been wrecked and swept away. Profane, wet miners were coming from downstream to report their sluices smashed and scattered in the willows.

"Anybody hurt?" Romig asked.

"Just you." The whites of Arnold's eyes appeared enormous in his muddy face.

"You and Luki got me?"

"Mainly Luki," Arnold said. "He had you by the hair. I had him by one arm, and we all rolled downstream until Greene caught me by one leg."

Old Malcolm took Romig's arm. Romig never remembered the trip to the merchants' living quarters in the back of the store. Lying there on a bed sometime later, he vaguely heard Old Malcolm growling about ashes dumped on the floor. He heard Arnold say, "Hmm. That wasn't the only bump you took. It's a good thing your head is like a piece of oak."

Then Charity was looking down at him, and he saw in her eyes everything he had fought against in himself. He tried to smile at her, to reach up with his arms, but her face became misty and disappeared.

For two days Arnold kept him lying still in Old Malcolm's bed. Then the Mormon told him, "I'm not going to battle with you any longer. Unless that headache comes back, you'll be all right."

Gorham had been in several times to report every-thing that was known. Someone had blown the beaver dam with a keg of giant powder. There had been a miners' meeting. "If you think the camp was howling mad before," Gorham said, "you ought to hear it now. Sixty-some miners below the island lost their sluices."

Luki's Hawken rifle was never found. The Ferguson had been recovered with a bent barrel. A quarter of a mile below the island Roberts had picked Arnold's mahogany case off the willows, and Greene had found the Mormon's black bag lodged against a broken sluice.

During the excitement someone had walked into the open store and made another try for gold held there. This time Old Malcolm's choice of a hiding place had been a sack of rice, and the thief had not made good his try.

Romig went up to the beaver pond to have a look with the eye that wasn't black and shut. What had been a beautiful reservoir was drying desolation. The surge of water had uncovered the fact that one dam had been built on top of another. Deep silt that would have been rich meadowland someday had gone down the Blue. Pick points were gleaming as a group of Irishmen attacked a huge beaver house.

"There'll be a million b'avers in there, sure!" one worker said.

Timmy was wallowing in a muddy pool, trying to catch stranded trout with his hands.

Romig opened his good eye wide when he noticed men gathering in force before the Shenandoah. He saw

Garrison moving briskly, giving orders. Presently the group trying to crack the stubborn beaver house gave up and joined the crowd. A bartender came out and locked the doors of the saloon, and not long afterward, surrounding teams of mules and oxen, the miners of Moonbeam moved downstream, a jostling mass of juggled tools and shouting men.

They built a dam that day where the rock dam had been. Sull was in charge of gangs that loaded wagons. Haring directed movements of the teams. The McAllisters and twenty others framed timbers for earth-filled cribbing. Earth flew from wagons standing in the Blue. Broad-footed oxen tamped the fill. There was a central opening for a headgate to be raised and lowered by means of a windlass set on huge posts.

There were too many men, and they bumped into each other; but the work went rapidly, and through it all ran the crisp direction of Barney Garrison, who did not seem to hurry but was everywhere.

Arnold and Marmett took seventy men downstream to rebuild the sluices wrecked below the island.

By midafternoon the dam was built. Haring drove into the river with a wagon carrying all the men who could get on it and a headgate of two-inch planks, double thickness, bolted with wagon-tire iron strapped on the downstream side where the gate would be forced by water pressure hard against peeled-log rollers.

Romig was standing on the hill with Mrs. Marmett. He had tried to load wagons until miners took the shovel from him and told him to watch, that this was on the house.

Charity came up the hill. She smiled at Romig and said, "Aren't you a pretty sight!" She looked at the sleeping baby in Mrs. Marmett's arms. "She's getting more beautiful every day, Martha."

The two women exchanged a look that left Romig alone, completely without understanding of them. He had called the infant a whopper, and now he glanced dubiously at it again—and whopper was all he could think to call it.

Mrs. Marmett smiled at the baby, and the smile took much of the pale tiredness from her face. Then she looked at Charity and glanced briefly at Romig. "I'm a little tired," she said. "Excuse me, please. I think I'll go on back to camp."

She walked down the hill slowly, smiling at the baby.

There was a level scrutiny in Charity's eyes when she came close to Romig and said, "I haven't seen much of you lately, Jonathan."

Considering her tone and look, he decided she had made a statement with no intent of levering for an explanation.

"I guess I have been busy," he said.

Charity was looking down at Roberts and Muchow carrying a windlass from shore, wading because the dam was so crowded men were bumping each other into the water.

"It won't take you island men long to work your two claims now, will it?"

You island men. That sort of setting apart reminded him of Garrison.

"No, I guess it won't."

A shout went up from the dam. The windlass was in place, and the headgate was being lowered. It went down smoothly to a log sill on the bottom of the stream. The river beat against it with swirling fists. Water spread along the face of the dam, began to rise and flow into the old bed; a trickle, and then an increasing stream as the Blue was completely blocked from its normal course except for small leaks around the headgate.

"No doubt you'll be moving on soon," Charity said.

Romig studied her face. It was impersonal. She might have been talking to a casual acquaintance. That hurt him, even knowing that it was he who had been at fault in their relationship. He wanted to tell her now the things he had avoided.

"Charity—"

The miners below sent up a bellowing cheer. Silt was rolling in a dark stream around the loop of the old river bed. Garrison gave one glance, then started up the hill, his manner plainly indicating that he considered the project accomplished and forgotten.

"Charity," Romig said, "I have to tell you—" There might have been a breaking in her manner then, he thought. Something changed in her eyes. She was waiting to hear what he had to say.

Then Garrison was close, and in a few moments he was with them. The flashing glance of his green eyes read their faces. "There's your dam," he said. It came to Romig that he was talking to Charity, that Garrison had directed efforts below because she had asked him to.

"We owe you thanks," Romig said.

"Anything to help you on your way, Romig."

The two men measured each other, and Romig knew he hated Garrison as much as Garrison hated him. The coldness and sureness of the man caused anger to rise in Romig as combers climb a shelving beach. His cheek and swollen eye throbbed with a charge of blood.

Garrison smiled. "Can I see you back to camp, Charity?" He did not wait for an answer. He took her arm and guided her downhill.

Later, when Romig was inspecting the headgate at the dam, Roberts said casually, "My offer is still good." He raised his brows at Romig's black look.

CHAPTER 23

WILL GREENE was away on hunting detail, but all the other island men were at their sluice the morning Old Malcolm caught the man with Leibee's buckskin poke.

There was angry shouting in the store. Old Malcolm's voice rose mightily and brought silence. A man ran from the store, shouting at the islanders, "We got the killer! We got the killer!" And then he sprinted toward Moonbeam.

The island men dropped their tools. They went to the store in a silent rush. Six or seven miners were facing Old Malcolm and Eph across the counter, the latter with his Starr in a knotty fist.

"Fair play, boys," Eph said.

Between the merchants was Charley Stoker, the youth who had reclaimed a stolen watch the day Garrison arrived in Moonbeam. His face was white, defiant, the freckles standing out like dead leaves on a snowbank.

Old Malcolm lifted a large poke from the counter near the gold scales. It seemed to have a few ounces of gold in it. "I think it is the one Luki described to me. This mon just brought it in, but—"

"I told you I found it in the cabin I bought last week!" Stoker said.

Teteluki examined the poke. "It is Leibee's. I made it."

"And Stoker *found* it! The lying bastard!" a miner shouted.

"I did, I tell you! God knows I did!"

"We don't know it," Roberts said.

Arnold waved his arms. "Let him talk."

"It was jammed between the ridge log and the roof of the cabin I bought last week," Stoker said. "I—"

"That's the cabin Hartwein and Fitch built," a burly miner said. "And it wasn't even built when the Dutchman got murdered. You're a dirty liar, Stoker!"

"Hartwein and Fitch wasn't here then," someone else said.

"Who's in with you, Stoker?" Muchow asked.

"Would I be idiot enough to bring a poke in here—if I'd taken it from a murdered man?"

"Maybe," Young Malcolm said. "None of us but Luki could identify Leibee's poke, as far as I know. I see you gambling pretty heavy."

"Wait a minute!" Romig said. "We're not trying this man. He's got to have a chance."

"Sure!" a black-bearded miner said. He was still holding in his hand the poke he had brought in to deposit. "Give him a chance, and then let's hang him."

Boots rushed across the porch. More miners entered. They accepted the evidence at face value and called for a rope.

Teteluki said to Romig in a low voice, "Let's get him away from here. The store could be wrecked."

"So help me, I'm telling the truth," Stoker said when they took him to the tent on the north bank where Romig, Teteluki and Arnold now lived. He looked at Romig in appeal.

Gorham arrived soon afterward, pushing through the gathering crowd. He appointed men to help guard the tent. About half of them complied. Seth Marmett was one.

"No hurry, boys," Seth said. "He won't get away. Let's hear all sides."

"Yeah!" a miner shouted. "You had Wakarusa John too—and look what happened!"

Gorham went inside to talk to Stoker. He was not there long, but when he came out the crowd was doubled. "Charley Stoker ain't guilty," Gorham said. "I'll stake my life on that."

"You'll have to if you try to stop us!" someone yelled. The mob was there, stalled now by opposition, but hanging fire, needing only a little push or leadership. The rumble of its spirit made Gorham look small and futile. He raised his hands for silence and got it.

"Here's what he says: He found the poke stuffed between the roof and ridge log of the cabin he bought. He—"

"Where'd the gold in it come from?" someone wanted to know. "His claim petered out a long time ago."

"He found a rich streak of gravel a few weeks ago," Gorham said. "He was keeping quiet about it. That's reasonable enough, considering all the hell that's been going on. Suppose—"

"What kind of a story is that!" a miner yelled. "Even with my neck in a noose I could beat that!"

Romig raised his voice and let it roll. "There's a man's life at stake here! Let's have order. We've got a district and laws to cover this. Let's operate by law in a fair court!" The thing was to delay, to give the miners' tempers a chance to cool before Stoker went to trial.

His voice and manner held them for a moment; his beaten, swollen face gave him savageness that helped his purpose. "Good God! He's ugly," someone muttered.

"Let's send a committee to Stoker's claim to run a pan or two," Romig said. "That will be that much toward finding out part of the truth."

Arnold acted instantly, appointing four men to the task. They left. The mob waited. It was not waiting on the report, Romig realized. It had already convicted Stoker.

On a slow patrol around the tent Ruthven stopped beside Romig. The black bars of his brows were drawn tight. He murmured, "If they start, they'll go over us like a snowslide. Talk to them some more." He moved away.

Sunlight caught the golden lights in Jake Rutledge's crinkly beard as he stuck his head from the tent flap. "Stoker wants to see you, Romig."

"A fine thing!" a miner growled. "The judge trying to do the defending too!"

The Rutledges were standing. Muchow was sitting on a box, his face like a hatchet. They all were watching Stoker, seated on Romig's cot. Outside the mob grumble rose. From somewhere at the back of the tent Young Malcolm said in a voice that invited trouble, "Step back a ways, bub. You can hear everything when the time comes."

Stoker looked at Romig. "You believe me, don't you? You can help me, Romig. You know I'm telling the truth."

What was the face of evil? This square, frightened visage with its freckles standing sharp where blood had drained away? So long ago Romig had pushed that face, contorted, its lower lip stuck out, away from a helpless thief. That memory was vivid now, and with it came the thought that there had been born in Stoker a basic indignation toward wrong. That thought, vagrant, powerful, and the appeal of Stoker's eyes brought Romig to decision: The man was innocent.

Outside, he'd begged for decision based on facts, on investigation, on careful weighing of the evidence; inside, he had made his own decision on the basis of things that could not be put in words. He looked at the

Rutledges: noncommittal, watchful; at Muchow: hostile, mind set.

"Help me—somehow," Stoker said. "I've told the truth."

A high-pitched voice shouted, "Hyar's the rope, boys!"

That was Cotton Denby, Romig thought, a cousin of Ashfield, the murdered South Carolinian. A stir of sound, a feral tightening and rising, ran through the mob.

"We're doing all we can, Stoker," Romig said.

"No. No, you're not! You've got to get me away from here until they cool off. I'll come back. I won't run away. But I ain't got a chance right now. You know it!"

Gorham was trying to talk again, but he was being shouted down.

Eph came in. He took the Starr from his belt and put it under a cot.

"So you won't try to protect me!" Stoker was talking to them all.

"Not with guns, lad," Eph said. "Not now." He looked at Romig. "Better go out and talk; do something. She's running short. The Carolinians can touch it off any minute."

Ruthven stuck his head inside. "Romig."

Sull and Garrison ducked through the flap. Sull looked at Stoker and shook his head. "He never made more than a dollar bet on anything."

"Go out and tell them that," Romig said. "Tell it loud. Tell it slow."

Sull nodded. He left.

"We've got to get him out of here," Romig said. "Maybe take him to Breckenridge."

Garrison took out a cigar. He clipped it with ivory-handled clippers and lit it unhurriedly, his eyes flashing around the tent. "What do the rest of you think about that?"

"It's best," Eph said.

Jake' Rutledge nodded. Art stared straight ahead. Muchow shook his head.

Sull was talking. The miners were listening. Sull seldom spoke more than a few words, so now they were listening.

"It's up to you boys," Garrison said. "Charity is bringing two horses." He let his face and manner show that he had no interest in the matter. "Work out a plan before she gets here"—he looked at Stoker—"if you think he's worth it."

"He's worth it," Eph said. "Go out and hold 'em off, Romig."

Romig went out and looked at the crowd. There was reason in them, he thought. There was reason in all men. Sull had finished speaking. Arnold and Ruthven looked at Romig for help. There was a tiny wedge of silence for an instant, and Romig put his voice into it.

"All of us have an interest in justice. Some of the men standing around this tent"—he named them, taking time—"came over the mountains with Hans Leibee, and they, as well as Joe Ashfield's friends, and the friends of the other men injured by evil in this camp, have a particular interest in seeing that justice is done—"

"Damned right we have!" Cotton Denby tossed his rope. The long knot was in it.

"—but it must be justice and not the ruin of a mob. We are all men with a grievance, and mine is as great as the rest. Look at my face!"

"I can't stand to!" a miner shouted. A laugh sent another wedge into the tension.

Romig held them, using all the little tricks that go with public speaking: the pauses, gestures, the raising and the lowering of the voice. But mainly it was the terrible sincerity of his words that made them listen. He saw Eph move among the guards, rubbing his nose, speaking softly from behind his hand. Garrison came from the tent, smoking his cigar, staring at the sky.

Romig went on talking, and if he had not seen the same thing before, he might have thought that he was driving reason into the miners; but he had been in a pulpit just long enough to know that when he had finished his words would be forgotten—and Denby's rope would toss again.

He saw Charity riding down the road and—the devil's hind leg!—Olga Munson on the other horse.

"—Stop and think a moment, all of you! If someone had hidden Leibee's poke in *your* quarters, then what . . ."

The horses came around the flank of the crowd. Madam Olga was wearing a blue-velvet gown, her high-piled hair bright honey color in the sun.

"Make way for a lady!" she said.

Romig let her have the stage as eyes went from him.

"Let's get over there near the tent so we can hear what's going on without getting these here horses polluted by the smell." A few moments later Madam Olga said, "Well, Art Rutledge, get the hair out of your eyes and help me off this brute. The way you stare a body'd think you never seen me before." She glanced casually at Romig, and he knew she was giving the stage back to him.

Young Malcolm, the devil of adventure riding high in his eyes, gathered in two sets of reins after Roberts helped Charity down.

Romig started to speak again, but he did not get far.

A cleavage developed at the back of the crowd. Several men began to shout.

"There wasn't a color on Stoker's claim! We panned in four, five places!"

The word was repeated. A low animal growl ran through the crowd. It was a mob once more. Denby tossed the rope and howled. "What are we waiting for!"

From somewhere on the flank a miner yelled in alarm. "Stoker's making a run for it!"

Malcolm was up, his horse moving nervously. Stoker came leaping toward the second mount. The man who had shouted the warning picked up a rock and sprinted toward them. Stoker went into the saddle clumsily. He had trouble trying to turn the horse. Roberts slapped its head around. Young Malcolm reached out to grab a rein near the bit. The frightened horse tried to rear, but Malcolm pulled its head down, and then it started with a lunge.

A rock spun through the sunlight. It struck Stoker in the side of the head. He rolled from the saddle like a sack of loose hay.

The mob was moving then with infuriated howls. Romig ran toward Stoker. Someone tripped him. Boots trampled him. He saw Eph and Roberts trying to lift Stoker to his horse, and then they went down. The guttural sounds of fighting beasts rolled over Romig.

Charley Stoker choked out his life on a clean yellow rope hanging from a tree limb while Romig was staggering toward him. It was not far from the graves of Sampson Greene and Hans Leibee.

The mob broke apart as quickly as it had formed, men scattered in little groups, some walking alone as if they had no use for their companions.

Ruthven and Old Malcolm cut the body down. The old Scot's face was blazing white. One of Ruthven's ears was dripping blood. His eyes showed a sickness of the world.

Olga Munson touched Romig's arm. "We tried. You tried awful hard, preacher." She tugged at the shoulder straps of her velvet gown and went up the road.

Charity came up with Sull, who had carried her to safety when the rush started. "You're all right, Jonathan?" she asked.

Romig nodded bitterly.

Garrison limped up. One eye was closed. There were livid marks on his forehead and jaw, and blood was trickling from the tangle of his curly hair. He ripped away what was left of a shirt sleeve. "This is the *second* time I've fought for principle—and got nowhere either time," he said tonelessly, looking at Charity.

Arnold had not been hurt. Men had pushed him aside, but even in their insane anger they had not hurt him. He shook his head in wonder. "Those same men laughed and built a dam for us."

"Those same men crucified Christ." Garrison dabbed at his face with his sleeve, then flung the rag away. He took out a cigar. It was broken. He threw that away, and walked up the road toward Moonbeam, where Sull was already going with Charity.

Soon there was no one left at the body but some of the island men and a curious few who had taken no actual part in the hanging, except to watch and not protest.

Gorham and Young Malcolm had suffered the worst beatings, and now Young Malcolm was in a fearful rage. Gorham was quiet, sick inside. He sat down on the ground and held his head. After a while he looked around and asked, "Where's Luki?"

"He picked me up and carried me away from the fight," Job Davis said. "And then he just walked off."

"He went out again to look for Wakarusa," Gorham said. "That's what we got to do." He glanced at the body. "It won't help him none now, but—"

"He didn't go after Wakarusa," Davis said. "He didn't have no gun or nothing. He just walked down the river like he never wanted to see another human being."

It was little Ephraim who gathered all the details of

the aftermath and reported them an hour later. "The men that went to pan Stoker's claim got the wrong ground," he said. "Stoker was right. He did have a mighty rich streak of gravel." He spat and looked at the mountains. "Troy Haring is gone. He left on one of Charity Megill's horses just after the hanging; and now that kid, Timmy, swears up and down he peeked through a window and saw Haring hide something on the ridge log of Stoker's cabin the day after Charley bought it."

"Why didn't he say something sooner?" Ruthven asked.

"The kid was up the river fishing this morning. He just came in." Eph spat again and went on talking unemotionally. "Here's the worst. Olga Munson had sort of suspected Haring, but not enough to turn a mob loose on him without being sure. Haring, for one thing, had a hell of a fight with Stoker over a woman in Olga's place—and lost. But the gal was sweet on him, all right, because he was promising her a lot of things that no wagon-swamper could have delivered. He dropped several hints that he had plenty of gold to spend when the right time came.

"You're wondering why Haring flew his kite? After the deal today Olga went back and kicked the truth out of the gal, and then she made the mistake of leaving her alone while she went over to tell Sull. He was the closest member of the secret committee. In the meantime the gal gets words to Haring, and he skips."

"What a fouled-up mess!" Muchow cried.

"Sull never said anything," Ruthven said darkly.

"He told me," Eph said. "We both figured there'd been enough half-cocked ruckuses for one day, so instead of starting another prairie fire, we did all the checking we could. Seth Marmett and some others went up to Stoker's claim. That's when we found out the first bunch hadn't even panned the right ground. Sull and me went over and talked to Olga's girl." Eph nodded. "I think we got some truth out of her. She mentioned, among other things, that Haring had talked a lot about Canon City. It seems he has some friends there."

"Canon City?" Romig said. "We came through there on our way to Oro."

"Uh-huh," Eph said. "And you might have to go back through there and then some before you catch Troy Haring."

Young Malcolm leaped up. "Let's get started!"

Eph frowned. "Let's do a little planning first. Where's Gorham?"

"Looking for Wakarusa out in the timber some-place," Muchow said. "I was going with him, but he rode away too fast."

"He's wasting time," Eph said. "If Luki couldn't find Wakarusa, nobody can. Now—those of you who want to go after Haring, get your loot together. Ride light. Arnold, you'd better arrange for the mules. Get all mules if you can. Get the pick before those jugheads up there start on the warpath. I'll find Luki. He knows an Indian trail that will save us time."

The island men were moving.

CHAPTER 24

NOW THAT IT WAS TIME TO GO, Romig wished that he could stay here in Charity's cabin, talking to her, looking at her, trying to forget that this day had ever been. He waited tensely, on his feet, reminded by the ticking of the Venus clock that time has no regard for man.

Charity stood looking at him, waiting. There were no words to say, for truth much older than words was in their eyes. Romig put out his arms, and together they moved against the little space between them. It would have been so easy long ago, he thought.

After a while he again heard the busy clock, the loud talk of men at the corral behind the Shenandoah.

Charity was crying softly in his arms. "I've loved you ever since that day in Oro City."

He saw her as she had been that winter-hard day on the lee side of a cabin. He saw her standing with him long ago when he had looked musing on storm-clawed heights and again when he had looked back on his way to the pass.

He held her hard and tried to kill the thought that he would always be walking toward Shining Mountains, looking back at a lonely woman. And for a while he succeeded, blotting out the steady ticks of time, feeling that here was all the personal peace and happiness he wanted.

"I love you, Charity."

It was their world for a while, but the shouts at the

corral broke through at last, and the little clock kept nagging.

"What held you from me so long, Jonathan?"

He told then of his father, of the eternal whispering promise of vague things beyond the next blue barrier.

"I'll go with you, Jonathan. I understand only a little of what drives you on, but I love you. I'll go with you."

Romig looked over her head at the room. It represented a woman's way, a settled way, and it brought him an uneasy knowledge of what could be and what could not be. But he loved Charity, and there was in that a great compromising power.

Outside, Young Malcolm shouted Romig's name.

Charity clung harder. "Don't go. The others will be enough. You have no real desire to kill a man, no matter what he did."

"It's still possible he isn't guilty. I might be able to give him the help I failed to give Stoker today."

She pushed her hands against his chest and looked up at him with a tenderness that hurt him. "If you failed Charley Stoker, the whole world failed him. Don't go away, not now, Jonathan!"

Young Malcolm shouted again. "Christ's sake! Romig, we're coming back—if we ever get started!"

"And then," Charity said softly, touching Romig's battered cheekbone, "we'll go together—wherever you want."

His mother, Romig thought bleakly, must have said those very words when she was young, believing them no less strongly than this woman in his arms. But time and the restlessness of Romig's father had worn cruelly against that honesty.

"We'll be together," Charity said. "After all this wasted time."

He pressed his face against the sweetness of her hair. He kissed her for the last time, then put her from him and went to the door.

He looked back once. She was watching from the doorway with the strength and understanding bred from centuries of women who had watched men march away, ride away, go with determination toward right, toward wrong, toward horizons unexplored, toward change instead of permanence.

Twenty men had ridden furiously toward Hoosier Pass, the way Haring had gone, as soon as Sull had passed the word about the Kansan. They had left, Eph said, without plan, provisions or leadership. Once they lost the trail and became cold and hungry, their purpose would suffer considerably. They were on horses too, Eph pointed out, and you couldn't expect too much from horses. His plan was to cut across the mountains on the Indian trail that Teteluki would show them, cross the same pass where Eph had left the island men the spring before, and then go down the Arkansas to Canon City.

"Let's go!" Malcolm had his bagpipe slung in its carrier.

Heber Arnold had no gun, only his medical kit.

Romig took the carbine Old Malcolm had provided, and swung up on a mule.

When they paused to rest the animals on a bare ridge

high above the Blue, Romig borrowed Muchow's telescope and looked back at Moonbeam. He could just
make out the twin cabins where Sull and Charity lived.

"All right," Eph said. "Another lift."

They went up toward the alpine firs.

CHAPTER 25

O N KNEES AND LEGS that groaned Romig let
himself down on damp sand beside the
Arkansas. He plunged his hands into the
stream and leaned over to drink. It was a few hours
before sundown the day after Stoker's death.

According to Eph, they were about ninety miles from
Moonbeam.

This thing called justice had to be served; but if Eph
and Luki returned with word that the three men
stopped ahead did not include Troy Haring, Romig
knew he would be relieved.

It was hot, even here in the cottonwoods where the
river ran in a great gravel slash. Romig dipped his face
into the water again, and then, with his wrists still
making protests against the current, he raised his head
toward pinion-dappled hills to the north. They looked
warm and smug, as if they had never known the touch
of winter. On his left, the peaks rose clear and shining.
Running toward them was a long mesa, so smooth and
straight it had the look of being man-made. A ramp to
the sky. What lay beyond those gray summits?

Romig pushed himself up against the tug of saddle-
weary muscles. He went into the trees and sat down

beside Job Davis on a log. Haring and Wakarusa John, perhaps. The other . . . ?

"You figure it's them, sure enough—the gang?" Davis had asked the question several times of other men sprawled or standing in the cottonwoods. "Haring met Wakarusa, say, but who—"

"I don't know," Romig said. "We'll see."

So long ago he had left her standing in the doorway. It was coming to him now that during those last few minutes he had seen an understanding in her eyes beyond what she had spoken. It might be . . .

"Watch that mule, Luki," Roberts said. "He wants to go downriver."

It had been steady riding. Oro City at dusk, with only Eph riding into the gulch to ask a question. Miners at Cache Creek and Georgia Bar had tumbled out when the strange music of a bagpipe roused them. No rider, they said, just a group of discouraged greenhorns walking down from California Gulch.

Even Young Malcolm had been grumpy with little Ephraim when the hot morning sun began to make them sag the next day. They should have taken the direct route toward Canon City, the Scot said. That afternoon they passed two ranches in green valleys that pointed toward the Arkansas. With the suspicion of property holders for hard-eyed roving men, the ranchers held their rifles ready. No rider had passed, they said. One of the ranchers wore a brass belt buckle with C.S.A. on it. Roberts stayed a few minutes to talk to him after the others rode on.

Where the river began a great swing from south to

east to run beside the Sangre de Cristo, Eph led them off the hot mesas of rabbit brush and along the edge of the water where the going was slow, but where they could not be seen for miles.

At intervals Teteluki and Muchow walked up the high banks to scan ahead with Muchow's glass; and thus it was they saw three riders coming from a slash in the pinion hills, two mules and a horse. Teteluki, not using the glass, said the horse was Charity Megill's, the one Haring had ridden out of Moonbeam.

That slash in the hills, Eph said, was the Ute trail to the inland buffalo grounds of South Park. Haring might have swung down this way. Eph went up the bank himself the next time, returning to report smoke ahead at the mouth of the Indian gulch. A quarter of a mile from the place, Eph and Teteluki went ahead to scout.

The island men waited.

The Arkansas ran its endless song. Above the cottonwoods, magpies worried a cruising hawk. A flight of pinion squawkers passed, going toward the north hills, their hoarse cries fading slowly.

"What makes you think Haring might be innocent?" Davis asked.

"I think he's guilty," Romig said. "But we don't know for sure."

Roberts spat a short oath with contempt enough to dam the river.

"Happen one of them men is him or Wakarusa John, I ain't worrying about them being blood-guilty," Art Rutledge said.

Romig looked at his dusty boots. There was going to be little chance to know about right and wrong, the way things were.

"There they come!" Malcolm said.

Teteluki and Eph came through the trees swiftly, almost silently. Eph nodded. "Wakarusa John is under a big cottonwood on the hill, watching the valley. The other two, we figure, are near the mouth of the gulch, with the animals between them and Wakarusa."

Teteluki went to the river for a drink, and afterward he stood there looking at the western mountains, taking no part in the council that followed.

"How do we move in?" Jake Rutledge asked.

Eph looked at Young Malcolm. "It's all yours, fire-eater. Go ahead."

Malcolm sat down on the log beside Romig and Davis. He looked slowly at his companions, and there was more of Old Malcolm in him at the moment than Romig had ever seen.

"Describe the ground," Malcolm said.

Grim men with bloodshot eyes squatted around a place where Eph pushed twigs and mold aside and sketched with his finger in damp soil. Malcolm gave his plan immediately.

The island men nodded. They settled the details of assignment quickly. Teteluki said he would stay with the mules.

"Before it starts," Romig said, "I'm going into that gulch unarmed and talk to them."

"Great Jesus Christ!" Art Rutledge said.

Ruthven nodded soberly. "I'll go with you."

"One fool's enough," Roberts said. His slender fingers were tapping his rifle barrel. His cold eyes stared at Romig, and he shook his head gently.

"I wouldn't do it, Romig," Jake Rutledge said in an odd, soft voice. "I'd be a-scared to do it, but I know how you feel."

"You'll mess up everything!" Malcolm cried.

"No," Eph said. "No, he won't. Nobody's coming out of that gulch alive unless we want 'em to, so Romig can't hurt the plan."

Malcolm scowled. "All right, Romig. Put a handgun under your shirt—"

"I'll go unarmed. If it's the men we want, I'll talk to them—and maybe we can take them back to Moonbeam for a fair trial."

"Hell's fire!" Muchow said. "Who wants to take them back!"

They went downriver. Teteluki, standing near the mules, watched them go with no expression but somberness.

The plan was almost cocked. Romig stood behind a cottonwood on the upriver side of a green fan of grass near the mouth of the gulch. A small clear stream was running from the gulch into dense willows along the river. Limp green against dry hills to the north, the top of an enormous cottonwood raised above all other vegetation. Wakarusa would be under that tree, about a hundred yards away.

Davis, Arnold and the Rutledges had gone up the left side of the gulch with Eph. They would close in on the sentry and block escape toward the hills. All but

Arnold. He was armed with nothing but his medical kit. The Mormon had said nothing at the council, only squatted there with his brown eyes watching faces.

Romig licked dry lips and watched the little fan of grass where clear water ran. All at once he was tremendously thirsty.

Malcolm tapped him on the shoulder, pointing with his eyes. Ruthven, Roberts and Muchow were crossing downstream. Water sparkled as it broke against their legs. Screened by willows, they had gone down the south bank, and now would take positions on the east side of the gulch.

There was nothing wrong with Malcolm's plan, Romig thought, except that a plan to kill was always easier than a plan of living.

"Still want to go?" Malcolm whispered.

Romig nodded. There was no safe way to do what he had to do. Those who had stood and watched Stoker choked to death in Moonbeam had taken the safe way.

". . . we'll go together—wherever you want," Charity had said. Romig stood there looking at the little stream, remembering all he could about her.

Malcolm tapped him on the shoulder again. Romig blinked and brought his thoughts back to the moment. So soon? Were the others in position already? Romig put his carbine on the ground. He stared at the wet splotches where his hands had gripped it. There was security in that black piece of steel, and now he had parted with it; but it was the security of those who had let Stoker hang, of those who would kill the men in this gulch without asking a question.

The grass mat pulped down under his feet. His heels broke through and made sucking sounds that trailed him. First, he saw the striped backs of two mules, and beyond them, browsing bunch grass on the gulch banks, the black horse Charity had ridden into Moonbeam. He went around a turn and saw between him and the animals two men sleeping in the shade beside wet ashes. Their rifles lay between them.

One was Troy Haring, open-mouthed, ugly in his sleep.

The other was Leo Gorham.

He was on his back, his youthful face relaxed and dirty, one knee drawn up and leaning outward, his left hand resting by his head with the fingers curled like an infant's.

Romig stared. There was an acid taste in his mouth and a sickness coursing through him. He heard himself calling softly, "Gorham! Leo!"

He called several times before Gorham's eyelids twitched. They steadied. The Kansan came alive. He grabbed his rifle and put it on Romig all in the motion of sitting up. Defensive animal savagery glinted deep in Gorham's eyes before the man in him took over, and he realized that Romig was standing quietly, unarmed.

The Kansan's eyes leaped past Romig, to both sides of the gulch. He glanced behind him, and then back at Romig. "How many of you?"

"All of us," Romig said. "All your friends, Gorham."

That did not hurt. Gorham merely smiled, with the tightness running in his eyes.

Haring wakened then, as catlike as his companion.

He grunted deep in his chest, and his bloodshot eyes went wide. He drew a pistol from under his shirt and brought it up deliberately.

Gorham pushed the pistol down and cursed Haring tonelessly. "You want to start shooting before we know anything?"

His eyes as vicious as the red glare of a questing weasel, Haring put the handgun inside his shirt and picked up his rifle. He jerked toward the mules when one of them stamped under the bite of deer flies.

"No, Romig," Gorham said. "We don't go back like good boys. You don't hang us."

"You have no chance to leave here alive."

"Eph with you? Luki?" That was the only time fear touched Gorham's face. And then there was an insolence and hardness in his expression that must have run clear through his being.

This was the face of evil, this was the face of murder, youthful, tense, direct.

"All around us?" Gorham asked.

Romig nodded. Gorham and Haring exchanged quick looks.

Gorham gestured downgulch with his rifle. "I always liked you, Romig—you and Arnold and the Rutledge boys. Go on back."

It was time, Romig knew. He had to force the question out. "Hans Leibee? Ashfield?"

More spirit-bruising than a direct admission was the look of cold amusement in Gorham's eyes. Romig turned and walked away.

He heard Gorham say, "No, Haring, damn you!"

Malcolm's bruised face showed relief when Romig walked into sight. He looked closer and asked no questions. He fired one shot into the air, and like an echo came two more from somewhere up the gulch.

"That takes care of Wakarusa!" Malcolm said. "Who else is in there?"

Mechanically Romig picked up the carbine. "Haring," he said. "And Leo Gorham."

"Gorham? How'd he catch up—Gorham! Jesus Christ!" The significance of that ran through Young Malcolm's mind as quickly as it had through Romig's, the whole foul working of the Moonbeam gang. "Gorham. Sure! The dirty sonofabitch!"

They waited. Hoofs slashed rocks and gravel somewhere in the gulch. The sounds receded. Jake Rutledge yelled hoarsely, "Up the gulch! They're heading up!"

Three shots came close together. A horse screamed.

Malcolm could not stand the waiting. "They're breaking back the way they came! I'll miss everything. Stay here, Romig!"

The Scot ran into the trees at the side of the gulch. Silence began to grind at Romig's nerves.

Muchow shouted something, and a voice answered. A little later Romig heard the same sucking sounds he had made going into the gulch. Gorham walked into sight, crouched at the shoulder of a mule. He glanced at Romig, then whirled toward a sound in the trees on the east side of the gulch.

Roberts was there, pushing his way through a limb tangle. Too late he saw the head and rifle rise above the animal's shoulder.

Not knowing whether he aimed or not, Romig shot. Gorham fell against the mule. The animal whirled, knocked Gorham down and went running back into the gulch. The Kansan was sitting up, grasping with both hands near his crotch when Romig reached him. Blood was coursing in the channels between his fingers.

Another shot came from upgulch as Roberts rushed from the trees. He picked up Gorham's rifle. "I should have killed you on the trail last spring, Gorham."

Gorham lifted a gray face. "If Sull hadn't trailed you home—one night when you were drunk . . ." He turned his head toward Romig. "I didn't think—you had the guts—to shoot, Romig. Made a mistake, didn't I?"

Gorham was trying to smile. He was utterly unafraid, and yet there was appeal in his eyes. "I didn't blow the dam, Romig. Haring did that against my orders, and he planted the poke on Stoker. I didn't want an innocent man to hang, Romig, so help me God."

"Where's the gold you stole?" Roberts asked.

Gorham ignored him. "I bossed the rest, all of it." His face was pinching grayer as he talked. "Haring ruined things, for a chance to drown you, Romig, and a chance to rob the store. Wakarusa was all right. He was smart, and followed orders." Gorham looked at his hands. They were not doing much good. "You'll never hang me, boys."

Muchow came in leaps. He looked at Gorham. "I let him walk past me," he said. "I didn't realize—I couldn't believe . . ."

The Rutledges and little Ephraim came out of the trees on the left side of the gulch. Art's hat was gone.

His dark hair hung wildly, swinging across his fore-head as he limped. He stopped to wipe the butt of his rifle in the grass, and then he saw Gorham.

"Leo!" he cried. "You're hurt! Who—" Art looked at the grim faces of his friends. "Not him!" he yelled.

"The same mule-sticking bastard," Roberts said. "Tell your musical chums all about it, Gorham."

"I'll get Arnold," Romig said. He yelled the Mormon's name.

"Let him die," Muchow said. "To hell with him."

Art Rutledge dropped to his hands and knees beside the wounded man. "They ain't right, Leo. Tell me . . ."

Gorham's eyes were getting blank and glassy, but they met Art's long enough, and the Kentuckian saw enough. He rose slowly with hell riding his dark features. He picked up his rifle and started to raise it as a club; and then all vitality left him. He stood there bewildered, staring.

"Arnold!" Romig yelled again. He started up the gulch.

Jake Rutledge caught his arm. Spiderwebs and leaves were tangled in his curly beard. He shook his head slowly. "We got Wakarusa the first crack. Ruthven or me shot Haring off his mule when it started to break up the bank. Arnold ran up and was kneeling over him to see how bad . . . Haring got a pistol out'n his shirt and took Heber through the heart before Art could use his rifle butt."

A terrible shout of protest gripped Romig, but he had no power to utter it. He saw Jake's blocky face and tangled beard sink away as the Kentuckian sat down. He heard Muchow cursing bitterly.

Art was still staring dully at Gorham. "I ought to smash you dead, Leo."

"Go ahead," Gorham whispered.

He took futile hands from his leg and settled on his side with a sigh. His beardless, cleanly chiseled face grew sharp as life ran from him.

CHAPTER 26

DRAINED OF SPIRIT, Romig sat beside a spring where thin gold plaques of aspen leaves floated. Among the frost-touched trees, the mule drowsed, jerking portions of its flesh at insects.

Yesterday they had buried Heber Arnold. The others . . . it did not matter. The earth would receive them all in time.

Ruthven, Young Malcolm and Davis were sitting near the body when Romig walked up the gulch. Davis was sobbing. Arnold's brown beard was shining in the sun . . . his face gray, still gentle . . . one hand reaching toward his medical kit.

Yesterday.

Romig was still grasping for something in experience or faith to overcome the taste of bitterness and failure.

It was sunset when they buried Arnold. They did not speak much except to insist that the fragile chain of circumstance had not been altered by Romig's preliminary act; but still the thought jeered him. Afterward, they tried to find the answer to why such things could be, and Jake Rutledge spoke as closely to the truth as any when he said, "Heber ought to knowed that a tromped snake lives till sunset."

They went back to the river, dragging from weariness and the plunge from tension, and there they camped.

Unusually quiet, Malcolm said, "I never look at flames without thinking of the fireplace Leibee and I built—and now I'll think of this."

One by one they went to their blankets, except Teteluki, who walked in the darkness somewhere, returning late and startling the mule guard.

That was yesterday, and it had passed forever. . . .

Romig sat a long time looking into the sun-filled valley. Far to the north, the mark of dust showed where his friends were riding toward the headwaters of the river. Down there where the valley turned, somewhere close to a conical, pinion-covered hill, the little part of Heber Arnold that had died was under rocks in a sandy grave.

The living, greater part of Heber Arnold was here at the spring with Romig. So long ago, one evening in the island cabin when the Mormon had been squinting under candlelight, experimenting to see if vinegar would wilt the barbs of porcupine needles, he had said, half musing, "Luki says there is a Christ Child in every man. It's a beautiful expression that I never heard before."

Gorham and Arnold . . . They had left the earth together. Teteluki's thought would serve them both in Romig's mind. The face of evil? No, only a sickness because the Christ Child had not been nurtured. Think then of Leo Gorham fighting to save the life of an innocent man, of Gorham saying no when Haring would have shot.

There is a Christ Child in every man.

The sullen tides of doubt rolled through Romig. He had lost too much, and he was only a man; no thought would serve him if he sat and cuddled it. He rose quickly.

Romig wanted movement, vastness, the chance to fill his hands and mind with the primitive work of survival. It was his only hope. There was peace in elemental work.

Teteluki, Ephraim and Ruthven had understood most of all. They had spoken no final word of parting, merely shaken his hand and let him go.

Jake Rutledge had said, "I always think about that funny prayer you said when we were freezing, Romig. I sort of got you figured out now. Once I thought you was just running around like a sow with a straw in her mouth, but now I guess there's things inside you that won't let you do what folks think you ought to do."

Young Malcolm, scowling fiercely like his father, had made a gift of his brand-new rifle. "You might meet a bear—or something," he said. "Take the no-good thing."

And Roberts, his smile as insolent as ever, shook hands and said, "Good luck, Sir Galahad."

Romig rode through the dying foliage of the aspens above a booming stream that came from somewhere on the planes of rock ahead. He did not look back, but he knew the little conical hill would now be merged with greater hills behind it, and that the dust up the valley would be gone. He let the mule set its own pace on the dim Indian trail.

Cut with the sharp jewels of memory, Charity's face was before him. It would always be there, like the spirit of Heber Arnold, like the somber eyes of Teteluki. But for Arnold's death, Romig knew he would have returned to Moonbeam. What might have happened then there was no way of knowing.

This was best, he thought. He had to go on and find himself and come to peace as Teteluki had done in his way. Perhaps he had seen that knowledge in Charity's eyes even as her love made her say other things. He did not feel strong and wise in his decision; he had a haunting fear that he might be wrong. But stronger than that, driving him so that he had to go now or later, was a belief that someday and somewhere he would find the values and peace that all the restless Romigs had yearned to find.

Jonathan Romig rode on toward a nameless pass. Shining Mountains closed around him.

Center Point Publishing
600 Brooks Road • PO Box 1
Thorndike ME 04986-0001 USA

(207) 568-3717

US & Canada:
1 800 929-9108